Praise for Treva Harte's *Why Me?*

"Ms. Harte once again gives [illegible] an enlightening tale sure to please.

—Michel[illegible] *nce*

"Treva Harte constructs a wonderful romance coupled with the fast-paced suspense of finding and eliminating the potential danger. Sizzling sensuality lends further depth to the story, but does not overshadow the primary love story. Explicit scenes are sprinkled throughout the book, placing this book firmly out of reach of the faint-hearted reader."

—Julie Shininger, *Escape to Romance*

"Treva Harte has yet to disappoint me with one of her stories and *Why Me?* is no exception."

—Flora for *Sensual Romance*

"The suspense lacks for nothing. Clearly described, each step perfectly choreographed, *Why Me?* is a delight for the reader searching for that perfect suspenseful encounter. The sensualist will delight in the erotic scenes, and lose nothing through the wonderful constructed scenes."

—Shadoe Simmons, *All About Murder Reviews*

"What would it be like to have a man know your every thought? Well, Ms. Harte shows us the pros and cons of such a feat, making *Why Me?* intriguing and enlightening. The romance between Wynn and Cassie sizzles, it's wonderful and refreshing."

—Tracey West, *The Road to Romance*

LooseId

ISBN 10: 1-59632-130-X
ISBN 13: 978-1-59632-130-4
WHY ME?
Copyright © 2002 by Treva Harte
Originally released in e-book format in June 2002

Cover Art by April Martinez
Edited by: Catherine Gilbert

Printed in the U.S.A. by
Lightning Source, Inc.
1246 Heil Quaker Blvd
La Vergne TN 37086
www.lightningsource.com

WHY ME?

Treva Harte

Chapter One

"Must warn Art about Lida."

Cassie woke up with a start in the murky half-light of early morning, already groping for the telephone to make her call.

She almost knocked over the telephone before she finally found the thing. Her fingers were ready to punch in numbers when she stopped and gave a quick, embarrassed laugh.

"That must've been some dream." Cassie shook her head once, sharply. "Who are Art and Lida?"

The tiny furred body next to her hissed at Cassie's sudden movement, furious that the human dared to disturb her sleep. Cassie automatically petted the cat, who accepted the apology with a lazy feline stretch.

That was when Cassie realized her hands were shaking.

She lay back down, but the sense of urgency wouldn't leave her. She couldn't go back to sleep when her dream refused to fade like normal ones did. She was sure that Art would be in trouble, terrible trouble, if she didn't let him know.

Maybe she should just get up.

Cassie looked at the alarm clock and almost snarled. Yeah, she ran her own business and could keep her own schedule, but that had never meant starting work by four-thirty in the morning. She was more the type to putter around the house and edge out to work around ten.

Still, there were a few folks on vacation who wouldn't mind if she cleaned their places ahead of schedule. Then maybe she could head for the beach early and enjoy herself. The pristine isolation of a not-quite-spring beach always made for a perfect weekend.

After long, painful years of forgetting to make time for play, Cassie had finally learned to reward herself for doing good work.

"Even if I don't go to work right away, I'm good and awake now," she mumbled to the cat as she got up. "Might as well get ready."

But things still didn't feel right. Damn that dream! Her stomach was in knots. She hadn't felt this bad since—no, she refused to feel that bad over any dream. She'd promised herself she'd never feel that bad again.

She turned on the television, mostly for its soothing background noise. She carefully spooned out her yogurt and blueberries even though she wasn't very hungry. That was what she normally ate for breakfast. Today wasn't going to be any different.

She started the coffee. Healthy food was fine, but she believed caffeine was the most important part of any meal.

Cassie got out her list of things to do for the day. Another thing she'd finally learned was to consult her list rather than her memory before starting work.

She leaned over and stared at the paper, tracing the names with her finger. The first house should be easy. Mr. W. Harmon lived alone and, as far as she could tell, never stayed long at his own home. At least nothing was ever out of place. She cleaned for grandmothers who had more interesting things going on in their houses. That was too bad, since he was really good-looking. He was good-looking with a beautiful, pristine house and—

"Boring," Cassie said out loud.

Unless maybe he really lived with a girlfriend? Cassie felt a little interest stir at the thought. Yeah. A girlfriend who never came over to his place. That might be pleasant. God knows Cassie's ex-boyfriend still came over far too often.

No. Bad thought. She decided she didn't like the idea of that guy being attached. She needed to come up with a new reason.

"At a press conference held yesterday, Senator Hornsby garnered still more support for his presidential bid..."

Cassie took a spoonful of the blueberry-yogurt mix and almost forgot to chew as she stared at the TV screen. The fear she'd been fighting swept over her again and she didn't know why. There was nothing in the scene to frighten anyone.

A serious-looking man and a smiling younger woman strode together down the sidewalk. Several other suited men, all talking among themselves, closely followed them. It was the sort of news story she usually tuned out and she decided she'd tune it out this morning, too. This was just an ordinary morning, after all.

Pandora wasn't interested in the news, either. However, the black cat eyed Cassie's breakfast with a definite gleam in her eyes. Making her move, Pandora leaped onto the table. Cassie glared. The cat glared back, then deliberately lost interest and jumped down. Cassie went back to the news and breakfast.

"...as Senator Hornsby arrived at his hometown yesterday. Hornsby appeared at his local party's fundraiser with several well-known politicians, including Representative Lida Chatham. Chatham, who recently dropped out of the presidential primaries herself, expressed support for Hornsby's presidential..."

Cassie swallowed hard.

"Oh, no."

The two politicians had no reason to look familiar. Other people might care about who was running for president, but Cassie didn't care about politics, not even national politics. Besides, he just couldn't be—but her inconvenient memory supplied Senator Hornsby's first name. Arthur. Art. "Art and Lida."

She went back to glaring at Pandora, as if this new information was somehow the cat's fault.

"What am I supposed to do about *that?*"

Cassie forced herself to relax. Nothing, of course. She must've remembered the names from a news report. That explained her silly dream.

She wished the feeling of worried urgency would go away completely with her rational answer, but it seemed that the nervousness lodged in her stomach was stronger than reason today.

* * *

He woke up aching. For a moment he just lay there, feeling aroused and confused. He moved his wrists, cautiously. They weren't tied after all.

She'd done things to him with her mouth that had made him beg. Begging did no good, though. At the first plea, she'd drawn back, almost touching but not quite. When he felt her breath on his damp skin, deliberately blowing a puff of air over his too bloody hard, too damn sensitive cock, Wynn knew he was in trouble. He couldn't move because of his bonds, but he'd been ready to try and rip the restraints off the bed. The woman had been—she'd been—

She'd been a dream. No real woman could get a man that crazed. Not this man, anyhow. Could any woman be that enticing? That hot?

He snorted and sat up, ignoring his arousal. This wasn't the time to rediscover his teenaged wet dreams. He had adult problems. He bent down and picked up the envelope again.

Wynn Harmon would've looked out the window, but he knew whoever was spying on him would wonder why he was awake at four-thirty in the morning. As he sat on his bed, he absently stroked an old envelope. Now he was certain the paper was something more than just trash to him.

Wynn blinked once, his brooding suddenly interrupted. Something had connected in his brain, just like it had earlier. But now that something was gone. Even so, he tried again, reaching out for—for something. For a moment he thought he felt a click. Then nothing. The feeling was a little like a car battery that had been slowly fading and finally died.

Wynn stopped trying. He couldn't force this. Still, he was sure somehow he had been near someone recently and made contact with them. He'd known something was going to happen once he'd picked up the discarded envelope on the floor and felt a sudden alertness. He'd never gotten hard when he made the connection before, though. Wynn didn't know what that meant and didn't have to time to wonder right now. He needed to ignore his cock and think logically.

He'd connected previously through objects he and the other person had both touched—but he'd always known who the person was.

Who the bloody hell could it be? Damn, he needed to know *now*.

He forced that urgency away, too. No. Things weren't quite that bad yet. No one would kill Art immediately. At least not unless they absolutely had to.

And Wynn was safe as long as his watchers thought they could control him. He'd let them control his actions. For now. That's what he'd done when he was a teenager, to lull his guards.

But they couldn't control this. Wynn stared thoughtfully at the envelope. Both the message and the envelope that held it should've been trash. Meaningless trash. He would've destroyed any mail that someone else might have found important.

Who would have handled his trash and why?

He shut his eyes to concentrate, moving impatiently past the strange sexual tension he felt when he touched the envelope. He'd been at home far too much in the last week and there hadn't been anyone else in the house. There rarely was.

One of the watchers could have slipped in, though his security system hadn't recorded anything suspicious. Of course, they could work around even his system. There was the mail carrier. But neither of those explanations felt right. There was...there was his cleaning woman.

He felt just the way he did when the right pieces of a jigsaw finally fit together. For a minute he savored his triumph. That had been difficult but—

His cleaning woman? He was going to have to depend on rescue from his *cleaning woman?*

Cassie shifted gears in her BMW. She'd used most of her savings long ago—what she had of them, along with the tiny inheritance from her mother—on her car. She knew what her family, particularly her stepmother, would and did say about her "squandering" her money.

She wasn't her family, though, and she didn't care what any of them thought. When she'd bought the BMW she'd loved it because it was a sign she was on the fast track. Now she loved it because the car reminded her she wasn't on that track anymore.

She came to a quick stop in front of the overgrown driveway. She liked this house. In fact, among all the houses she cleaned, this place was one of her favorites. She wasn't sure why. Other people she cleaned for were nicer—she had met this owner exactly once and that was when he hired her—and other houses were certainly easier to clean. This one had a million quaint little nooks and crannies to navigate and tidy.

"I ought to charge more than I asked for this one," Cassie told herself, even though she knew she charged plenty for every house. She cleaned plenty, too, in exchange. It was a matter of pride with her that people tended to be willing to pay and to keep her on once they got her.

She intended to give W. Harmon his money's worth, but her goal for the day was to be done with all three of her houses near noon.

"Starting work at six does have its advantages," Cassie said aloud as she mentally calculated how much time each house would take. "Not that I intend to find out what they are too often."

She hopped out of the car and grabbed her cleaning supplies and then took the key labeled *W. Harmon* on the ring.

For just a moment the lock hesitated, and then gave way without further trouble. Cassie stepped in, ready to put in the security code.

The system was already off. Cassie wondered what was up. This guy was a security nut. He'd never forgotten to leave the alarm off before. Still, it made her job easier. She was always afraid of doing the wrong thing and having clients' alarms go off while she was cleaning.

Cassie felt herself relax. Arlington was a crowded northern Virginia suburb, with tiny yards and plenty of traffic. But this house contained its own special world inside, one where jarring noise or light refused to intrude.

Maybe that was why she enjoyed cleaning here so much. The place should impress rather than comfort her since it was certainly furnished to seem imposing. But she liked it despite that.

At least she didn't have a lot of furniture and clutter to deal with along with all those nooks and crannies. There was very little in this house, but what was there was expensive and old. The effect was maybe a little pretentious, but still impressive.

Cassie had always wondered how a relatively young man, especially one who didn't show off any old family portraits, had collected these antiques.

She had also wondered whether he had a lot of family money, earned a lot of money on his own or just plain stole what money he had. But she was sure he had some. The house contained too many expensive items. Just the Chippendale sideboard, which sat in solitary splendor in the dining room, was worth more than all of her furniture combined.

How did a person live with expensive antiques and no clutter? But then this client didn't seem to have a life. For example, she knew the bedroom closet contained a neat row of expensive suits, a rack of silk ties and neatly ordered polished shoes. No sweat pants, no T-shirts. The man dressed for success but not normal life.

She walked purposefully through the half-empty house until she got to the kitchen counter. She picked up the check there and then she began her routine. With headphones on, rock music blaring, she started to empty trashcans. Once she was following her usual pattern, she let her mind drift.

Art and Lida. Lida and Art. Assuming something was wrong with Lida, what would it be and how could anyone ever get through to Art? No. This whole problem was too stupid. She forced herself back into her usual day's routine again.

Cassie automatically checked the envelopes in the trash. She always did that in this particular house.

She liked to know about the people she cleaned for. Maybe people would call that snooping but usually it was really easy to find out things. No snooping required. Most people left plenty out in the open and never thought about what their things told an outsider. She'd found drugs, love letters, pornography and more in homes where anyone could see them.

But W. Harmon was different.

She was actually a little ashamed of how hard she worked to find out things about him. He didn't make it easy. She never could find out much about him even when she looked more carefully than she usually did—

Someone tapped her shoulder.

"Oh, my God!" Trash spewed out of the can.

Cassie whipped the headphones off and, still breathing hard, whirled to face... W. Harmon himself.

Though she'd only met him once, she couldn't mistake him for anyone else. He had dark hair, direct, intense dark eyes and he dressed then as now in a tailored black suit.

That answered one of Cassie's questions about him. Even first thing in the morning he was dressed perfectly for the day.

On anyone else the suit would've just been another dark suit. On him it was memorable. He had one powerful aura. That's the only word Cassie could think of to describe it, even though she tried not to use such a California term too often.

Cassie blinked, trying not to act mesmerized by his gaze. She'd felt that way when she first met him but had hoped she had exaggerated the effect he had. Now she realized she had, if anything, minimized the hypnotized feeling he gave her.

"I didn't expect you to be here." Cassie winced as she heard herself stating the obvious. Maybe she'd been talking to no one but herself for too long.

But he was never home. Ever. She'd cleaned his place early—though not this early—and late. No one was ever around.

She wondered if he realized she had been picking through his trash. She decided the best thing to do was to not offer any apologies or explanations. Perhaps he'd just let the whole thing slide without question.

And maybe she should be grateful he wasn't still in bed at six in the morning. Hmmm. Maybe not. She liked the images she was conjuring up. She'd always thought he was sexy. She just hadn't been close enough before to discover he was as sexy in person as she'd imagined. And as formidable. She'd had no idea she could be turned on by intimidating men.

"I didn't expect to be here today either."

He should've looked harmless and ordinary as he bent to help pick up some of the spilled trash. He didn't. He looked like he was waiting. Cassie didn't know what he was waiting for, but she felt sure it was something important.

The man of mystery didn't offer any other explanations. Well, obviously he, too, knew better than to apologize or explain. If he didn't say any more—well, his silence was consistent with his enigmatic lifestyle.

Cassie really had nothing but speculation to offer about this client's line of work. After her half-hour interview with him, he'd given her his business card. Along with his phone number it said only "W. Harmon, Consultant."

In the D.C. area, anyone who wasn't an attorney or a computer expert was a consultant. Whatever that meant. Oh, well. Cassie had spent many fruitless hours thinking about W.

Harmon ever since she had met him. She saw no point in continuing to gape at him.

Cassie scooped the rest of the trash into the can and accidentally brushed the man's hand.

"Sorry—" she began and then stopped.

An alien, impatient emotion swept over her. She clutched the trashcan hard.

Art is in trouble, for God's sake! We have to hurry.

She stared up at the only other person in the room. His face didn't change expression. He clearly hadn't heard anything.

She hoped she didn't look as terrified as she felt just then. He didn't seem concerned, but that could mean anything given who he was.

"I'm sorry. I need to sit down for a minute." Cassie thought she said that before she sat down, hard, on the wooden floor.

"Are you all right?" He sounded no more than mildly interested.

"Yes. I just—uh—got winded for a minute."

He didn't ask anything more. He didn't offer to help. He just stood there, his hands in his pockets, looking at her with that intent stare.

The man looked spooky. Handsome as the devil, but spooky.

The whole situation was spooky. She had never felt or heard anything that clearly in her mind before. She knew the voice hadn't come from her thoughts.

What was wrong with her? The answers that came to her were either laughable or frightening. So she came up with an easier question.

Why did this have to happen in front of this guy?

Cassie wondered what she looked like, sprawled on the floor in front of this suited stranger. She didn't like the contrast of his looks and hers. She suddenly wished she was dressed in anything but her usual cutoffs and faded T-shirt. She wished, instead of being just over five feet tall, that she could loom over people the way the man in front of her did. She wished that she'd highlighted her hair with blonde streaks a little more recently. She wished—she wished he would stop staring at her as if she was some kind of strange zoo exhibit.

Cassie very carefully stood up again.

"I'm feeling much better now."

Even if it was a lie, the lie was worth it. The strange, panicky feeling was still there, but she felt better on her feet.

"Are you prone to these spells?" the man asked her in a faintly accented voice.

She couldn't quite tell what the accent was but his accent, combined with his deep voice, made his speech incredibly attractive. Almost hypnotic. Damn, there was that hypnosis thought again.

I can't believe this. How did I get you, of all people?

"Not at all." Cassie dismissed the idea briskly. A housecleaner better sound brisk or people might see her as having potential problems doing her job. "I can't imagine what came over me. Believe me, I'm just fine now. Never better." She forced herself to stop talking and just looked at him.

His eyes narrowed, studying her again. "Indeed."

"Mr. Harmon—"

"Wynn."

That was his first name! She hadn't even known that after all these months. She'd figured it had to be William, though that seemed a bit ordinary for someone so—so atypical. Win. That suited him better.

"With a y, then double n." The man's words broke in smoothly on her thoughts. He said it as if he had spelled his name to people far too often.

"Oh. Unusual name."

"It's Welsh."

That might explain the accent. Cassie gathered herself together.

"Cassie. Cassie Majors. Oh. I guess you know that. Seeing as you write checks to me all the time."

"Cassie isn't short for Cassandra, I trust." Wynn still sounded indifferent but polite. "I always thought Cassandra a rather unlucky character in the myths."

"No. It's short for Cassidy. I never use the full name but my mother thought Dad's last name should be put in somewhere. That was only fair."

"Ah—theirs was a very modern, feminist marriage?"

"Oh, no."

"I see. They weren't married."

"Oh, they were married. Just not to each other. And not to anyone at that particular time."

Cassie couldn't believe she was actually discussing this with a near-stranger. Not only that, he was her client. She shut her mouth hastily but feared the impression had already been made.

How is anyone going to believe this flake? Why of all possible people did she have to be the one to get through? A security guard is going to take her away before she gets within a mile of Art—

"Hey!" Cassie yelped, indignantly.

It was bad enough to be hearing strange things in your head. Things were going too far when your strange thoughts began to criticize you as if you weren't even there.

"Excuse me." She retreated to the hall closet where the vacuum was kept.

Cassie didn't wait to see how he was going to respond. She turned on the vacuum since the noise made any sort of thinking difficult. That was just the way Cassie wanted things before she ran into Wynn Harmon again.

Flipping out in front of clients who were near-strangers was not high on her list of smart career moves. She wasn't sure why, but she was determined to appear somewhat sane until she could finally get out.

"And I'm not a flake," Cassie muttered to herself as she dragged the vacuum back and forth rather viciously. "How many flakes know the term supercilious?"

I said flake. I didn't say illiterate.

"That does it." Cassie concentrated on not thinking anything at all. She thought about black, black holes. No light. Only darkness. No sounds, no smells, no messages—

That's too much effort. Why don't you just listen to me and do as I say instead? I promise to stop just as soon as you tell Art and get him to understand.

"How do I do that? I don't even understand." Cassie bit her lip after saying that.

This not thinking wasn't working. In fact, the situation was getting worse. The voice was already telling her what to do. Soon she would be having heart-to-heart conversations with it. Next she'd be stripping her clothes off, running down the street, and predicting the end was near. And it would be. Someone would cart her off to the nearest mental institution. The End.

None of that has to happen. You don't have to understand, either. You just have to listen to me.

"No!" Cassie turned off the vacuum.

She had made it to the kitchen but, unfortunately, there was her client, Wynn, sitting at the kitchen table, sipping coffee as he read the newspaper. No, probably tea. Seeing as he was British.

She hoped the vacuum had been noisy enough to muffle her yelling from her client.

"I'm going to need to mop here." Cassie tried to sound courteous. She had to remember it was his house. He could be wherever he wanted, even though she was having a personal crisis right now.

"All right."

He gave her another assessing look, got up and strolled out of the room, cup in hand. Cassie took time to admire his walk since he couldn't see her check him out. That made her feel a little less subordinate. And his rear wasn't bad to look at, either.

It was too bad he was so…so…unapproachable. She was actually getting a little sexual tingle from watching that butt.

A few moments later she heard a computer switch on in another room.

She was a little surprised he had actually understood that she needed him away from her when she cleaned. Wynn, with a y double n, Harmon didn't seem like the type to care about what other people wanted or needed. She couldn't figure him out at all. Then again, why should she? All she had to do was clean his house.

She corrected herself. All she had to do was clean his house without cracking up while she mopped the floor.

She was profoundly grateful that he'd left her alone before she did something really weird. Of course, poking into someone's trash and talking out loud to a voice in your head might already qualify as weird to some people.

I'll give you time to get used to the idea. This must be upsetting for you, I know. But I don't have much time to give. You need to understand that. And, believe me, I wouldn't use you if I didn't realize you're all that I've got to work with right now.

"Damn it, you need to stop insulting me! I'm certainly not doing anything for a voice that can't treat me with a little respect." Cassie paused with the mop.

The sick feeling in her stomach told her the truth. She wasn't dreaming now. She knew that. No, she was awake, and she'd not only heard a voice in her mind but she'd had conversations with the damned thing.

"Oh, God. I'm in big, big trouble. This may be even worse than last time. What do I do?"

Chapter Two

"So, Ned, I've started to hear these voices. Well, just one. A guy's voice. I think. I don't know why I think it's a guy... Anyhow. That isn't important. What is important is that it's already telling me to do weird stuff. Uh—Ned, are you paying attention?"

Ned turned his head toward her and looked earnest.

"Yeah, Cassie. That's, like, so strange. Hey, were you on anything? That could cause you to hear and see stuff."

"No! Ned, of all people, you ought to know I don't do drugs!"

Cassie couldn't believe she was sitting in her sunny, bright little kitchen having this conversation. Ned, on the other hand, seemed unfazed. She wondered what it would actually take to faze him.

"Well, you could've changed your mind. Hey, did anybody give you anything? You know, like you were at a party and someone slipped something in the food or a drink..."

"I didn't even see anyone that whole day. Except my client. And he was the one who was drinking. Tea. Well, probably tea. Anyhow, I wasn't at any parties and I didn't eat or drink anything except what I made for myself at home."

"Whoa. Really, really strange." Ned blinked at her.

Cassie could have sworn he looked a little respectful. Oh, damn, why had she actually thought Ned could help her think through anything?

"Yeah, well it really spoiled my trip to the beach, I can tell you that." Cassie had discovered she didn't like walking the beach wondering if she was crazy and, if she was, what to do about it.

She toyed with the idea of telling her family. No. They already thought she was way off center. This news would just confirm all their worst suspicions. They'd have her institutionalized in a second.

Ned stood up and stretched. Cassie paused for a minute to admire him. You couldn't say much for Ned's mind, what there was left of it, but his body was still in fine, fine condition. And Ned meant well. Most of the time.

"Well, Ned, what should I do?" Cassie couldn't help asking.

Someone who looked as strong and tough and masculine as Ned should have a strong, tough brain to go with the body. Somehow she still thought that. Well, she thought that in her weaker moments.

She felt weak now. She felt vulnerable and weak, weak, weak.

"Wow, Cassie. I don't know."

Ned returned to the kitchen table with the bowl of sugar in his hand.

Yeah. Great. That's why we've dated each other off and on for years, Ned. Because you're such a rock for me to lean on.

No, she didn't want to think about that. She'd wondered why she'd put up with Ned far too often. Right now she had more important concerns.

"Like, maybe you need help."

"Help?"

"Yeah. A professional. You know."

Ned poured a huge amount of sugar into his coffee cup and stirred it.

"A *shrink?*"

"You don't have to shout. That's what shrinks are supposed to work on, right? People with voices in their heads?"

"What would my brother say if he found out I was going to one? And Dad?"

"Why should they know? You can hire a shrink yourself, right? And the psychiatrist has to keep things confidential. Right?"

"Oh. Right. Yeah. But what if this shrink makes me do something awful?"

"Like what?"

"I don't know. Undergo hypnosis or something. Or talk about my childhood. Whatever it is that shrinks do."

"You hired him. You fire him."

"Oh." It was frightening when Ned began to make sense.

He gestured expansively. "Therapy can be real helpful, you know. That's what all the magazines say. I had some done on me once. A while back. Sometimes they give you drugs, too."

"What was that like, Ned?"

"Some of the drugs were OK but the therapist didn't do a thing for me. On the other hand, nothing hurt, either."

"Nothing much ever does hurt, does it?" Cassie resisted a patronizing pat on his hand. "Well, I'd have to find a good one. One that could help. That can't be the easiest person in the world to find."

"Well, yeah, of course. Why not ask your step-mom for one?"

Cassie stared at him again. She wasn't sure just how Ned's mind came up with ideas but—yeah. How had he managed to connect her stepmother with a psychiatrist?

Even worse, he was right. Cassie would bet big money that Tasha would know a good shrink. She might never go to one herself but she would know the best in the area. Tash always knew how to get the best of everything everywhere. For years Cassie had fought the annoying tendency Tash had of knowing the right thing to do and the right person to do it with.

Maybe this was the time to stop fighting and use her.

Now all Cassie had to do was come up with a way to ask without having Tasha run to her dad, screaming that poor Cassie had finally admitted she needed help. Her stepmother had probably been waiting for that moment ever since she married Dad.

Cassie began to rub her forehead. Oh, boy. This would be very, very tricky. Who did Cassie and Tasha both know who Tasha would believe needed a shrink?

Ned scraped the kitchen chair against the floor before he got up again, the way he always did.

Well, that was easy. Anyone would believe Ned was in desperate need of psychiatric assistance.

Just faintly, in the back of her mind, Cassie thought she could hear a protest. She didn't know why. She decided not to listen. Listening to what was in her head had gotten her into enough trouble.

"I need a second opinion," Cassie said out loud.

Ned shrugged and drifted back to the refrigerator.

When you started relying on Ned for his brains, you were in trouble. She needed someone bright.

Emily.

Cassie hesitated. How long had it been since she'd called Emily? Cassie tried to remember.

They'd been really close in boarding school and college. After graduation, though, Emily had gotten engaged and married and Cassie hadn't. Then Cassie had kept going to school while Emily started work as a high-pressured, low-paid advertising flunky. Cassie had started work just when Emily stopped work and started having kids. They'd been out of synch for a long time.

Cassie figured she hadn't talked to Emily in over a year. Wasn't it after Emily announced she was pregnant for the third time?

She needed Emily. Emily was bright. Emily was stable. She still had the same husband, she sent out Christmas cards with those photos of smiling, normal kids. She couldn't think of anyone more rational than Emily. Better yet, Emily didn't talk when she knew she shouldn't.

Besides, right now Cassie was out of other ideas for second opinions.

"Ned."

"Yeah?"

"I am calling someone now. When she picks up, I want you to go away." Cassie spoke very distinctly, the way she might to a five-year-old. Subtlety was wasted on Ned. On the other hand she figured he might actually get upset if he heard he had just developed a psychiatric problem.

Ned grunted but she was pretty sure he'd heard.

Then, before she could think any more, Cassie punched in Emily's phone number. The disembodied telephone voice informed her that the phone number had been disconnected but was gracious enough to let her know what the new number was.

Cassie scribbled it down on her list and put that one in.

Another disembodied voice then allowed her to leave her name and telephone number. Cassie snarled her message into the receiver and then hung up.

She had to admit that after a year apart, it was stupid to feel annoyed that Emily wasn't there when Cassie needed her. But now Cassie was annoyed and without a second opinion.

* * *

Where the bloody hell was she? She had to pick up!

The biggest problem with sharing his gift with others was there was no guarantee that they'd use it wisely. And Ms. Cassie Majors looked like a person who could never be counted on to do anything wise.

He thought about the unexpectedly vulnerable look she'd had at times, especially when he'd sent out his most powerful message. He'd made the transmittal stronger and more urgent than he needed to, obviously. But Wynn hadn't known how receptive Cassie was to him.

When he thought about her reaction, he fought down the sympathy he felt. He imagined Cassie found it easy to inspire sympathy and interest. The woman looked like a sexy waif—he judged she usually was more waif-like than sexy, but either one could work on a man's feelings. Not on him, of course. He had no time for either waifs or feelings.

Still, when she had sat down on the floor she had looked, literally, punched in the gut. She was sensitive all right.

She was small, too, so it seemed worse somehow that she looked so hurt. Wynn knew he'd done that to her and he couldn't do anything about it. He'd wanted to, though. At the same time he'd wanted to push her further down on the floor, too, and bury himself inside her. That hadn't been sympathy urging him on. He could imagine her face, dazed with longing and delight, as he pushed his way into—

Right. As if he always dazed and delighted women when he had sex with them.

Wynn scowled. His prowess and her sex appeal made no difference. What was important was that she was receptive to his gift—although Cassie Majors looked totally unsuitable for any of his purposes. He could only hope he was wrong about how useless she would be.

On the other hand, even if she was useless, his gift was valuable for sensing danger. Wynn knew that danger was getting closer. He was sure he was right about that. He had tried to play innocent for two days and that had worked. But that ruse would fail soon.

This morning he'd heard crashing sounds in the driveway. When he went to his car, he found his laptop computer had been smashed. Wynn didn't see anything obviously wrong with his car but he didn't need to. His plan to drive out fast when they weren't expecting it wasn't going to work.

Damn. How would he get in touch with her if he had to leave the house?

She was unreliable, unpredictable; the communication he shared with her hadn't been established long enough and it sputtered out too easily. It was always difficult finding someone whose mind was receptive to him. Also, while it was fairly easy for him to read receptive minds, it took more time to allow him to project his thoughts. If she were nearby, or he could touch something of hers, he was able to strengthen the link—Lord, if she were nearby he could just talk to her and explain somehow. Or maybe he could just get away with everything without explanation. He preferred that.

Meanwhile the prickling on his neck was getting stronger. He ought to know to pay attention to that after all this time. Wynn hesitated, then moved to the closet and pulled out a small, worn-looking bag. He'd used that bag before to escape. He could do it again. After all, that was what he'd been doing all his life.

Once he was gone, how would he find her? Wynn shrugged. He'd try the easiest way first. He pulled her business card out of his wallet. But, as he had figured, the response he received came from an answering service. Somehow he didn't think he could leave this message. He took a quick look but of course her name was unlisted in the telephone book. So much for easy.

He paused and concentrated. Yes. He remembered the license plate number on the BMW. Hesitating no more, he moved to his desktop computer. The Internet could be just as useful as telepathy. While he punched in the e-mail address and his question, he could feel the prickling grow stronger.

C'mon, man. Hurry.

Waiting for a response seemed to take forever. Logically he knew that demanding an answer that required a little—work— in what were supposed to be inaccessible files took time. But he also knew he didn't have much time.

When he finally got the answer on the screen, he grunted once. Urgency was pulling at him to go faster yet, but he cleared the history, then the cookies and the temporary files. They'd check on what he had been looking at, of course. He was going to make sure it was going to be a lot more difficult for that to happen.

Even if they know how to trace all this it would cost them time. Not that he usually kept anything dangerous in his computer. He was well aware that Internet activity was usually traceable.

His information request popped up. Hmm. When Cassidy Majors had first come to work for him, he'd had her screened, of course.

Her references had been enthusiastic about Cassie's abilities. That was all he'd needed to know then.

Now he knew more. In fact he'd learned a good bit about Ms. Majors from his informant. She appeared law-abiding, healthy and had a better credit history than one might expect. She certainly hadn't lied about having someone named Cassidy for a father.

Who her father was had made him raise his eyebrows a bit, but there was nothing wrong with having a wealthy father.

And he knew where she lived. Now that he had erased his quick message, he was reasonably sure he would be the only one to locate her.

Wynn looked outside. Ah, almost dusk. The human wolves after him probably liked the dark. But so did he. So did he.

He looked around his house with a sudden regret. What a pity. The antiques he began collecting years ago, only to put in storage, had finally had a place to be displayed. As time went on, somehow he'd found himself buying more things that seemed to go with the house.

Wynn stared at the huge gilded mirror he had placed in the living room. That would be incredibly difficult to move and almost impossible to hang anywhere but in a room like this. What had he been thinking? He didn't even own the house.

But this place had been part of his whole grand scheme to finally turn completely respectable. Respectable? No, he wanted more than that. He was going to be important.

And the house had become something more. Wynn lightly touched the spines of some battered books in the built-in bookcase. They weren't expensive. He'd just enjoyed having them around.

Now that he was leaving, he could admit this house was more than a symbol of what he wanted to become. Oh, bloody hell. He could find other houses. Now that he'd figured out how to create a home, it couldn't be that hard to make another.

Importance, acceptance, permanence were all still close enough for him to see and obtain once he took care of his immediate problems. Wynn turned off the light in the living room and then moved to the kitchen, flicked on more lights, and turned on the stereo in the library. Then he returned to the dark living room and efficiently pushed up the window and slit the screen with his pocketknife. He could almost hear the sounds of quiet feet drawing closer. Time to go.

Bag in hand, he slid himself outside and flattened himself against the wall behind the shrubbery. Nothing yet. He saw a car drive by. The car's headlights went out. Hmmm. A strange car was parking not far from his house. No one ever did that. He lived on the end of a cul-de-sac.

It could be some teenagers giving each other a very long good-night kiss but somehow he doubted it.

He began to move. He was unhurried, but every move was calculated and quiet. Behind him the house waited, lights on, faint music coming from the back. Everything there looked welcoming.

Wynn fled that light and noise, picking the densest shrubbery, the darkest passage away from the house. A car door clicked shut, quietly, as he got near the street. While he waited in the shadows, he watched the two people walk toward his house.

He could tell at least one had a holstered gun, which hung awkwardly under the man's jacket. Probably the other one had a weapon as well but was better at concealing it.

Only two goons? They'd underestimated him again. As they headed for his house, Wynn walked out from the brush and then continued, unhurriedly, down the street.

He had a plan. He always had a plan. When you had the gift, a plan, and plenty of cash, everything was possible.

He was already far enough away that he wasn't sure whether he heard the sound of breaking glass or imagined it. But he had already made his good-byes to the house. What happened next there was simply what was going to happen. Wynn concentrated on the future.

The first thing he had to do was find a way to get to that flaky woman without anyone following him. He'd been getting faint distress signals from her. She must be a good link.

Of course she also might be one of the enemy. He hadn't picked up on any danger of that in her thoughts but he couldn't deny she had been rooting through his trash. That hadn't been just cleaning.

Why did she need to do that? What did she want to find out about him? He thought about what he had just learned from her from the computer. She didn't seem dangerous. Whatever had made her look at his trash probably was innocent enough.

Nonsense.

She was trouble. Wynn wasn't sure what kind of trouble she was, but he absolutely knew in his gut that she was. Not just his gut told him. His cock reminded him that she made him as hard as that faceless woman in his erotic dream.

Bloody hell, Cassie wasn't even his type but he kept imagining her in all kinds of fascinating positions, doing all kinds of fascinating, erotic things...when she wasn't driving him insane with some maddening bit of illogic that ran through her head or into her conversation. All of that added up to trouble ahead.

Unfortunately she was trouble that he had to deal with. Soon. He began to walk just a little faster.

Chapter Three

Cassie looked at the telephone. Emily still hadn't called. After all these years Cassie had finally neglected her last girlfriend long enough. Emily wasn't going to call.

Cassie realized she was pacing again.

"I can't wait anymore," Cassie finally muttered. She dialed a second number.

Tasha would be there. She was always around when Cassie wasn't sure she wanted her to be.

"Tash? Hiya. I need to ask a favor." Cassie had worked on her lines for a while.

But Cassie couldn't continue because Tash didn't need to work on lines. She always had plenty to say and was more than willing to say it.

"Darling, how fortunate it is that you called."

Cassie listened, envisioning the woman on the other end of the phone.

Tash was about as short as Cassie was and her mom had been. Dad had a weakness for petite women. But that was where her resemblance to Cassie's mom ended. Tash had fluttering eyelashes and a soft voice and hair that wisped around a heart-shaped face. If a person didn't know her, that hapless person would swear she looked harmless and sweet. Once you did know her, you realized she was about as harmless as a hungry piranha.

"I'm so glad you bothered to contact us, dear. What a relief! I was sure you had forgotten your brother's birthday celebration is going on tonight."

"Oh, yeah, sure. Hank's birthday. Tonight?" Cassie tried to keep the squeak of dismay out of her voice. "I didn't realize it was tonight!"

Tash's voice grew firmer.

"But you'll be there. Of course. I'm sure you don't have any other plans."

Tash knew Cassie and her lack of a social life only too well.

"Yeah. Of course I'll show up. Why would I miss Hank's twenty-first? I know how big a deal that must be to everyone. But, listen, I did want to ask—"

The phone clicked off. Tasha wasn't interested in questions.

Cassie put her phone down hard.

She should have known this wasn't going to be easy. If she hadn't called, she could have gone on about her own business. Tash would never have called Cassie to remind her about the party—her stepmother would have preferred to point out to Dad how flighty and forgetful Cassie was.

Tash'd told her about the family get-together a month ago, and Cassie had made a note of the date on the calendar. Then Cassie'd—well, sort of deliberately—forgotten about the whole thing.

She didn't want to remember family obligations and her family had gotten used to her sometimes ducking out of them. Due to her ill-fated call, now she had to dress up and visit the family and act happy about her half-brother's birthday.

Hank was going to graduate from business school in the next year or so, go off and make a zillion dollars and never need to worry about anything in his life. Cassie'd been there and done that for awhile. No big deal. He'd probably be a lot better at that life than she'd been.

But just because it was his birthday she had to get him a present to celebrate. What did you get the guy who was about to get everything?

And, after all that effort, then she still had to wheedle some information about psychiatrists out of Tash. What a long evening this would be.

Cassie sighed. No matter how she tried—and she had tried, even though her family might not realize that—she would never fit in with them. They were always nothing but trouble for her.

But they were trouble that she had to deal with tonight.

* * *

"Darling, we're so pleased you're here. A little surprised you remembered us, but pleased." Tash's smile was frighteningly pleasant. "I'm sorry you didn't have time to dress before you ended work."

Cassie smiled back. Both of them knew what her cleaning wardrobe looked like and both of them knew this wasn't it. Cassie was glad she'd worn her jeans and Gap knit shirt. They were her best jeans, the type she'd wear to any party—if she went to parties—but Tash wouldn't care about that.

She figured her ensemble was just offensive enough to irritate Tasha, but not so outrageous that Tash would take action. Cassie still remembered her teenaged years when Tash would make her go change outfits. She wasn't sure what would happen now that she was an adult.

Tash, of course, was in some kind of designer pantsuit that sparkled subtly. Sequins would have been too tacky, but Tash knew how to make an appearance.

"Hey there, Hank." Cassie kissed her younger brother on the cheek.

They smiled a little tentatively at each other. There was nothing terribly wrong with Hank. There just wasn't anything particularly compelling about him, either.

"Hey, Cass."

That was it for her conversation with Hank.

Cassie gave Tash a quick peck on the cheek and then looked consideringly at her father. She never knew quite how to greet him. They settled for their usual half handshake, half hug.

"How's business, Cassie?" Her father always emphasized that she ran a business. He was less likely to tell people it was a cleaning service.

"Good, Dad. How's yours?"

"Booming. Keeping me busy."

Cassie tried to think of more clichés to help her dad out but lost interest in the conversation. That was her dad's family. A mix of boredom with a dash of unpleasantness. Her father might've made Natasha accept Cassie as a family member but he'd never made her like it.

Still, if not for Tash throwing in a few barbs now and then, Cassie might fall asleep. She would've certainly been able to do the family get-together thing by rote. Maybe Cassie should be grateful to Tash.

Naaaw.

"Gotcha a present." Cassie knew what was expected next and passed on a wrapped present to Hank.

She wondered what the family would've made of some of the less than legal things Cassie had come up with to hand to him. Hank was a challenge. She always gave Dad Scotch. Tash got perfume. Usually Chanel. Hank hadn't quite fit into the right pattern yet.

"Hey, thanks."

Hank looked at the silk tie Cassie'd bought.

"Thought it would help for your entrance into the business world," Cassie said.

If she'd had a passing thought about how impressive a certain client of hers looked in his power ties, she kept it to herself. As it was, she might've hit on the perfect annual present for Hank. Impersonal but inoffensive. That was about the best she could hope for with her family.

Things dragged on until dinner. Cassie sat, staring at the family silver. Well, Tash called it the family silver. Once, after

Cassie had told her real mother about the expensive silverware, Mom had laughed and said the Bill Cassidy she'd dated hadn't inherited enough money for paper plates, much less silver.

There was a pause in the conversation. Cassie nerved herself. Now.

"Tash, I have something to ask. Something sort of personal. Well, not personal."

She'd rehearsed this, damn it! But with three people staring at her she was getting rattled.

"Yes, dear?"

"I need to know the name of a psychiatrist. It's for Ned." Why, oh, why had she thought Ned's idea was a good one? She could've looked up a shrink in the Yellow Pages. Had someone check one out on the Internet. Anything but this.

"Ned needs a psychiatrist?"

"Yeah. Well, you know Ned."

"Oh, yes." And Tash didn't care for Ned at all.

"He's been hearing things. Voices."

"Good God, that sounds like he could be dangerous!" Bill Cassidy leaned forward. "Do you still let him in your house?"

"Yes, of course. He wouldn't hurt anyone. They're just...voices. Sort of." She could feel an ache develop in the back of her skull. "Anyhow, I wondered if you could recommend a specialist for him. I told him I'd arrange and pay for it."

Oh, God. Why would Tash raise a little finger to help Ned, of all people? Cassie realized she should've thought this out a lot more carefully. To start with, if Ned thought a plan up, it was doomed to failure.

But Tash was watching her with an odd look. An almost pitying, concerned look.

"Of course. I know just the woman. She's very good." Tash's voice was gentle. "You can have every confidence in her, Cassie."

This was playing all wrong.

Why was Tash's voice gentle? Too late, Cassie knew Tash hadn't been fooled. She was awfully hard to fool at the best of times and this wasn't Cassie's best time.

Tash knew. Tash knew what had happened before and she knew it was happening again.

"I'll get her number and call you first thing tomorrow. Don't worry, dear. I'll arrange it all." Tash gave her a pat on the hand.

"I can take care of things." Cassie got the words out through her gritted teeth.

She forced herself not to snatch her hand away. Tash was being nice.

No. Tash was daring to feel sorry for her again. Cassie much preferred the hostile relationship they'd built up again after the last time Tash had felt sorry for her. Cassie would rather feel like the rebel daughter she'd been since her teens than the pitiful daughter she'd been for a while. She hated being the Cassie who needed Tash and Daddy's help and support. She hated realizing that she'd gone back to running to someone else to solve the problem. She'd wanted someone else to tell her what to do after all these years of refusing to let anyone do that.

Cassie had a distinct desire to go bite her stepmother and her patting hand. And then slug Ned for getting her into this.

And then kick herself for being stupid enough to walk into this without thinking things through.

* * *

"Cassie?"

"You came!" Cassie stared at the figure standing by the door. "Have you been waiting long? I was at Dad's."

"Not too long. I thought about calling you back, but then the kids were driving me crazy and finally I got them out of the house and I thought you sounded like you could use a visit. I came over before I chickened out." Emily sounded hesitant but friendly. She sounded almost like the old Emily.

"I'm really glad. I think I've messed up again. You always cleaned up afterwards for me. Oh, come in, silly. Don't hang out by the door. I'll fix us a drink." Cassie was pleased with the last inspired sentence.

She hadn't had a friend over for drinks in ages. Maybe since Emily last came over. How long ago had that been?

"What do you have to drink?"

"Nothing."

Emily laughed.

"I figured. I stopped at the store on the way. Gin and tonic, Cass? You do have glasses, I hope?" Emily held up the bottles and came through the screen door.

"Yeah. Sit down and let's talk." Cassie felt a sudden sense of happiness come over her.

Emily was back. Maybe things weren't as bad as Cassie thought.

Cassie poured gin and tonic.

* * *

"You should've waited," Emily told her. "You never could lie to Tash. I always had to come up with how to deal with her. Remember?"

Cassie bit her lip. She recalled some of the ways Emily had managed to deal with Tash. And both Dad and Tash had thought Emily was a good influence on Cassie. They still did, deluded creatures.

"Thanks, Em. So where were you when I screwed up this particular time?" Cassie kept staring at her buddy as if Emily wasn't real.

Maybe Em wasn't real. She didn't look the same. Or maybe she did. She looked a lot closer to the Emily that Cassie remembered from college. But the last Emily had been Mom and Wife Emily. Emily didn't resemble that slightly matronly, carefully made up and wardrobe coordinated Emily.

"By the way, you look good. You've lost weight."

"Cassie! The last time you saw me I was pregnant with twins and Jill was under a year old. Of course I weighed more!" Emily sniffed and then paused. "Not eating after Jim gave me the "Big Announcement" worked better than Weight Watchers, though, for dropping the pounds. It took me weeks before I could believe he meant good-bye when he said it."

"Oh, damn, Emily, here I am running off my mouth and you're telling me you and Jim split up? You were so h…" Cassie thought about her next word. "…well, not happy, maybe, but so settled. Yeah. The two of you were settled. I thought you were going to be married forever and ever."

"Me, too. But the idea scared Jim. Four kids *really* scared him." Emily's smile trembled at the ends. "Of course now we have joint custody and he gets all four of them to deal with every other weekend and on the holidays. That's more than he did when he was married to me. Serves him right."

"Bastard," Cassie said.

"And you're worried you're crazy? You make perfect sense to me!"

The two them both started laughing.

"God, Em. I'm sorry I haven't talked to you since forever. I missed you." Cassie looked down at the gin and tonic she was drinking. "I haven't had one of these since we last met. They aren't bad. But I just never drink them without you."

"I haven't done a lot of things we used to do together, Cass. I was too busy trying to keep everything together. Whenever I saw you in the last few years, you were always such a free spirit. I was probably envious. Oh, hell. Of course I was envious."

"And I thought you'd figured out how to be a grown up! I envied you!" Cassie had forgotten the fun of confessing all your deepest hidden feelings.

"Man, were we stupid."

"Yeah, and now we're just drunk." Cassie stared at the glass she'd refilled more than once. "I haven't been drunk in years."

"Me, neither. I'm sure glad Jim has the kids this weekend. And I never thought I'd say that and mean it." Emily began to laugh again.

"But Em, what should I do?"

"Well, you don't seem crazy to me. Drunk and feckless, maybe, but not crazy. But I'll admit this voice sounds serious."

"I'm scared this will be like last time," Cassie muttered, at last.

"Well, is it? By the way, I still contend you weren't cracking up then. I mean, then everything piled on top of you and you needed out. How about now? Does your job stink? Are you engaged to some new jerk that you want to run away from?"

"No. None of that. I've been really careful not to make the same mistakes. So I don't understand what's wrong and I don't know what to do."

"Well, you can't do much about Tash suspecting something, so don't worry about it. You do need to go on with the shrink appointment, I suppose. Hmmm. What can I do to help?" Emily sized Cassie up. "I know. I'll dress you properly for a visit with the psychiatrist. You never could dress right for important occasions."

"I've been dressing myself for years, Emily."

"Now let someone who knows how do it," Emily answered. "And call me when you're done with the doctor. I want to know if things are going to be all right."

"I don't think one visit will cure everything, Em."

"Well, it's a start."

Chapter Four

Cassie fingered the pearls around her neck. Her dad had given them to her when she turned twenty-one. She wore them on special occasions. Special occasions like job interviews, funerals and, now, first visits to the psychiatrist. Cassie lumped them all under "Things You Don't Like Doing."

For a moment Cassie wondered if she'd like her pearls more if she wore them to different types of events.

Naaaw.

Cassie studied her surroundings, trying to ignore the knot in her stomach. The reception area was tastefully decorated. The walls were off-white, the abstract swirls of the one painting on the wall were soothing, and the gray leather chairs were surprisingly comfortable. Everything was designed to make you relax.

The whole place made Cassie very nervous.

"Ms. Majors?" The woman who stepped out didn't make Cassie feel any better. This woman didn't dress carefully for special occasions. She just dressed that way all the time. Cassie could tell. "Dr. Blessingham."

Cassie stood up, carefully smoothing her silk skirt.

The woman held out a nicely manicured hand and gave Cassie's hand a measured, firm shake. Then she dropped her hand to her side and stepped aside just enough to let Cassie into the inner office.

"Well, then." The woman looked her over. No soothing bedside manner here. "What can I do for you?"

"Well—uh—" Cassie willed herself not to stammer in the face of authority. "Actually my stepmother recommended you."

"Natasha Cassidy. Yes. You mentioned that on the telephone. A delightful woman."

Cassie was sure that was why she had gotten an appointment so quickly with such a popular doctor. Using Natasha Cassidy's name tended to move things along.

"She said you're a specialist in a problem I may—I am having. But I don't know much about you." Cassie knew that wasn't quite as forceful as she wanted it to be, but in the face of the other woman's formidable courtesy that was the best she could do.

"You'd like my credentials?" The woman smiled. Once. Nicely.

Cassie wished she had that professional niceness down herself. It must come in really handy.

The only problem was that all that professional niceness didn't warm up those eyes of hers.

Cassie was getting the same feeling she did at banks. It was her money but somehow she always got intimidated as the bank officials waited, patiently and politely, for her to make her case as to why she needed that money. Cassie mustered her courage.

"Yes."

"Of course. I graduated from Yale, went to medical school at Duke, I worked several years at the Mintzer Institute..." She moved smoothly through all the right steps. Cassie started to tune out. "...where I began to develop a particular interest in a number of severe psychoses. For example I have written a number of papers on auditory hallucinations..."

Psychosis? A psychosis sounded pretty severe. Auditory hallucinations? The doctor sounded plenty qualified, but none of this was reassuring Cassie at all.

"But I'm sure you aren't paying by the hour to hear about me. Something has brought you here. Would you like to discuss it?"

Dr. Blessingham had finished her spiel. She was waiting for Cassie to talk. To produce. To make it worth her professional time to listen to her new patient. At least that was the way it felt to Cassie.

She couldn't start talking about a voice that was telling her to chat with someone who might become president. That was just too out there. Maybe she could lead up to it with talking about a mere congresswoman. Oh, yeah. That would make everything much more reasonable.

"I keep thinking I need to talk to someone I don't know." Maybe she shouldn't even mention the voice at first. "I have to tell someone about a person named Lida. I think Lida might be an important person, actually—"

What the bloody hell are you doing, woman? Are you insane?

Cassie almost welcomed the voice back. In fact, that voice sounded like an island of reason right now.

"Well, I probably am insane. Why else would I be here?" Cassie answered.

"Well, people have many reasons to consult a psychiatrist. That would be one." Dr. Blessingham blinked, once, but spoke smoothly.

No. No, no, no.

You're an idiot. But you're not insane. You're only going to get yourself into worse trouble if you stay there. Get the bloody hell out.

"You may have a point." Cassie knew that when the voice started to sound reasonable she was in trouble, but her gut was agreeing with that voice. She trusted her gut.

Besides, the shrink had on a pearl necklace that looked way too much like Cassie's, and anyone who voluntarily wore pearls just wasn't Cassie's kind of person.

"Thank you. Now would you care to pinpoint your problem just a little more? Most people don't think they are insane. If they do, they usually have a reason. Maybe several reasons."

"I must be insane to be here." Cassie tried not to giggle. "At least that's the way I'm hearing things right now. I'm sorry I wasted your time, doctor. But I did pay your bill up front and now you have at least forty unoccupied minutes that you didn't have before. They're my gift to you. I hope you enjoy them. Good-bye."

Cut the sarcasm and leave.

Cassie stood up. She didn't bother to shake hands in farewell. She just walked out as fast as her pinching high heels would let her.

* * *

All the strange elation Cassie had felt after her exit had long since faded by the time she got home. After all, what she'd really done was paid a lot of money for ten minutes of nothing. As she unlocked the door she thought about the cleaning she had rearranged in order to make time for that stupid visit.

"What a waste."

"I totally agree." Cassie stopped, her hand still on the dead bolt lock, and then turned. The voice she'd heard wasn't inside her head. This voice was attached to a real body.

"What? Who—"

Wynn Harmon, dressed in jeans and a Hawaiian shirt, of all things, was sitting at her kitchen table. His sunglasses were tossed on the table and his long hair, no longer tied behind him, swept down to his shoulders.

He looked...different. Not as aloof. He looked a little wild. Oh, God. Her throat was getting dry just looking at him. And other parts of her body were getting wet. How did he *do* that?

Cassie looked at her cat. Pandora was curled up in his lap, something she never did with strangers. They both looked disapprovingly at her.

"That lock is a total waste. Your security could use a bit of work," he told her, as if it was her fault he was inside.

"Your manners could, too." Cassie heard the words come out her mouth before she could stop them. Well, there went one cleaning job.

But wait a minute. Forget the cleaning job. Why was he here at all? Most clients didn't make house calls to their cleaning people. And none of them ever made uninvited house calls.

For one minute his mouth moved up in a quite charming grin.

"Sometimes my manners do."

Cassie couldn't help herself. Against her better judgment, for just a minute, she was charmed. She had never seen him smile. That simple gesture had transformed his face and made him look—well, not spooky but attractive. Approachably attractive instead of good-looking-but-keep-away-handsome.

Then the mouth flattened back out again as if the smile had never existed. Maybe she had taken to seeing things as well as hearing them.

"Well, why the hell are you here?" Cassie figured the time for politeness had long since gone. "And how did you get in anyhow?"

"I'm here to see you. Getting in was absurdly easy. That dead bolt won't help you if anyone seriously tries to enter this place."

"I don't have anything worth stealing. Most everything here is from yard sales."

She saw him glance around and her heart sank.

What she liked to think of as a cheerful, bohemian interior suddenly looked like a disorganized mess. The brightly painted, mismatched chairs looked cheap instead of cheerful. The old sofa with the serapes thrown over the stains on the back looked shabby rather than comfortable.

Then something clicked.

She couldn't believe it had taken this long. The accent wasn't quite the same, but the timbre of the voice was. The snotty attitude expressed by those two voices was exactly alike. And "bloody hell" was something Wynn would say, wouldn't he? Her voice had said that, too.

"You rotten little swine."

"Ms. Majors?"

"I don't know how you've done it and I don't care. You can just stop doing it right now. And if I could figure out how to do it and have people believe me, I'd sue the hell out of you for this little trick."

"Pardon me?"

"Pardon me, my butt. You're the voice! You've been talking to me!"

Congratulations. You're smarter than you look.

"Stop it!"

Make me.

For one long moment Cassie contemplated all the ways she'd like to make this jerk stop. *Very* painful ways.

Then she took one, long breath. Calm. She needed calm.

"Fine. I don't know if I can make you quit. But I assume you didn't do this to show off what a great party trick you have. What do you want from me?"

"That's easy, Cassie. Art."

"Oh, no. Art."

"I need you to help. No one will suspect you if you give him my message since there's no reason for you to know anything about him."

"Yeah. Right. Why don't you just tell him?"

"Because Art and I would be dead before I got the chance. Or at least by the time I got out the door. Men with guns came after me in my home last night. They aren't sure when or how, but they know I'm going to send a message. They're waiting for me to do that. So I have to do the unexpected. I have to use you. By the way, that reminds me. I believe I'll need to stay here for a while. Once again, no one has any reason to connect you with me. I'll be much safer here than anywhere else I can think of."

"Why don't you just mind-zap Art?"

"He's not a person I can—uh—mind-zap. His mind isn't receptive to me."

"Good. E-mail him instead. See, I'm being fair. I'm assuming phone calls are monitored. Right?"

"I think so. And I plan to e-mail him—after you give him our code to let him know when to get the message. I'm not letting it sit on a computer where God knows who will read it before he does."

Cassie rubbed her forehead hard.

"Maybe you better talk to me a little bit more about this. In coherent sentences. Out loud. And slowly. I'm not understanding a word."

"Fine. But one more thing—"

"Yeah?"

"No more psychiatrists. They aren't going to help. You don't have a problem anyhow."

"Oh, yeah, I do. The problem may not be the one I thought I had originally, but it's a big one. A big, annoying Welsh problem."

"Ah. Yes, I see your point. But that problem isn't going away. Not yet."

She opened her mouth to explain to him exactly how she intended to get rid of her problem but he wasn't looking at her. Or, if he was, he wasn't looking at her face.

His gaze swept her up and down and a whole new wave of indignation took over. It was indignation that was making her so warm, right? Yes, of course. Cassie got angrier just because of that momentary cheap sexual thrill.

"God. I finally took a really good look at you. You may do after all."

He sounded both stunned and pleased.

Somehow that was even more insulting, though Cassie wasn't sure why just yet.

"Do for what, pray tell? And why are you looking at me like I'm a—a prize at auction you might want to bid on?"

"What? No. I'm just surprised. You look, well, respectable."

"I *am* respectable. A lot more respectable than people who break into other people's homes. Listen, bucko—"

"No, no. I just meant that you look like someone who could go to a senator's office without being pounced on by security first."

In fact, she doesn't look too bad at all once she is out of those cleaning rags of hers. Rather fetching, even.

Cassie paused. So many different types of anger were now pushing at her she wasn't sure she could express any of them.

"I—I—"

Calm down. You know I'm not here to do anything but get Art, me—and you—out of a mess. There's no need to get in a snit.

Cassie opened her mouth to blast him out loud. She shut it again.

Wynn blinked at her, looking genuinely surprised.

"Hey!"

"Yes?" Cassie crossed her arms.

"That was an evil thing to say to me."

"Yes."

"Totally uncalled for."

"Oh, I thought it was very justified. And Wynn—"

"Yes?"

"I didn't actually *say* anything."

"No. No, you didn't. *Oh, my God.*"

"I think I can do it, too. You know, your party trick. It isn't so hard. And, by the way, Wynn, besides being able to talk to you I think you should know I can hear what you're thinking. I hear your voice. Literally. Even when you aren't trying to send me a message. Got it, jerk? I can hear the thoughts you don't mean to transmit."

Of course. How could I have missed that? I just wasn't expecting—no one has ever been able to do that before with me...

"Shit." Wynn said out loud.

Cassie couldn't help grinning. It was gratifying to surprise the high and mighty Wynn.

Despite his words he didn't look angry. He looked surprised, then thoughtful and finally concerned.

Cassie stared in fascination. He had just shown more emotion in those few seconds than she had seen on his face in their whole previous acquaintance.

Then the thoughts came flooding in.

I suppose I'll have to trust you now. But you need to understand something. I picked you to help me because you could receive my thoughts and do what I want. Now you're both more useful and more dangerous, Cassie. And I'm afraid you're probably in more danger.

Cassie stopped smiling.

Chapter Five

"Quit that squirming. You aren't making it easier, especially since the last time I did anything like this was four years ago. To a dog."

"That doesn't reassure me."

"I'm not reassuring you. I'm shaving your hair off."

No, it won't be like Sampson, Miss Delilah. My gift doesn't reside in my hair. I don't think. It's been so long since I did cut my hair I can't be sure.

Very funny.

I hope I'm just being funny. What if we discover we can't communicate this way anymore?

"I guess we'd just have to go around talking like normal people do." Cassie squinted and then nodded. "OK. I think you'll do."

He looked at himself in the mirror.

"Oh, God. I haven't had my hair this short since I was a teenager and living at the—living where I was made to keep my hair short."

"Your hair doesn't look half-bad."

"It looks all bad."

Cassie looked again and disagreed.

Wynn was handsome, no matter how he wore his hair. The long hair made him look aloof and mysterious and untamed.

The buzz cut made him look tough. Lean, mean and dangerous. She wouldn't mind jumping him either way.

"Nonsense. You look like you're in the military. You should fit right in at the Pentagon. Well, I guess maybe you look like you just started in the military with all that white skin showing on your head. But still—"

"Wonderful. That's been my ambition for years."

"Listen, you look different. Really different. I thought that was your goal," Cassie pointed out.

"There's different and there's different. When it starts growing in I'll look even worse. Maybe I should grow a goatee."

"There's no pleasing some people."

He aimed one of those rare, lethally charming smiles at her. She felt the unwelcome warmth again as he did. She wished he'd stop that. She wished she'd stop feeling that way when he did smile.

"Thanks, Cassie."

But now we need to stop fooling around and get to business.

Cassie knew he was right. She'd been avoiding thinking about the whole situation—up to the point of accepting Wynn as an uninvited guest for the past few hours rather than probing for why he was here.

The frightening thing was that he seemed to be avoiding things, too. He had stepped into her house as easily as he had stepped into her mind and somehow he made everything seem right. But what was he going to tell her at last?

She looked at him as he brushed wisps of hair from his shoulders. She had a sudden urge to help him with his cleanup. Touching him, while giving him a haircut had started up all kinds of urges. Cassie kept her hands close to herself. But she wanted to touch him. She licked her lips, her mouth suddenly dry from less-than-pure lust.

Whoa, whoa, whoa, girl.

He was way out of her league. He was too handsome, too smart, just too much altogether. She'd have to remember that, even if he seemed more approachable suddenly.

His transformation came from more than a haircut. At some point—well, she knew the point had been when they both had suddenly realized she could enter his head too—he had changed.

Maybe it was hard to keep aloof and mysterious when you could mind-talk with someone. But, whatever the reason, she had the feeling Wynn had decided she was all right and he could show his real self. Wynn had a very nice real self that he kept hidden away for special people. That self had turned agreeable and open and rather charming.

Unless he was just acting, trying to make her trust him and go along with whatever it was he had planned. How could she tell? This mind-talking formed a bond, all right, but that didn't mean the person you had a bond with was trustworthy.

She didn't know this guy at all. She just gave him a buzz cut to disguise him from mystery bad guys, chatted with him via telepathy, and apparently was going to have him as a houseguest for an indefinite period.

Maybe she really was crazy, after all.

Will you stop that? You aren't crazy. You have a gift. You just don't know how to use it properly yet. I'll help you. I have to. It's an obligation. Besides, I need you to learn. You have to help me.

"I wish you'd stop walking into my mind unannounced," Cassie told Wynn. "It's like someone stepping into your bathroom while you're in there naked."

This time his grin was slow and wicked.

"Sorry," he said aloud.

I'm just not used to people noticing that I can do it.

That's a terrible excuse, Wynn.

"If you want to teach me how to use this—this ability, you can start now. How do I stop people like you from doing that to me?" Cassie asked.

"From getting into your mind?"

"Yes."

"Well—"

"Oh, no, Wynn. Don't try to make something up. You're the one who said I have to help you on this stupid mission of yours. If I have to help, I have to know what to do. I have to know how to do everything."

"I liked you better when I thought you were just a flake. Now you're getting logical on me."

"I never liked you. But since you're starting to pretend to be a human being, I guess I can pretend to be logical. And, let me tell you, until I can work this voice thing, I'd appreciate it if we communicate like two ordinary human beings."

"We are ordinary human beings. We happen to have an unusual talent, but everyone has a talent in this life. The use we make of our talent is what makes any human being extraordinary."

"Nice speech, Wynn. You give it often?"

"My mother gave the speech to me when she prepared me for what I could do a long time ago. I was impressed. I see that you aren't."

"Maybe it's all in the delivery. Or maybe your mother wasn't planning to use you on some dangerous escapade where she refuses to tell you much of anything that's going on." Cassie crossed her arms and glared.

"She wouldn't. Now Da would've had no problem with doing that to me if he thought he could've gotten away with it." Wynn didn't glare back. Instead he looked more and more cheerful and pleased. "Very well. What do you want first? To have your gift explained or to have the reason I'm here explained?"

"Whichever is the more urgent."

"Y' know, Cassie, for someone who looks like such a flake—"

"Careful, Wynn."

"For someone who seems as—as unconcerned with appearances as you, you often sound remarkably well-educated."

"For a cleaning person, you mean?"

"For any person."

"*Summa cum laude* from Williams. How about you?"

"Never went to a school in my life."

"You're kidding, right?" Cassie pushed back a laugh. "I mean, the way you talk and your house looks, and—Well, it seems so incredibly—conventional."

"If I have to stop name-calling, you do, too. No, my childhood was not conventional. We lived like gypsies when I was young. Da saw no reason to put me in school. We were never around anywhere long enough for me to go anyhow. Da taught me—well, he taught me everything I needed to know."

"I never would have guessed it."

"Appearances can be deceiving. I would never have guessed your educational background, either. Not, of course, that I would try to say anything disparaging about your appearance or your education."

"Of course not, Mr. Harmon. As interesting as I'm sure it would be for us to talk about our pasts—" Cassie deliberately refused to think about a certain part of her past right then in case someone chose to pry. "—I'm not as concerned about that right now as I am about our immediate future."

Wynn, who had been thinking about a man who had appeared god-like to his small son and about the near-escapes they'd had together both from the law and from those on the opposite side of the law, reluctantly pulled himself away from his memories.

Da had taught Wynn everything Da thought important. How to dress well and talk well. How to size up a situation and use it to advantage. How to use his gift to make people do what

Wynn needed them to do. Maybe that wasn't really everything, but it'd done fine for Wynn so far. After all, Da hadn't been all bad—at least not at first—and he'd never been stupid.

Despite everything, he missed his father. Sometimes.

He looked over the small woman in front of him. She wouldn't understand his past or what was going on with him now, but, by God, she was going to be shaping the future for them both. So it was time to explain what that meant.

He didn't want to.

Something had changed. She wasn't just some nutty free spirit who had managed to pick up on his mental signals. He didn't know her as well as he intended to, but there was intelligence there, and humor.

Bloody hell. He was starting to worry about her. He didn't want to feel that way.

Of course, even if she did agree, there was no danger for her. That was the whole point. She would simply slip in and out, and no one would be able to figure out who she was or why she was there because there was no logical reason for her to be part of this. No one would look for her afterward.

Even if they did, they'd never know where to look. It was that simple.

Despite those assurances to himself, Wynn knew things had changed. He had just wanted to get the job over with. Now he was afraid to start.

* * *

"Well, where is he?" Emmanuel Rauss looked at the two in front of him.

They looked at each other. They looked at the floor. They didn't look at him. Emmanuel took that as a very bad sign.

"We lost him for a minute. Sir."

Carter looked almost as miserable as he should about making such an admission.

But not quite miserable enough.

"If you lost him briefly, then you must have found him again?"

There was another long silence.

"Not yet." This came from Ullmann.

"Then he's gone. And you have no idea where he is."

"Well, we're looking. We have someone looking at his computer files. And, after all, we have all the contents of his house to find clues in."

"And you think Harmon is a careless man? After all, we are talking of someone who managed to escape you quite easily."

"There must be some clues somewhere. He left everything behind. He was in a hurry."

"Or he planned this very expertly. I may have underestimated this Harmon. I still don't understand his connection with the senator, so I couldn't use him properly. What have you found out about him so far?"

The two other men looked at each other again. Emmanuel began to think he was dealing with complete incompetence. He hated that. He could feel some anger beginning to bubble and strove to be polite. Perhaps he was jumping to conclusions. He would give them another chance to explain.

Still, his fingers began to drum, just slightly, on the chair. He was being patient, very patient, but he wanted something besides foolish looks. He dealt with intelligent people whenever possible. Stupidity was a waste of his valuable time. That was why he had long ago chosen to only be with a select few who understood what he needed.

These people were failing him.

"Well?"

"There isn't much." Ullmann looked even gloomier when he had to say that. "He doesn't seem to be the sort of fellow you can track easily. No school records, no steady girlfriend—or boyfriend—no insurance, no known living family—"

"The senator must speak to him regularly for a reason. We know he can get in touch with Harmon night and day from our surveillance equipment. At least he used to. Of course, we had to take that equipment out once the senator announced his candidacy, since too many people are now checking for bugs. So. What is Harmon's area of expertise?" Emmanuel smiled encouragingly, but wondered if they even knew that much.

"Well, we think… As far as we can tell, he's something of a mind-reader."

"What?"

"There are stories about him. Nothing we can pin down. Politics is new for him. What he usually does is a little mysterious. Wealthy people employ him to find things when they seem gone forever. Jewels, people…" Ullmann swallowed. "Naturally, people in power don't like to talk about hiring someone like that. One woman said he found her kidnapped granddaughter when the police weren't able to. We don't know how he does it, but there are rumors of some kind of E.S.P. Everything has been kept very quiet and confidential, though."

"E.S.P. Mind-reader. Oh, God. A clever charlatan? I thought better of the senator." Emmanuel frowned as he pondered the problem. "Maybe there's something more to this. Something you haven't found out yet. And, of course, why is the senator talking to someone like this at all? What has he lost?"

Whatever Art Hornsby wanted must be important if he was willing to risk using someone with Wynn Harmon's reputation. Emmanuel knew of nothing in the senator's background that would make him willing to risk ridicule for psychic aid.

That alone was worth some consideration.

"Perhaps your contact could find out," Carter hesitantly said.

He immediately stopped when Emmanuel looked at him.

"My contact with the senator is already working on the problem. She's getting very little help from my people outside, though." Emmanuel frowned, almost impersonally, at the two men.

They both shifted their feet.

"He has very little of a personal nature in the house and no correspondence. He didn't use much e-mail, either, for example. Not that we could find."

"Hmmm. I find that difficult to believe. When people watched him they saw him on the computer for long periods of time."

"We're looking."

Either his men were stupider than he had originally judged or Harmon was far, far more than Emmanuel had anticipated.

Emmanuel hated to believe he had misjudged his people, although they were giving many indications of their stupidity at the moment.

On the other hand, Harmon might be an even more complicated problem than he had originally believed.

"Look harder." His voice became even softer. Perhaps he would have to start looking for himself.

He didn't mind eliminating complicated problems.

Chapter Six

"Art contacted me about a year ago. Very privately, you understand." Wynn leaned forward as he spoke, hoping Cassie realized what this meant to them both.

"I had no idea who he was then or what he had planned. Art wasn't saying much. He knew that as soon as people heard that he wanted to run for president, things wouldn't be the same for him. And if they ever heard why he contacted me, he'd be laughed out of office."

"You don't have to look at me. No one would ever think to ask me, even if I wanted to tell." Cassie shrugged.

She didn't like the questioning she saw in Wynn's eyes. He shouldn't have to wonder about her.

"Maybe not," Wynn answered.

He moved back and away from her as his mind closed.

"He wants to be president. That isn't news now that he's announced. But Arthur Hornsby is a cautious man. He wanted to see what some of his potential advisors and confidantes really thought of him and his campaign before he committed himself to anything. He wanted to discover his potential opponents' weaknesses. And, somehow, he heard of me."

"And he believed in your abilities?" Cassie wasn't sure if she should be impressed or appalled.

"He doesn't know everything about me, of course. I never tell people everything. He just knows what most people do. I can find things out about people. Art doesn't ask how. I usually choose to work for people like that. If they don't know how I get my information, then they don't question its validity."

"So, even though he doesn't know how you do this, you became his little mind-tapper?"

"To some extent. He didn't know how useful I could be. I wasn't sure how useful I could be myself at first. I can't see into everyone's thoughts. Some people I can find no link with. Others have a weak connection with me. With some, I can have very clear pictures for limited amounts of time. And it's always been harder for me to project my thoughts into others' brains. I've never had anyone hear me thinking before you. But then, my gift can't always be commanded or forced."

"In other words, it isn't controlled?" Cassie asked, sweetly.

Wynn shrugged.

"So what do you do for the senator? Go to cocktail parties and hang out, listening?"

"Sometimes. I'm not very good at cocktail parties, I admit. Usually I find out other ways. I'm known to be flexible and resourceful on assignments. Art has been pretty pleased with what I've been able to come up with for him, especially when everything always checked out. Gradually what I've been doing, well—it's become pretty big-time. In fact, lately I've started having some delusions about becoming part of his staff somehow." Wynn swallowed. "That's a step up from what I usually do."

Cassie looked at Wynn. He seemed to be telling the truth, but he didn't look as pleased as most people in the D.C. area would be to make that announcement.

"Part of the president's staff? That sounds impressive. But? I can tell there is a 'but' coming."

"Very perceptive of you. I ran into something I didn't expect. You see, I began to get flashes of one mind that was intent on more than campaign finance or policy or cutting some political enemy's throat. I began to realize that someone was out to seriously use Art."

"Lida."

"Lida. She wants him to be elected president and she wants to be his running mate." Wynn stopped, abruptly.

"So she's ambitious." Cassie shrugged, too. "That's pretty common in politicians."

"She's evil. I don't say that lightly."

The old, spooky Wynn was back. The one who frightened her. She couldn't read his thoughts at all, and his face had become a blank mask. He looked at her with his intent stare as if he knew all the evil mysteries of the universe and intended to tell her just enough about them to scare her.

And he was.

"How is she evil?"

"She's twisted and she has a—a group of allies who are evil. They know that they could never get themselves into power directly, but Arthur Hornsby is a chance for them to get what they want indirectly. You see, he loves her. Or at least he loves the Lida he thinks he knows. And he respects her enough that he might just consider making her his vice president."

"Oh, man." Cassie rubbed her neck. "Well, there are a bunch of problems here. First, it doesn't say much for Art's—uh, Senator Hornsby's—judgment. Second of all, he's married. And third, if Lida is so evil, why is he involved with her at all? I mean, when you say he loves her, I figure you don't mean he loves her from afar."

"No, not from afar. That isn't general knowledge, of course. And as to the rest, well, it's not easy to find Lida out. But for my gift, I'm not sure I could see what she wants. All her life she's learned to conceal emotions and show what people want to see. You see, not only is she a politician, but her family has been involved in politics for years—her father is one of Art's oldest friends. In fact, he was Art's first campaign manager."

"There's more to this, of course, or you wouldn't be so worried. What does she want, exactly? Other than to sleep with Art and be vice president?"

"I'm not sure how much is safe to tell you. And I see this through her mind—sometimes—so what I understand may not be all accurate."

"How much danger will I be in if I go to warn Art?"

"Enough. I don't want there to be any, but that is a possibility."

"Then tell me everything. I'm not risking my life on just you saying that there's a problem. Besides, what can I tell the senator to convince him if I don't know anything?"

"I do hate it when you become logical."

Cassie waited.

"I think that Lida has more in mind than being a mere vice president. I just recently figured out that she's meeting with someone dangerous. She may have hired him to work for her, just like Art hired me. But he does other things for her."

"Things like—?"

"She ran for president and couldn't make it on her own. She may have decided she doesn't want to wait another four years to try again and possibly fail."

"I don't think I like the way I see this is going."

"Well, she was widowed and became a representative because of that death. I can't believe the idea hasn't occurred to her that Art could die in office." Wynn's voice was calm, but she saw him tighten one hand into a fist. "I can tell she wants to be president. And once I realized Emmanuel was involved..."

"Emmanuel? I don't understand."

"Of course not. You've never heard of Emmanuel Rauss."

"I've barely heard of Arthur Hornsby!"

"Not many people know Rauss. I do. Emmanuel's philosophy is that he is above all rules because he's the smartest man in the world. No, wait. He's probably God by now. After all, when we first met, Emmanuel wasn't his name. Anyhow, he has a small, handpicked group of those he's decided are intelligent and superior people. All of them do exactly what he asks them to. If Lida's willing to use him, then she's willing to be ruthless to get what she wants. And if he's willing to help Lida, then he'll do anything to get what they both want."

"Oh, boy. And she could be a heartbeat away from the presidency. If everything works the way she and Emmanuel have planned. That's what you're thinking."

Cassie didn't even have to use telepathy for this one.

There was another pause.

"Wynn?"

"Yes?"

"Why?"

"Why what?"

"Why bother? Why you? Why me? It sounds to me like Art is a two-timing politician who got fooled by the wrong person. Why do we have to fix it?"

"Because—" Wynn tried to think.

He couldn't come up with a simple answer to that. He hadn't even asked the question before. All he'd known was that he had to stop it.

"Because I don't want Emmanuel or Lida anywhere near power and I don't want them to win. And—and because I think Art is more than what you say. He trusts me as much as he trusts anyone. I don't usually get trusted much. I don't want to let him down."

Cassie let out a long sigh.

"Well, if you feel loyalty to Art, then I guess there's a reason for that loyalty," she said.

Did he feel loyal to Art? Wynn wasn't sure. Maybe that was what the sense of responsibility he felt was called. He just knew he couldn't let Art be destroyed without trying to stop it.

"Well, of course the bad guys are chasing me with guns." Somehow Wynn felt more comfortable with that reason. That sounded less—less altruistic. More real. He wished he hadn't thought of it last. "If Art or I don't get rid of them, I suspect they'll keep doing it."

"That one works for me." Cassie nodded. "What do we do next?"

* * *

"Darling, I'm so glad you could make it here tonight!" Lida ran to the man at the doorway and threw her arms around him. "I know how busy you are with the campaign."

Art Hornsby smiled. That was one of the many things he liked about Lida. She was reserved and professional in public and completely different for him in private. He wished his wife had learned that trick years ago.

"How could I stay away with the two of us in the same town?" he answered.

"I hoped you would think that way. That's why I made sure you knew I was in this hotel." Lida smiled at him. "I ordered something from room service. Would steak and champagne work for you?"

"You know it always does, dear."

Art settled into a chair while she adjusted the light near him. That was another thing he liked. She saw to his comfort. Not many young women knew how to do that properly. Perhaps it came from her late marriage.

She was young to be widowed, but she'd married an older man. When he'd died from a heart attack a few years ago, she'd been chosen to fill his term in office. That wasn't unusual. What was unusual was that she had been re-elected on her own.

She'd even made a much stronger showing in the presidential primaries than anyone had expected until the realities of campaign funding and name recognition hit her. Yes, Lida was young and deferential and, to top it off, a smart politician.

Too bad he was married. She would make the perfect first lady.

She kissed him, very lingeringly. Perhaps politicians and first ladies didn't need that particular qualification, but he liked that about her, too. In fact, he might even rank that higher on the list of things he enjoyed about her.

The phone rang and they both frowned.

"I'll only be a minute. I hope it isn't room service saying they're delayed—" Lida moved to the telephone.

"Hello, Sis."

Lida smiled. She didn't have a sister. Only one person called her that. Her sorority sister. They were as close—closer—than most sisters.

"What's up? I have a visitor with me."

"Ho. I understand. I just thought I'd pass on something amusing. No. Perhaps it wasn't something amusing. It could be a problem. At any rate, I'll make it quick."

"Yes?"

"I had a potential new patient come in. You're becoming popular. This one was obsessed with talking to someone about a Lida. I thought of you right away since it's a fairly unusual name and she said this Lida was important. She ran away before I could find out much more, but I thought you'd be pleased to know you are gaining your own group of special fans."

"She wasn't dangerous, I hope. I'd hate to have to alert some security."

"I doubt it, though I guarantee nothing. Being able to forecast which patient is a threat is an impossible business and not one I want to engage in. But she seemed almost normal. I just thought I'd let you know in case of any problem. Stay alert, but probably nothing will come of it."

"Aren't you violating some sort of patient-client code?" Lida almost smiled.

"Oh, please. This involves you, Lida. Besides, she isn't my patient. Anyhow, I'm sorry I interrupted. I didn't know you were busy tonight."

"Thanks. Believe me, I don't want to keep my visitor waiting."

Lida hung up and turned to Art.

"Anything important, dear?" Art asked as she came toward him.

"Oh, no. That was just a friend with a mildly interesting story to tell me. Now, where were we?" Lida slid into his lap and rested her head against his chest, close to his heart.

* * *

"Hey, Cassie!" Another, very familiar voice, interrupted before Cassie could say anything more. Maybe that was just as well. Cassie wasn't sure what to say. Ned ambled into the kitchen. "What's happening?"

"Oh. Ned." Cassie knew she was staring as if she hadn't ever seen Ned before. That wasn't too far off. She had actually forgotten about Ned's existence. "Ned, this is Wynn. Wynn, Ned."

She saw the two men eyeing each other. Ned, usually the most amiable guy in the world, looked like he was considering a scowl. Wynn had gone well past considering having one. His frown was a masterpiece in threat faces.

Oh. She hadn't even thought about this when she told Wynn he could stay. Well, she hadn't told him exactly, but he knew he was staying.

Ned was used to staying, too. He knew he could drop in whenever he wanted and be there as long as he wanted. At least he could up until now. Why not?

Cassie had long since realized that his casual coming and going meant nothing much, and she enjoyed his uncomplicated company. She was alone too much, and having Ned around was better than nothing. She was no longer sure if Ned had ever really meant anything more to her.

Cassie couldn't help contrasting the two men in front of her. Ned was still red-haired, tall, and good-looking. None of that had changed. She'd always liked that. What had always amused and infuriated her about Ned, though, was the lazy acceptance that whatever came along in his life would be fine since he had no control over what happened. That acceptance was in the way he moved and thought and spoke.

His current annoyance was unusual. Cassie knew that if she had thought at all about Ned's reaction to seeing Wynn, she would have thought Ned would have no problems with having another male in her house. Ned never cared about anything in particular.

Now Wynn was different. Some people might think he looked a little too exotic with his dark hair and direct, dark stare all combined with pale skin and a tall, thin frame. She thought he was breathtaking.

Now, even more than his looks, it was the alertness, almost wariness, coiled up inside him that made Cassie want to go and cuddle him, just the way she did Pandora, until he calmed down enough to relax and trust her.

She had a feeling he might lash out first, just the way her cat did sometimes. You could tell Wynn was used to fighting for what he wanted. Cassie respected that even though she wished he didn't think he had to fight her.

She looked at him again. He seemed aloof but watchful as he contemplated the other man. Something about his stance and attitude struck her as overwhelmingly male, territorial and sort of sexy. She fought a smile.

Maybe she didn't want to pet him exactly the way she would Pandora.

"Wynn is going to be a houseguest for a while, Ned." After admitting that fact out loud, Cassie turned to Wynn. "Ned and I are long-term...um..." What were they anyhow? "We've known each other for a long time."

Wynn grunted. He shot her one guarded look.

I don't need anyone else knowing where I am.

Ned is harmless.

No one is entirely harmless. Remember, I trust you because I must. But I intend to trust only you.

"Got any beer, Cass?" Ned opted to ignore the other man and wandered to the fridge.

"If you left some from last time, Ned." He didn't usually.

Ned pulled out a carton of ice cream instead and began to scoop some out into his favorite bowl.

"Cassie, are you going to help?" Wynn apparently had also decided to ignore the other man. "We can't fool around much longer."

Cassie knew she ought to say no. That would be the logical response. Whatever it was Wynn had in mind, she shouldn't get involved. She'd spent a good portion of the last five years making sure she didn't get involved in any way with anything.

Wynn might be tempting, but she wasn't an idiot. Cassie swallowed and got ready to say no.

Right then was an unfortunate time to remember some of the last advice her mother gave her.

"Cassie, I raised you to care. Logic will kill you. Don't smirk at me. You're going to die inside, child, unless you realize what you're doing and follow your heart instead."

Her mother had thrown herself into all kinds of causes. Cassie'd disliked that whole thing intensely and vowed she was never going to be that stupid.

She'd decided to follow logic and self-interest despite what her mother had told her. But Mom may've had a point. Logic had gotten her—well, what had logic gotten her? Cassie was living alone in a condo, cleaning houses for a living, and realizing that Ned was about the closest thing to a friend she had in the world.

Cassie stared at Ned, happily pouring chocolate syrup on top of the ice cream. Ned was doing what he always did. She was getting irritated like she always did. That was familiar. She let Ned hang around even after they had called it quits because—because she knew him. He was predictable and safe and someone to talk to besides Pandora. And he'd never presume to judge her. Not like her family always did. Judging Cassie was one thing her mother had in common with the rest of the family.

But Ned, and all the rest of her life, was boring. As boring as she had thought Wynn's life was, not too long ago.

Wynn was pushing her into something she knew nothing about, something scary, something unfamiliar. She hated being pushed. She knew this was going to be more work than she had taken on in years—maybe ever. And there was no logical reason to do it.

Cassie.

Wynn, don't. I'll make up my own mind.

"Cassie, you got any motor oil? My car's been having problems." Ned grabbed a spoon without asking. Like he grabbed anything of hers he needed.

"Check the garage."

Wonder of wonders, Pandora ignored Ned's food and chose to go rub herself against Wynn's legs. Wynn picked her up.

"I've never been around pets much. They certainly can attach themselves to you," Wynn said aloud. "I could get used to this."

Please, Cassie.

She could tell Wynn hated asking that. He wanted her to do something for him, all right, just like Ned did. But he was asking first and he was sorry he had to ask. At least that was different. And all of a sudden she wanted something different. She was desperate for something different.

"Believe me, my cat doesn't do that for everyone. For anyone. She was wandering around near my trash can when I took her in. I think she holds a grudge against most humans because one abandoned her."

All right. To hell with making up my mind. I don't have one. Logic never was my strong point, I guess. I'm already a pushover for every stray who comes in the door. Who am I to refuse to help save the world and life as we know it?

Mom would have been proud. Of course, her father and stepmother would be appalled if they ever found out. Well, she never could please all of her family anyhow. And they never would find out.

"I already did check the garage. Damn, Cassie, you mean you're out of motor oil? That means I'll have to go get some at the store. Are you sure? Can you run me over there? I've kinda been putting off taking care of things, and now my car is pretty bad. I better not use it."

Cassie had heard that excuse and that plea many, many times before. He'd at least learned not to ask to actually drive her BMW. She'd chauffeur Ned sometimes, but she'd only give him her car if it was a life-or-death emergency.

Unfortunately for Ned, though, the life-or-death emergency she was dealing with had nothing to do with him.

"Sorry, Ned. Can't help you this time. I'm going to be sort of busy."

Ned's protests became a distant whine in the background when Wynn turned toward her and began to speak.

"I appreciate your help, Cassie." Wynn's voice was soft. "I know you have your own life and I'm pushing things here. I understand. You have no reason to help me or even believe what I say. The worst of it is that I know I shouldn't ask this of you even though I am asking for your help anyhow."

"I know." Cassie kept the scowl on her face but could feel a little softening inside.

He sounded so sincere. Then she reminded herself that he wasn't just asking her for a ride to the local store. Wynn had already told her that this was dangerous.

But there is one other thing, Cassie. Something important. Something you need to know first.

"Now what?" Cassie asked, none too pleasantly.

Wynn leaned toward her. Cassie had to actually fight the pull he exerted. She wasn't sure if he was looking at her that way deliberately, but she knew she wanted to agree to anything if he would keep staring at her so intently. She'd almost prefer to think he was using some sort of hypnosis on her rather than know, deep down, one reason she was ready to agree to whatever he said was because she was attracted to him.

Emmanuel knows me—or he used to years ago. We both had different names then. I just figured out that he was involved and who he must be a few days ago. That's when I realized I needed to get out of sight before he figured out who I was. If he finds out I'm still around, he'll know I'm not just a threat because I'm Senator Hornsby's employee. He'll go after me, and he'll go after you, too, if he finds out about you.

Why?

Because Emmanuel is like us. He has our gift, too.

"Fine. Wonderful. Guess he can join the crowd," Cassie said with disgust.

There was a second of silence while Wynn looked blankly at her.

"Bloody hell, woman, you need to take this more seriously!" Wynn sputtered into a laugh.

When he stopped laughing but remained smiling, Cassie smiled back.

"Oh, I am. Much too seriously to do anything but laugh about it." She held out her hand. "So we're in this together now, partner?"

Thanks a lot, Mom. Look where all your integrity and values have gotten me.

Wynn took her hand and, instead of shaking it, just held it for a moment. She could feel the warmth of his hand, the thumb he nestled in her palm. Cassie liked the feeling.

If this guy could make her enjoy just handholding, what else could he make enjoyable for her?

"I guess so," he agreed with her reluctantly, almost as if he hadn't been the one pushing the idea a few moments ago.

Ned was looking at them.

"You two are weird," he announced. "And you're not making any sense."

"No kidding," Wynn muttered. "I'm afraid we may've even gone beyond that."

But his smile was still there.

Chapter Seven

"You're quite insane, woman. I've never heard of this Harmon person, if he even exists, and I've never heard of you."

Art Hornsby's face looked sterner and more menacing by the moment. His politician's mask was completely gone. She'd done the unforgivable by disparaging the woman he loved. And Wynn wasn't around to help her out.

"Cassie? Wake up. You must've fallen asleep on the couch."

Cassie woke up and almost wished she hadn't. Wynn loomed over her. She didn't feel much better awake than during her nightmare.

"Isn't it bad enough you march in and out of my house and my mind constantly? Do you have to regulate my sleep, too?"

"Hey!" Wynn scowled. "We just need to get ready. This is the big day. If this goes well, I can be out of your life in less than twelve hours."

"Listen, I'm sorry if I snapped. I have a headache. A bad one." Cassie thought about that a minute and then said, "No, I'm not sorry I snapped. You caused the headache."

"Huh?"

"I told you to not mind-talk me so much all the time. It hurts, OK?" Cassie shut her eyes a minute. "It's a little like trying to talk nothing but a foreign language all day."

"Oh." It had been so long since Wynn had learned to use his gift that if he ever had known that, he'd forgotten.

"And when you enter my mind, it hurts, too."

Wynn blinked. He'd never thought of that. He'd taken for granted his gift and his right to use it. Da had encouraged him to do that—but then, he'd learned long before this to be careful of what Da approved of. He hadn't meant to hurt her. "I try to be careful. No one else even knows I do it."

"Well, I know. And it hurts. Not as much as when you started but...it's not always pleasant." Cassie thought about what she said and shrugged. "I guess it's like sex. While it can be fun, the first few times aren't always great."

How had she known about his first... Then he realized what she meant.

"I'm sorry."

He was more than sorry. If what he'd been doing all these years to others was even close to what he'd felt back when he'd first been with a woman or, worse yet, how he'd felt at the Institute—The idea had never even occurred to him until now. "Cassie, I can stop. Everything. If you want me to. I really am sorry."

His mother had tried to tell him to be careful how he used his gift. But that had been so long ago that sometimes he got confused or didn't remember everything. He'd blanked out so much after she left. What he remembered he'd tried to live up to. Mostly. As soon as he understood what she meant. But he'd never thought of this.

He was an idiot. And more like his Da than he should be.

"No. It's all right, Wynn."

Cassie was looking at him, and he remembered again that she could hear his thoughts.

He couldn't remember when he'd last felt quite so awkward.

Really, Wynn. I'm getting pretty good at this. And now it's sort of fun.

She touched his cheek. He almost flinched. People usually didn't touch him at all except for a handshake or maybe a slap on the back.

"Are you all right?" Cassie looked concerned.

"Yeah."

He wished her touch hadn't been meant casually. He hadn't been with anyone for a long time. But, no, that wasn't what he wanted exactly. He didn't need just anyone's touch. He wanted to be with a particular someone right now. He wanted Cassie and no one else. Strange. He couldn't remember ever feeling that way before.

Wynn closed off the thought. No. He didn't have time for a need like that now.

"You had a phone call." Wynn finally remembered why he'd shown up in her bedroom in the first place. "Emma? No, an Emily called."

"Really?" Cassie bounded off the couch so fast that she got a little dizzy when she stood up. "She's waiting to talk to me?"

"She left a number." Wynn shoved the paper with a number at her and watched while Cassie ran for the telephone.

"Emily?"

"Cass? I've been working but then you didn't call and I figured I better check on you!"

"I'm glad you did." Cassie hesitated. How do you ask someone for advice about a person who is standing in front of you? "How are you?"

Fortunately, Wynn wasn't Ned. He began to back out of the room but he mouthed, "You need to get ready."

* * *

Cassie didn't look like she was paying attention. She looked engrossed in conversation with this Emily. Wynn scowled. Cassie never did look like she paid attention.

He hoped she would. He hoped she would manage to look all right. They needed to pull this off. And then, for all kinds of reasons, he needed to get out of her life.

"Don't push me." Cassie covered the telephone as she spoke to him. "I've already gone through a lot for this."

"Right."

"I had to contact my stepmother for the second time in a week for help! Believe me, that's a lot!"

Cassie's headache throbbed again as she remembered.

"You want me to contact someone so that you can see Senator Hornsby?" Natasha's eyebrows rose slightly. She did the eyebrow thing really well.

"You and Dad are the only ones I know who could get me access to the senator on short notice." Cassie spaced her words evenly.

"And why do you need to see him on short notice?"

"There's—there's this guy I met who works for the senator." Cassie had really had to think about this one. Everyone in her family knew how little she cared about politics.

"Yes?"

"He told me about what a huge supporter Senator Hornsby is for the environment. And—well, I just won a little money from the lottery and thought I could donate some."

"Cassie, darling! You don't still play the lottery, do you?"

"Well, just sometimes."

"This is so typical. You finally win a little money back from all you waste and then you go and fling it upon some ridiculous liberal political hack! I suppose I should be grateful you don't donate to some Third World organization."

"Well, that was my second choice." Cassie couldn't help it. Tash always pushed her buttons. "If you can't help me with this, I probably will."

Her stepmother sighed. But Cassie could almost see the wheels turning in her mind. A donation to a political figure had to be more useful in her scheme of things than a donation to some poor country.

"I'll see what I can do." Tash then looked at her. "And how did the visit go?"

"Huh?"

"The visit with the psychiatrist."

"Oh. Oh. Um. OK. I guess." Cassie's brain scrambled for a minute. "No one will tell me, of course. That's between the doctor and patient."

"Yes. Yes, of course. Cassie—"

"What?"

"Never mind. I'll see what I can do." But Tash didn't sound happy about things.

Cassie turned her back on Wynn as she began to concentrate on this new, hopefully more enjoyable phone conversation. She barely heard the click as he shut the bedroom door.

"What's going on, Cassie? Have you heard anything I've said for the past two minutes or so?"

"Not exactly. Listen, Em. The situation has changed. The good news is that I'm not crazy. No more than usual. But now let me tell you the bad news. Well, as much as I can safely tell you. Oh, yeah. I also need some more advice on how to dress."

* * *

"Do I look all right?" Cassie bit her lower lip.

Wynn studied her carefully. She straightened her posture and tried to look assertive. She used to be good at that, back a million years ago. Wearing her best old power suit was reminding her of then.

She didn't like remembering what she was like then.

"You look—" he bit off the word he wanted to use and blocked his mind.

She looked endearing. She looked like a kitten trying to be a tiger. She looked like easy prey if anyone wanted to pounce.

"You look fine." He finished the sentence.

She did look fine. She was dressed perfectly correctly, just the way a visitor to a presidential candidate should look.

But she also looked vulnerable with her eyes fixed anxiously on him, waiting for him to pronounce judgment on how she was dressed. Why was she worried about his opinion? She shouldn't have to worry.

He held her by the elbow, escorting her, as they got in the car.

"Maybe I should do this." Wynn said the words before he could think too much about why he was changing his mind.

Cassie stared at Wynn.

Cassie couldn't tell Emily everything, of course, but what she had said had been more than enough. Emily had told her not to get involved in any man's problems. Of course, Emily had her own reasons to say that. No one would feel too good about men if you had four little kids and no husband around.

Now Wynn was telling her the same thing. She probably ought to take their advice.

Cassie was bad at taking advice she didn't want to hear.

"Wait a minute. You're the one who got me into this because you absolutely can't be seen walking into Senator Hornsby's office anymore. You know you'll be spied on, or stopped before you get to him and then followed and taken away. These guys tried to get you at your house already, right? You know that if Emmanuel ever sees who you are he'll get the word to Art that you're a telepath and you'll be thrown out. That's what you've told me. You've spent hours convincing me that I'm needed to thwart the bad guys. Now you say *you* should do this?"

"I could disguise myself."

"Like the Secret Service or Art's guards couldn't spot you? Don't start with me, Wynn. I didn't dress up like Little Ms. Executive to be told you think I can't do the job. Listen, it was hard enough to come up with a reason for an appointment with the senator. Don't change the plan on me now."

"Yes, but—" Wynn didn't like this feeling. Maybe that was why he never liked working with other people. He never knew how to handle them. He'd been feeling very confused ever since this morning.

Cassie looked like she was going to yell at him but then she stopped and suddenly smiled at him. He liked her smile.

"Hey, wait a minute. You're worried, aren't you? About me. That's—that's sweet, Wynn."

"Bloody hell." *He wasn't sweet and he was never worried about other people. Let them take care of themselves.*

"Thanks. I should be insulted, but—thanks." Cassie suddenly gave him a hug.

For just a second Wynn was tempted to hang onto her. He let the feeling pass. Almost. He could still feel a little itch of temptation to show her what a real, serious bit of physical contact was all about. Instead he grunted and started the BMW.

He was crazy. This whole thing was getting to him. Or maybe the prospect of danger was getting him horny. Maybe that was what was bothering him so much about Cassie. Of course. Sometimes adrenaline did that to him.

Wynn thought it over and decided he might do something about that itch. After all, Cassie was attractive, especially when she cleaned up. She could grow on a man. Maybe he wouldn't leave immediately. He might just explore some possibilities. Later. When they were safe.

Or maybe he wouldn't. He might not even get the chance to try. He knew how women acted around him once they got to know him better. And he had said he was going to get out of her life as soon as possible.

"There won't be any place to park anywhere near but I'll circle the Capitol. I won't be more than ten minutes away, I swear."

"OK." Cassie's smile was still sweet and focused on him. Then she straightened up and stopped smiling. "Well, let's get this over with."

"All right. Let's." Wynn shoved aside the stupid last minute urge to keep Cassie far away from this mess and concentrated on getting out of the driveway. They had to do this.

* * *

"Thanks for letting me see you, Senator." Cassie kept herself from wiping her hands on her skirt. She stopped herself from fiddling with the pearls. She stared hard at her folded hands.

"Anyone who is interested in my contributions to the environment is more than welcome to my time, Ms..."

"Majors. Cassidy Majors." Wynn had wanted her to have an alias, but Cassie couldn't come up with any plausible reason to tell Tasha to do that for her. Besides, once again, using the Cassidy name meant something. Tash had gotten her an appointment in just a few days.

Cassie wondered if there had been the slightest emphasis on the word "contribution" when Art—the senator—spoke to her. If so, it was hard to tell. He was being pretty subtle about why he had agreed to see her. Oh, God. Maybe he wasn't interested. What had Tash said to him? Or had she even spoken to the senator? Maybe the secretary had mangled the message when she delivered it to him.

Cassie fought panic. His interest or lack of interest didn't matter. He had agreed to talk to her for some reason. Money was one very good reason why the Cassidy name got people access to places. That had to be why she had made it here. Art didn't know that she didn't have any of that Cassidy money.

Besides, all he needed to do was be just interested enough to listen for a few more moments.

"Yes. My friend, Horace Jones, told me what a strong supporter you are." That was the name that Wynn had told her was their code.

Art Hornsby's face didn't change. But he did lean back to study her a little more carefully.

"Yes. Horace. I haven't heard from him for a while."

"He's wanted to contact you. But he's been prevented. So he told me to be sure to mention his name to you. He hasn't forgotten you at all, believe me." Cassie felt like someone in a bad spy movie. "Anyhow. I would like to just write down how much I would like to contribute to your campaign. Tell me if this would be helpful."

She quickly wrote: WATCH OUT FOR LIDA. HORACE WILL BE IN TOUCH BY E-MAIL. USUAL TIME. DELETE EVERYTHING. DANGER.

"That would be generous, Ms. Majors." The senator casually picked up the paper and crumpled it up before he put it in his pocket.

"I know how busy you are, sir. I won't take up much more of your time. But I hope we can see each other again and talk over our mutual concerns." Cassie hoped that sounded like what a real contributor might say.

"I'd be happy to invite you to some of our functions, Ms. Majors. And thank you."

"You're very welcome."

Cassie stood up, smiled as nicely as she could—thinking of professional shrink smiles compared to professional politician smiles and how hers compared to them both—and left.

* * *

Art Hornsby stared for a long moment at the door after the woman left. Then he made his decision and picked up the telephone.

"Hey, Jock. I had a potential security risk in here. Tail her."

He settled back in the chair. He knew he didn't need to say any more. Jock was a damned good security officer and had been taking care of him for years. He trusted Jock more than the Secret Service detail that had recently been given to him. Jock would be quiet if he asked him to be.

Something fishy was going on. Who was that woman? And where the hell was Wynn anyhow? That fellow was too damn elusive for Art's taste.

Then the pain that he had carefully contained burst. He sat down, heavily, in the chair. Lida. His perfect woman. What was wrong with Lida? Did he have to question her, too? Or was something going to happen to her? Had he put her in danger somehow? Either possibility hurt.

His face hardened. There was at least one or two other possibilities to consider. Was this message the truth? Was someone using Wynn? Or was Wynn using him? He'd known Harmon for a far shorter period of time than he had Lida. Whatever the hell was going on, Jock better find that woman and get some more answers than he had now.

* * *

"I think it went OK." Cassie wanted to giggle as she hopped into the car. She would have wondered how Wynn had known to drive up just when she needed him except that she had signaled for him. This mind-reading stuff could be awfully useful. Too bad cab drivers didn't respond to telepathy. "I know he paid attention."

"God, I hope he understood." Wynn concentrated on the traffic before pulling back out. "He isn't a stupid man but this situation is a little...unusual."

"I think I made it clear enough."

Maybe it was because she was so busy congratulating herself on a job well-done that his next move stunned her. He suddenly pulled her hard against him.

Before she could react, he gave her a very warm kiss. His mouth was just the way she'd imagined. Tasty. Exciting. She had wondered if she'd like kissing him. She did. Yes, indeed she did. Once she got over her amazement, Cassie tried to deepen that kiss. Mmm. Tasty, exciting and—over. Just as abruptly as when he had pulled her against him, he pushed himself away.

What happened? Cassie stared, trying to recover.

"I'm *very* glad you got out of there." Wynn didn't say any more as he pulled the car smoothly away from the curb.

Cassie thought about that. He'd given her a great kiss because he was relieved? Naw. He had to have some other reason besides that.

Cassie opened her mouth to say something, anything, but then realized something else. "Hey! You missed our exit."

"No, I didn't."

"We take 66 out of here—hey! Wynn! I thought you knew this area."

"Like the back of my hand. And so does the driver following us."

"Oh, man." Cassie shut up. Sort of. How had Wynn managed to give kisses and keep an eye out for someone tailing them?

Where're we going?

Not to your house, that's for damned sure. At least not now.

Cassie hugged her knees. Weaving through Dumont Circle and heading for Georgetown didn't seem like a smart idea. Then Wynn doubled back. They were somewhere near Foggy Bottom—she thought, though she wasn't sure herself now—when Wynn suddenly made a sharp turn into an underground parking garage.

He hastily gave the keys to the attendant and almost pulled her out of the BMW.

"I think we've lost them for a bit." He fastened his sunglasses on his face and walked them out fast.

"Now what?" Cassie's legs began to ache from trying to keep stride.

"Now this." Wynn made another quick turn and then they were hurrying down the Metro escalator. "If we've lost them for just long enough, they won't be able to follow this."

"But—"

"I hope you weren't too attached to that car, Cassie."

Cassie thought about all the money and time and effort it had taken to get and keep her precious car. She damn well was attached to that car.

"Maybe we can pick it up from whatever impound lot they tow it to. In a few weeks. If all this is over." Wynn glanced her way and then shoved his newly bought Metro ticket into the turnstile. "I'm sorry, Cass."

Cassie swallowed and followed him into the city subway system. There had to be some way out of this. Wynn had to be wrong.

Gone. Her precious car.

Bloody hell, that's better than your life! We can't go back. They'll be looking for us. You'd better hope they don't find the damned car and trace it back to you.

"But you switched the numbers on the license plate," Cassie reminded him.

"I know. But if they look that hard they'll know some of the numbers were tampered with. They'll be able to figure out what it said originally. Bloody hell. We should get out of the area for a while. That was too close."

She slumped into the seat, too dispirited to do more.

She could see Wynn, for all his relaxed slouch in the Metro seat, was keeping an eye out for who entered the car. Fine. Let him keep watch. He was the one who had gotten her into this.

Suddenly she wanted to make him as unhappy as she was.

"You run away really well, Harmon. Running doesn't seem to bother you. Some of us like to stick around for our jobs and our houses and things like that."

Cassie didn't even try to keep the bitterness out of her voice.

"You've lost a car. For a while. Do you want to lose more important things?" Wynn kept his voice low and not too unpleasant. Still, Cassie shivered. The anger was oozing out of her, leaving just the unhappiness. "I've run most of my life, yes. And I've stayed whole and alive. You'd do well to follow my example."

I spent a lot of time running in the past, too, Wynn. I like it better when I can stay somewhere for awhile.

I'm sorry, Cassie. Not this time. I can't let you. You may not realize what would happen but you wouldn't want to get caught.

"Can I go home long enough to pack some things?" Cassie tried not to sound as hopeless as she felt.

"I think we'll be safe enough to do that. It'll take a while to trace you to there."

Not just her car, then. She'd had a feeling that was what he had meant before but had hoped she was wrong. It was her house, too. Her identity. Everything she'd built up after almost losing them all so many years ago.

"Cassie, for God's sake, don't cry. I'll fix it. I promise."

"Some things can't be fixed. Not a second time."

She was going to cry in another minute. He knew it. He could hear it. He had no idea what you were supposed to do when that happened. He hated for women to cry. Nothing made him feel more helpless.

He opened his mouth to babble out anything to stop the tears that would come next but what came out instead was "Maybe you need to talk about that."

No. Please. I didn't mean that. If we start talking, you'll cry for sure.

He heard Cassie hiccup out a laugh instead.

"You need to work on your sincerity around me, Wynn."

"No. It's OK. I mean, it isn't great if you want to talk about what's bothering you, but it's OK. I can handle that. Tell me."

"How about if I promise not to cry? I don't really like telling people usually, but I'd like to tell you."

Cassie wasn't even sure why. She never told people about her past if they didn't already know. And the only people from her past that she still talked to were in her family. They certainly didn't make her feel any better about what had happened when they discussed things. But she knew Wynn would be different.

"Sure."

"Try to sound just the slightest bit enthusiastic, Wynn."

"Right."

They exited the Metro and, once they got to the sidewalk, Wynn raised his hand. A taxi stopped and opened the door. Taxis never stopped that quickly for Cassie when she tried that.

Cassie looked at Wynn. She knew why. She was going to tell him because she would have to trust him with her life. He might as well know what her life had been like.

"See, I wasn't always a cleaning person. A really sought-after, well-paid cleaning person, might I add."

"I've had to pay you. I know that."

Cassie gave that hiccupping laugh again.

"In my previous life I was a lawyer. A trial lawyer. My career in litigation didn't last long, but it sure was memorable. I got a job with a big firm right after law school. That was impressive. My dad and my step-mom were bragging about me for the first time in their lives. I knew I was going to be a real hot shot. I got my car with my first paycheck. That was just going to be the beginning. My second and third paycheck went for a deposit on a fancy condo. But I wasn't going to stop there. I was willing to put in the sixty-hour work weeks—shoot, the seventy-hour work weeks. I was going to make partner."

"Impressive."

"I thought so. Except that I hated it. Somewhere around then my mom died. Maybe that contributed to the problem. Her death made me think more about what I really wanted. She had never followed the crowd in her life. I never figured out why she was ever interested in Dad. Well, anyhow. She told me I was more like her than I knew. Did I tell you she went and lived in a commune for a while when I was a baby?"

"I could see you doing that."

"Yeah? I never thought that was like me at all. That's OK. Once Dad married Tash and the commune folded, I got sent to a boarding school in New England to be shaped up. 'Polished' is how Tash phrased it. That wasn't me, either. To make a long story a little shorter, I disagreed with Mom and what she thought I wanted out of life. We drifted apart while I went to college and she got married to some hippie leftover. She'd always said I'd hate law school and working as a lawyer when Dad told me to go for it. Then she died. I wasn't even there. I was working on a trial."

"That must've been hard."

Cassie nodded. But she wasn't done yet. He might as well know the part that would really make him wonder about her. After all, he had to trust her with his life, too.

"Soon after that I began to forget things. Where I put depositions, phone calls...deadlines. Deadlines aren't the best things to forget when you're the most junior associate in the firm. I just couldn't keep my mind on what needed doing. I'd blank out. My stepmother said I had a nervous breakdown. Maybe I did. Or maybe I'm just a flake."

I didn't mean the word that way.

Yes, you did.

Well, I don't think that way about you now.

"Anyhow, I ended up taking a leave of absence from the firm. A leave of absence that has lasted until today, by the way."

"You were stressed."

I was scared, miserable, confused, always doing the wrong thing, alone, drinking a little more than I should, sleeping less than I should, unsure of what to do about anything...

"Yeah. Stressed. I decided I wasn't going to ever be that stressed again. Cleaning houses isn't too stressful. I used to envy my cleaning lady when I was at the firm. She could come and go when she wanted. So I decided to become her. After my up-and-coming fiancé moved out, I sold the condo, got my stepmother to swallow her pride and recommend me to a few people, and—here I am. But I always remember to write everything down that I need to do. Just in case I start losing it again."

Cassie wondered what Wynn would say to that. All of it. Everything she hadn't talked about for years.

"You seem to be happy now."

"Happier. Yeah. I'm happier. At least no one tells me what to do. I'm sick of that. I let my dad tell me, then the partners tell me. Now I do what I want. I've learned to manage on my own, without help, and that means I'm never going to need to conform to anyone's rules and expectations again."

"I can understand that."

He kept staring at her. Cassie couldn't tell what he was thinking right now. Then he smiled.

"Tell me some lawyer words."

"Huh?"

"You don't look like a lawyer. You don't sound like a lawyer."

"I have a perfectly good diploma hanging on my bedroom wall at home to prove it!" Cassie retorted, trying not to smile. "Mmm. *Res ipsa loquitur.* Pro se. Jurisprudence."

"Sounds like dirty talk to me."

"The bills can get obscene when you have to use too many of those words in one brief."

Cassie was laughing with Wynn when the cab stopped. Cassie blinked and stopped laughing. She'd forgotten until now, but they were at her home. The place that wouldn't be her home for much longer.

"I don't want to go in." Cassie made a decision. "It'll hurt too much. I've been so proud of this damn place. Of everything I managed to get after deciding not to be a lawyer. I'm afraid I'm a little too—too attached."

"Do you want me to go and fetch you some things?" Wynn's voice was very gentle. She nodded. "You can stay outside. Driver, wait here for just a few minutes. I'll be out shortly."

Wynn returned with two bags. He tossed one her way and had the driver go back to the Metro.

As the taxi let them off at the station and drove away, Cassie looked at him. They were on their own now, just the two of them.

"All right. Now what?"

"We're going to the airport."

Cassie felt totally confused.

"Where are we flying to?"

Wynn looked the least bit impatient with her question, as if she should know the answer already.

"We aren't. I'm going to charge two tickets to Miami on my credit card. Then we're borrowing a friend's credit card and renting a car."

"But—I'm not following. We're not going to drive to Miami, I take it? And what kind of friend just loans you a credit card?"

He looked at her again. Even though he said nothing, she could tell he was impatient. She'd just made another stupid comment? This was starting to feel like the first year of law school when she gradually began to believe she didn't know anything.

"That was a euphemism, Cassie. There is no friend. I have a charge card with another name on it. I rarely use that card, but I don't know of any rental agency that just takes cash. We'll look like we're flying to Florida. But we're going…someplace else."

"Jesus, you know a lot of tricky moves. You seem really used to a life on the run."

He could lie and he could run away. She'd seen him do that. Why did she think she could trust him with her life? You shouldn't go around blindly trusting guys just because they were great kissers and they made you feel like you wanted to jump their bones. Or just because sometimes they looked so alone and you knew how that felt.

Oh, God. And you couldn't think about those things in case they were listening in when you thought it.

Wynn gave her an odd look before he replied to what she had said.

"I told you my childhood wasn't conventional. Maybe I should be clearer. Da was a con man. I know a lot of tricky moves, Cassie. Well, don't stand there and stare at me like you're half-witted. Come on, then. It's time for me to show you a few of those tricks."

Chapter Eight

"The Bide-A-Wee Hotel?" Cassie couldn't stop chortling. "I can't believe I'm actually staying at a place that really calls itself that."

She wasn't even totally sure what state they were in. Wynn had just shrugged when she asked and told her it was probably better if she didn't know. He was just driving randomly—if he didn't know, no one would.

"Get used to life on the wild side with me, Cassidy Majors. This is only the beginning."

Cassie looked at the air conditioning unit in the window that had kicked on with a roar of sound but very little cool air to show for its efforts. She could see Wynn was silently studying the dust on the bureau.

"Yeah. I can tell life as I know it will never be the same again." Cassie's laughter stopped.

That wasn't much of a joke after all.

Wynn switched on the one dim working lamp near the twin beds. He sat on one of the beds. Wynn wasn't laughing either. He was staring at her.

All of a sudden her mouth felt dry.

"Cassidy?"

No one ever called her that.

"What, Wynn?" She tried to sound casual.

She didn't feel casual.

Everything she had been trying to ignore was bubbling up. They were in a motel room together. Just one room. Now that could mean nothing. They could be just buddies who happened to be sharing a room. There were double beds in the place.

On the other hand, it meant something to her. Wynn wasn't just the guy with an aura, just her mind-talking buddy in telepathy. There was a definite physical side to him. Oh, shoot, he was the sexiest guy she'd ever met. Cassie wasn't sure why but she'd given up trying to figure out why. Obviously tall, thin, spooky guys with intense stares and slow smiles turned her on.

She might as well admit that she wanted to have more than a telepathic link with him. What she couldn't figure out was why she was suddenly getting the feeling he was interested in her, too. She hadn't ever felt that before.

Cassie looked at the two beds and then looked away. What would he say if she just told him she wanted more from him? That she'd like to go to bed with him? Before he'd probably have just laughed or stared. She thought. Now she wasn't sure.

Wynn couldn't help looking at Cassie. He tried to play it cool, but he couldn't. She puzzled the hell out of him. He almost thought she was interested in—well, she seemed interested in him.

She was oddly appealing, sure, but he'd been interested in women before. He could get them, too, sometimes, especially if he let himself peek into their minds.

The problem was, he had no confidence in actually keeping a woman interested. They didn't know about his gift, but something about him was different. Sooner or later they began to retreat from him. They always did. He wished he knew how the difference showed so that he could camouflage it more, make himself fit in better, but he never had.

Usually that difference kept women away from him unless he made a real effort to be with them. Usually the effort wasn't worth it.

But Cassie kept thinking he was sexy without him even trying to interest her. He had actually doubted his—her—thoughts at first. But she kept thinking it. She was still thinking it now. He didn't know why she believed he was some kind of stud, but he finally gave in and admitted to himself that he desperately wanted to live up to her expectations.

"Wynn?" She spoke it aloud this time. Oh, God, he could tell he was making her nervous now. "What do you want?"

And he could smell her. In this small room he couldn't escape. Wynn wasn't sure he'd ever been this near, this long to a woman in his whole adult life unless he was there for sex. He knew he couldn't remember ever before noticing what a woman smelled like. Not even when he was there for sex. He couldn't describe Cassie's scent but by now her perfume made him hard.

He imagined her clothing littering the room, him touching them and smelling them, and he swallowed. How could he stand being in a motel room without trying to sleep with her? By now he could tell when she was close to him, just from her scent.

Bloody hell, all his senses told him when she was aroused and the whole thing drove him crazy. Everything about her drove him crazy.

Whether he failed her or not, he had to try.

I want more from you, too. I'd really like to go to bed with you. No. That's not right. I'm dying to go to bed with you, Cassie.

* * *

"Johanna."

The voice was familiar even though it had been a very long time since she'd heard it.

"Is something wrong?" she asked, uneasily.

Emmanuel never called anyone. She certainly never expected he would call her.

And then she felt it again. That tug at her subconscious. She had almost forgotten the feel of what Emmanuel was able to do.

Back at the Institute he had become amazingly good at entering her mind. But she had developed some skill at realizing when he did it. He must be doing it again. There was no reason for her to remember any of this otherwise—

"Oh, yes. Yes, I did mention to Lida about a patient who had some compulsion that made the poor woman think she had to talk about Lida to someone... Well, she didn't get as far as saying why she needed to talk to Lida. I suppose she could have heard a voice. Often such people do."

But Emmanuel wasn't through. Johanna could feel her mind moving to another subject she would never think about ordinarily.

"Yes, I remember the other boy, though I didn't work as closely with him as I did with you," Johanna told him, as calmly as she could.

His ability still made her hands sweat. His powers could make her nervous and awestruck at the same time.

"You two were the only ones we felt truly certain had telepathic abilities. No, the name wasn't Wynn. But that does sound familiar. Let me think."

She scowled and felt a sudden surge of impatience smash at her brain.

"Wait, I said. Please. It's been years…it was a Welsh name. Owen. Owen Powell."

"Owen. Wynn. Of course." Emmanuel's voice was deeper now, more mature. But it had always had that seductively hypnotic quality to it. "Thank you, Johanna. As always, you've been a tremendous help."

"Of course I am. After all, I introduced you to Lida, didn't I?" She suddenly had a desperate need to remind him how much he did owe to her. She should be worth something to him. "I warned you when the Institute planned to run those tests on you and the other boy. That Owen."

"You've always been my very favorite psychiatrist, Dr. Blessingham."

"And you were always my favorite patient."

She almost hung up and then heard herself forced into saying, "The woman who came to my office? Oh, yes, I'm sure of her name. Majors. Her name was Majors."

"Ah. The woman Jock told me about was also named Majors. Yes." Emmanuel sounded faintly gratified. "Thank you, Johanna. Thank you very much. You've been far more helpful than anyone else around me. You know, I'm sorry you decided not to join my group. You could have proven to be remarkably useful."

"I didn't decide not to. You told me I wasn't welcome!" Johanna Blessingham protested.

She remembered how it hurt that she been excluded. If it had been anyone but Lida and Emmanuel, she would have been angry at them.

"How foolish of me."

Johanna smiled at the next questioning thought that slid into her mind. He just couldn't help thinking that.

"Of course not. I never studied the other boy much since we tried to keep the two of you separate up until that last study, but, of course, you had the better telepathic abilities."

And the telephone clicked. Johanna blinked in confusion.

Long ago memories of a beautiful young man swirled in her mind…she had embarrassed herself by the way she thought about him and then realized he could read her mind…of course, nothing could come of it since he had been her patient… Then her mind went blank.

She stared at the telephone. She wasn't quite sure. Had someone just called?

* * *

"Cassie?" Wynn moved a little closer to her. "We're going to be together—closely together—for the foreseeable future. I don't want to make you uncomfortable, but I've been thinking about you. You and me. A lot."

"But you don't like me!" Cassie had to point that out. "I'm a flake, remember?"

"No. I'm a jerk. You don't like me. Remember? You told me that you didn't. Back at your house when I broke in."

"I don't remember." Cassie wasn't sure she could remember anything at all. And the idea of her ever telling Wynn she didn't like him didn't make sense. Not anymore.

Wynn took a step closer to her and stretched out his hands.

Cassie looked down and then, tentatively, put her hands in his. The surge of feeling almost knocked her over. Damn, he was good at giving her overwhelming emotions. Not panic this time. She sorted it out—he projected lust, tenderness, a little fear.

Fear? Why was he afraid? She was afraid. He was Mr. Masculine Sexiness personified. Why should he be afraid of her?

Because you know me better than anyone in the world does, Cassie. I'm afraid you won't like what you get with me.

I don't know much about you at all.

Wrong. You know an amazing amount. But—what do you need to know?

Oh, no. You're too tricky. You tell me what I should find out about you.

Very well, Cassie. I was brought up to be a con man by a con man. We never stayed anywhere long enough to have a routine. When I got old enough for Da to see I didn't want to follow him and help out with all his little games, he sold me.

Cassie jerked back in surprise. No, he wasn't kidding. She could see that. Without further thought, she moved forward and held him tightly. This wasn't sexual. Wynn needed a hug.

He stayed in her arms a moment, then shifted away.

Tell me, Wynn.

Cassie knew Wynn didn't want to go on, but she waited. She could feel him picking his words carefully before he finally spoke again.

"Da and I never got along once my mother was…gone. I realized things about him I didn't want to know. And he realized I was never going to be what he wanted. We argued. As I got older, we argued more. Bloody hell. We didn't argue. That sounds civilized. We fought each other, any and every way we could. And then one day, a few years later, he dumped me off at the Institute. He'd had enough of me."

"You mother left you to face all that?" Cassie wanted to bite her tongue out once she said it.

Wynn shook his head, but almost as if she'd hit him rather than to merely indicate no.

"She *didn't* leave me. I won't believe that. Never. Something went wrong. I don't know what. But after she did— things got confusing. I don't remember it all. I suppose I don't want to remember it all."

And she could feel the old fear and confusion and outrage of a dark-haired boy, big for his age, but still a young boy. And she knew he wasn't going to tell her more about that. His mother must be an even more painful subject than his father.

But, to her surprise, she could hear his thoughts continue the conversation.

Technically, I suppose you could say Da gave up his guardianship of me to further science. But what he actually did was sell me when I was thirteen, anxious to strike out on my own, and about to be of no further use to him. I was bought by a bunch of shrinks and doctors and academics so they could poke into my brain and try to figure out my gift.

"I don't understand."

"Have you ever heard of the Mintzer Institute?"

Cassie frowned. She had. Where had she?

"If I have, I don't remember."

"It was in England. They studied the paranormal. That's me. I was a science experiment. Until I got myself out."

Now Cassie had a sudden vision of a desperate, dark-haired teenager hurling himself out of an upstairs window. She saw him falling down, wondering what would break when he hit earth. Even worse, she felt the underlying despair. He didn't much care if it was his neck, as long as he got away.

Her breath caught. *My God. Poor Wynn.*

"I'm sorry." Cassie didn't know what more to say. Maybe she'd already said enough.

No matter how miserable she felt with her family, no one had ever done anything remotely that bad to her. She doubted it would have ever occurred to anyone in her family to sell her off into—into something horrible—when she became inconvenient. Of course, no one would have wanted to buy her, either.

"So am I. It's a lousy seduction line." Wynn suddenly gave his charming smile and bent his head to her. "Let me try for something better."

Cassie wanted to protest, to tell him he didn't have to change the painful subject. Then Wynn's tongue flickered, just slightly, over her lips, and she forgot why she wanted to do— whatever it was she had wanted to do before.

"Oh." She breathed it out as she opened her lips.

That had been sweet. She liked that. She knew the kisses wouldn't stay sweet. She liked that, too.

Wynn slid his hands up under her shirt, just lightly reaching up. Cassie gripped his shoulders hard. Suddenly she knew she'd never had an experience close to this—how could she? She'd never been with someone whose mind and body were able to link with hers the way she and Wynn...

Her inconvenient memory kicked in again, right before her mind completely hazed over.

"I know where I heard of Mintzer Institute!" Cassie jerked her breast away from his lips.

"God, my seduction technique must really be lousy." Wynn's smile wasn't quite as charming and sincere as before. "Listen, Cassie—"

Cassie wasn't concerned with hurt feelings right at that moment. She gripped his shoulders again, but this time to shake them for emphasis.

"The shrink. The shrink I went to see. I told her I needed to talk about Lida. Dr. Blessingham. What kind of bad luck do I have? Of all the shrinks in the world, I went to see someone who said she had worked at the Mintzer Institute. I suppose it makes sense. I was worried about voices in my head. And that's what she studied there. With people like you."

Wynn's face didn't look seductive anymore. It looked a little frightening instead with his eyes narrowed and the fierce clench around his jaw.

"Then he'll know. Emmanuel must know who I am by now. And he knows you're around. He'll soon know where you live."

"Aren't you jumping to conclusions?" Cassie had to ask, even though she was getting a sick feeling in her stomach. "You act like this guy is all-powerful. Do you know Emmanuel? Like, you've seen him?"

"Yeah, I met Emmanuel. Once. Emmanuel's a smart man. We didn't see much of each other at the Institute—whatever experiments they were running required us to be kept separate—but he had the gift. I never knew which one of us was the better. But I'm good. Bloody good. He must be at least my equal. He'll make it his business to figure this out."

Wynn stood up and began to push his wallet back into his pocket.

"Come on, then. We need to do a bit more traveling before it gets completely dark."

"We have to leave?"

"I'd feel better with a few more miles between us and D.C., yes. I can feel... I can feel danger nearby. I know I can communicate with people better in my mind the closer that I am to them. I have to believe Emmanuel can do the same."

"But, Wynn!" Cassie couldn't believe he could just stop.

His smile looked regretful, but she knew he wasn't going to change his mind.

No seduction scene, then. Damn her memory. Maybe he wasn't that interested after all.

Then Cassie looked further down than his smile. Oh. That was a large bulge he was displaying. Very large.

Well, maybe Wynn's self-control wasn't the only thing he had that was made of iron. His discomfort made her feel much better.

"Cassie."

"Yes?"

"Should you hear any other voice—no matter if you aren't sure if you have or not, you'll tell me? I'm not sure the extent of Emmanuel's powers or what he's best at, but I have to assume he can do what I can do. He must be good at making people do what he *thinks* them to do. Hell. He must be damn good at that."

Maybe better than I am, Cassie. And he's definitely more experienced than you at using his gift.

"Oh." Cassie imagined her mind being invaded by a crazy man who thought he was God. Oh, boy. That could be…absolutely terrifying. Things had been bad enough when it was Wynn.

"Cassie."

"I'll tell you if I feel that happening to me, too. Or—or if it looks like it may be happening to you."

She did *not* want to think about the possibilities. Instead Cassie picked up her small suitcase and led Wynn out the door. She was beginning to want a few more miles between her and this Emmanuel herself.

Wynn watched her leave. Good. She understood they were in danger. He had been afraid she might not want to believe him. But she had.

The sudden fear that knotted his stomach wasn't for him. He was terrified for her. She had no idea what she might be in for if Emmanuel started to play mind games with her. He'd gotten her into this. Stupidly, he'd thought she would be safe from what was going on.

No, he'd started by not thinking about her at all other than a means to an end. She wasn't that. She was Cassie.

Cassie, who had let him into her mind and her home and had done what he asked even when he told her it was dangerous. Other people did what he wanted because he used his gift without them knowing or because he traded his gift for something they could give him in return.

Cassie'd done none of that. He couldn't think of anyone who had ever trusted him that much without any real reason at all. He didn't intend to abuse that trust. He was used to taking care of himself. Now he had to see she was cared for, too.

She was tiny. It was ridiculous to forget that when he loomed over her all the time, but she didn't act tiny. Half the time she acted like she could kick life in the butt and make everything do what she wanted. The other half she acted like she didn't know or care what real life was about and didn't need to.

He was starting to like both her attitudes.

But even though she didn't seem to realize it, even though he knew she had to do hard, physical work while cleaning houses, she was fragile.

Wynn thought of her small bones. He had managed to feel how little she actually weighed not too long ago.

He thought about the frightened look in her eyes she got sometimes, even when she was toughing things out. He swallowed hard. He didn't ever want her to realize how easily hurt she could be. Wynn didn't want to imagine a Cassie who knew she could be defeated or beaten.

* * *

Do you know Emmanuel? Like, you've seen him?

Yeah, I met Emmanuel. Once.

He'd heard of him. He wasn't supposed to have—the personnel at the Institute had tried to keep anyone they were testing separated from the other subjects. That way no one could compare notes or work out a con on them. So they said. Wynn had always figured there was more. There was always more to things than what they told him.

Wynn had first realized someone was trying to tap into his mind within a month of staying at the Institute. At first he thought it was a test.

The psychiatrists working with him had started with silly stuff—stuff he had known was designed to see if he was real or fake. Then what they asked him to do got increasingly more difficult. Sometimes he had no idea why they wanted him to do what they did. Sometimes the exercises they had him do seemed to make his powers stronger. They figured out what he couldn't do as well. He couldn't bend spoons or tell the future. But they never told him what was going on—at least out loud. But he got better and better at tapping into people's thoughts.

And when he first felt someone entering his mind, he could tell when someone was trying to make him do things he didn't want to do.

Still, when he felt a sudden inexplicable need to go to the Institute garden late one evening, Wynn's curiosity got the better of him. What did this message sender want?

He'd worked at looking like a good kid so far—quiet, responsible, well-mannered. Wynn had figured that would get him further in this setting than any other attitude. In this case, what the personnel thought he was like made it absurdly easy to pick the lock on his bedroom door and leave when it was lights-out in the Institute dorms.

The garden was darker than he'd expected. And deserted. As he waited, Wynn could feel something that felt a bit like terror inside him even though he tried to jeer it away with all the insolence a thirteen-year-old was capable of.

"Hello."

Wynn didn't want to jump. He almost succeeded but he could see—just barely—the person before him. That person had the trace of a smirk on his face. He'd known Wynn was afraid.

"Hello yourself." Wynn had been curt, his pride damaged.

The person who had summoned him, who'd made him start, wasn't much older than Wynn and not as tall. He was pretty much just a boy, like Wynn was.

"I've been told about you. I hear you can almost do some of the things I do."

"I wouldn't know. I'm new here."

Suddenly, without warning, Wynn felt a sudden force he'd never felt before. He fell to his knees. The other person laughed, sounding a brief burst of joy.

"You can kneel before me if you like. I can make you do anything."

"You took me by surprise," Wynn said, defensively, then bit his lip.

He'd had limited experience with people making him do things—mostly it was the other way around. Other than being summoned to the garden and now this humiliation, Wynn had never had to do anything he'd been mentally ordered to do.

But he figured out quickly how to block the next command. A slight jolt of what seemed almost a faint electric shock went through him but he shielded himself. He wouldn't do that. He wouldn't. But Wynn began to sweat.

"Hide if you want. I can do whatever I want," the young man told him. "I did it to you already."

"Because I wasn't prepared. It won't happen again." Wynn thought of picking himself up off the ground and decided it was safer to save his energy.

"I like a challenge."

And, just like that, the other person faded back into the shadows. Wynn, who was fairly good at that himself, couldn't help but be impressed.

Afterwards Wynn had made it his business to find out more about his mysterious rival. He was an American, shipped over to the Institute at the Institute's expense because they were amazed by what he could do.

While the people at the Institute weren't supposed to talk, that didn't mean Wynn couldn't enter the minds of at least some of them. He learned people weren't just impressed with his rival. He learned some were even afraid of him.

The other telepath was true to his word. Wynn got used to feeling sudden attempts at entering his mind. Wynn learned to how to block those attempts quickly.

But he hated waking up from his dreams, shaking, feeling sick to his stomach, wondering if this time he had bowed before the other man and actually obeyed that further command to unbuckle his belt and strip... But he hadn't. Wynn woke up each time, reassuring himself that he hadn't been humbled quite that much. He had to keep telling himself that he never would.

Wynn wasn't stupid. He knew there was something sick, something perverse, even more perverse than a need to embarrass him, in his opponent's desire to penetrate his brain and force him to do things Wynn had no wish to do. But Wynn managed to resist whatever power the other telepath had once they no longer were face to face. Sometimes he wasn't even sure how he managed to know and evade the commands.

What he couldn't seem to do was enter his rival's mind. At least not that Wynn could ever tell. No one ever talked about an Institute candidate suddenly running around half-dressed or any of the other things Wynn had tried to make the other telepath do.

Wynn assured himself that he was failing because he had too much to try to deal with. Between fighting off mental commands at night and the demands the Institute put on him during the day, Wynn knew he was reaching the end of his endurance.

Things were at a stalemate between him and his opponent until the week before Wynn finally left.

Wynn woke up that morning, feeling sick. He thought he'd had another bad dream, but his gut told him that what he remembered hearing was more than that. Someone had finally found a way to enter his mind again. Maybe that powerful someone had known how all along and had just been toying with him, waiting for the right time to strike.

I'm leaving, youngster. This place was all right for a while but I know what's going down and I'm out before it happens. Too bad for you. You'll never get out now. After my departure they'll watch you twice as carefully. It's not going to be fun. So long.

And, sure enough, it was just the way the younger Emmanuel had predicted. After the one telepath's hasty and unauthorized departure, the Institute had kept their one remaining telepath under close scrutiny.

His fellow inmate and tormentor had been wrong about one thing, though. Wynn had figured out how to make his escape. Anyone could escape if they were desperate enough. After all, if you failed and died—well, at a certain point, death could be considered just another way to get out.

* * *

Wynn brought himself back from that bad time. He stared blankly at the motel where he had just pulled up. Maybe he'd been driving too long. For just a moment he wasn't sure where he was, he'd been so lost in where he had been before.

But that time was over. Things were grim but he didn't feel quite that desperate yet. He didn't need to. He wasn't physically confined anywhere and so far he'd avoided the people he wanted to avoid.

Of course in some ways things were worse. Before he'd only needed to get himself out. There had been a time when he hadn't cared how. There was some freedom in that desperation. But that rather bleak freedom was gone now.

This time he was bound, somehow or another, to another person. Cassie had a hold on him. Wynn couldn't even explain how.

There was the possibility of sex, of course. Wynn shifted. Just remembering the start of their lovemaking excited him. That ought to be enough to keep him interested in her safety. He couldn't remember the last time he'd wanted anyone this much.

But there was more. Wynn knew he couldn't leave her alone right now and not just sexually. He needed to make sure she was safe.

He couldn't let her be harmed or made afraid. Not the way he had been. She was too important to him. Maybe more important than he'd ever been to himself.

Chapter Nine

Must call Ned.

Wynn woke up with a start, completely disoriented. He rarely slept so heavily, but after driving until one in the morning he had stumbled into the nearest motel and fallen face down on one of the beds.

He pushed himself up and sat, swaying a little, on the edge of the bed. Bloody hell, he felt almost hung-over.

Somewhere in the night he had a vague memory of Cassie curling up next to him in the bed. He'd liked that. He wished the memory was clearer.

Wynn could almost remember the dreams that disturbed him all night, too. A woman's body had been next to him and he'd been aroused, even while he slept like he'd been drugged. How could he help but imagine that body doing more than lying near him? He could almost taste how sweet her breast was in his mouth, how warm and clinging that pussy of hers was as he sleepily thrust into her.

Call Ned.

Ned?

Why the hell would he want to call that worthless druggie—? Oh, shit. That hadn't been the echoes of his own mind talking. That had been Cassie. And she wasn't next to him in bed now.

Wynn jumped to his feet fast.

"Damn it, woman!" He was vaguely grateful he hadn't stripped off his clothes as he ran barefoot out the door. "No!"

He reached her as she hung up the pay phone outside the lobby of the motel. He gripped the arm that was replacing the receiver but, of course, it was too late then.

"Cassie, we didn't drive all over creation last night so you could trot over to the telephone and tell everyone where the hell we are!" Wynn glared.

He had trusted her, by God. He thought she had understood what was going on.

She had run straight to the telephone without getting properly dressed. Her hair was still unbrushed and sticking up straight, and she was wearing the same clothes she had last night, but she stared at him as if he was the thoughtless one.

"But I had to have someone feed Pandora. And then I thought that Ned could go and get my BMW out of the parking garage and drive it home. I decided this was a real emergency. Because if he does, when all this is over I won't have to get it out of the impound lot somewhere in D.C.—"

"No. That's not an emergency. I'll tell you what the emergency is right now. All this may be over with one of us being dead. Bloody hell, Cassie! We can't be found. That means no one can know where we are. No one."

"But, like I've told you before, Ned is harmless."

"Ned can be used, just like anyone can be used."

"I didn't tell him where we were." Cassie's voice sounded very uncertain.

She hadn't done it deliberately. She just wasn't used to this. Wynn forced himself to calm down. Then he sighed and rubbed his hand over his face. The stubble scratched his hand.

He hated looking unshaven. He hated the dazed confusion still in his mind.

Bloody hell, he was tired. More tired than he remembered being in years.

"Get in the car. We haven't unpacked, so this should be easy. We need to drive some more."

"Wynn—"

Cassie felt awful. Wynn looked more exhausted and bewildered than she had ever seen him appear before. She saw him, as if by rote, pull his keys out of his jeans pocket. He was obviously sure that they had to do this. Damn, they had both gotten maybe four hours of sleep at best in the motel.

Of course she had napped in the car so she was feeling better than he did.

"We have to move."

"Wynn, let me drive. You'll get us killed."

Cassie bit her tongue. How many times had she said that to Ned, for different reasons? How many times had she then had to argue with his outraged pride?

"I can do it—" Wynn led them to the car and stared at the door a little blankly. "Hell. Maybe not. All right. Get us out of here."

"Where?"

"Surprise us. Just away from D.C." His voice already sounded a little slurred. "But when I wake up, I need to get to a decent-sized public library."

Cassie wanted to ask why, but he shut his eyes as he slumped into the car. As Wynn fell asleep in the passenger's seat, Cassie carefully started the engine. Guilt made her bite her lower lip as she began to figure out the unfamiliar controls on the rental car.

Whatever had possessed her to call Ned? It had seemed like such a brilliant idea when she woke up. Why hadn't she at least checked with Wynn first? Of course he had been sleeping like a dead man—no, she didn't like that image—he had been sleeping so soundly that she hated to disturb him...but still.

Cassie swallowed. What if it wasn't that she had been stupid and careless in calling Ned? What if Emmanuel had made her call?

"Now I'm getting almost as paranoid as Wynn," she said out loud.

Of course Wynn appeared to have good reason for his wariness. No. She hadn't been under any mind control. She had just been impulsive. How many years would it take her to realize that her impulsiveness could get her into a lot of trouble?

Cassie glanced over at Wynn. He really was sleeping. Another thought made her feel better. Despite everything, he trusted her enough to drive them out of here.

She wasn't going to abuse that trust. Cassie knew that Wynn didn't give it lightly. She wasn't sure he had ever given that trust to anyone before.

And Cassie began to remember what they had been doing back in the Bide-A-Wee. She wished they had managed to finish what they'd started.

Oh, well. Imagining how things could and should have ended ought to keep her awake for another hundred miles or so. That would be good, since she knew she wasn't going to turn the radio on to help keep herself awake. She couldn't do that while Wynn was asleep.

Cassie shook her head. She'd never felt this weird mix of emotions before. How was it possible to feel like you wanted to crawl into bed with someone to do everything but sleep and tuck him in for a long rest all at the same time?

* * *

"She didn't suspect anything did she?" Carter kept his voice threatening.

"Hey man, you ever heard of asking someone a question nicely?" The man acted as if he didn't know what was going on, but Carter saw the sweat beginning on his face.

This one threatened real easy. Carter knew he was going to really enjoy himself for the next few minutes.

"I don't have to ask nicely. Did she?"

"No. Nothing. She didn't suspect a thing." Ned's face shone with sweat now. "Honest to God, man!"

"Did you get a trace on the call?" Carter turned to Ullmann and thought about having to explain not knowing where the call came from when he spoke to Rauss. That made him feel a little sweaty himself.

"Pay phone in... Uniontown, Pennsylvania."

"Where the hell is that? Never mind, we'll find it," Carter said, hastily.

"Damn right."

"Now. What should we do with this little man?" Carter turned his attention to the twitching, fearful body in front of him.

"Rauss doesn't want people to know what's up." Ullmann looked dispassionate.

"Killing is easiest unless it makes the news."

"Why don't we have someone stay here with him? Maybe he'll get another phone call."

"Hmmm."

"At least for a while. He can go get that damned car, too, just like the woman asked. Of course we'll go along. Maybe there's something useful in the thing. And we can deal with him later."

Ned squeaked wordlessly. Carter almost laughed. This one was plenty cowed already. He wouldn't be much of a chore to keep an eye on.

"Ned? Is that you after all this time?"

The voice at the door was loud and overly cheerful. All three men jumped.

Ned blinked at the person speaking.

Everyone could see him pulling something out of his brain and puzzling over it. Finally he said, "Emily?"

Emily nodded encouragingly.

"Emily Logan."

"Don't push your luck, Ned. It used to be Lewis. I got married and changed my name to something without even an L in it. That doesn't matter anyhow since it will be Lewis again soon enough." Emily pushed her way into the kitchen, barely glancing at the other two. "Since Cass isn't here, why don't we go somewhere else and talk over old times?"

Ned blinked again.

"Huh?"

"We have so much to talk about, Ned. You know it's been years. And Cassie was always with us. We've never had the chance to be alone together, you know?" Emily tucked her arm under Ned's elbow as she urged him out.

"Hey!" Carter said.

He looked at his partner, confused.

"We know where you live, Ned. We'll come calling," Ullmann made his tone genial. "Or maybe you better come back and visit us here some more. When you're done with the lady."

Ned flinched again.

Emily almost shoved him out the door. Ned followed after her, clearly under the influence of a higher intelligence.

"Hey, thanks. Those guys were—"

"I know they're bad news. I'm not the idiot here, Ned. Let's go before they decide we both need to stay," Emily said through her teeth.

"Sure."

"Ned, where the hell is Cassie and what the hell is going on?"

Emily glanced at the man ambling along beside her. She had a feeling she knew what his answer would be. Ned hadn't changed much.

"So, like, you were interested in me back in the old days? Coulda fooled me."

Emily dropped her hold on Ned's elbow.

"No, Ned. No, I was never interested. Not then and not now. I never will be interested. I said that to get you away from those guys who looked like they wanted to kill you. Understand?"

"I always thought you were sorta cute, too. Not that I'd run around on Cassie or anything."

Emily sighed.

* * *

Cassie was just at the spot where she unzipped Wynn's jeans very slowly after she stopped the car on the side of the road when she realized that Wynn's eyes were open.

She hastily moved hers back to looking at the road. So much for fantasies.

Go on. Don't stop now.

"That's the problem with having someone read your mind. He can find out everything you think." Cassie hoped she wasn't blushing. "Of course, a gentleman doesn't have to comment on everything."

"Why not? I liked those thoughts. If you want, I'll help you with some."

Cassie began to think of warm hands stroking cool breasts, a warm mouth on—

"Hey, I'm driving here!" Cassie yelped.

"You started it. Hey, Cassie, where are we going?"

"I know a really, really good public library," Cassie told him, trying to keep thoughts of a mouth on her thighs far away. Damn him. "In New York City."

"The city?"

"It's easy to spot strangers in small towns like where we are now. It's harder when you're with millions of strangers."

"And New Yorkers get stranger every minute," Wynn muttered.

"That's not a nice attitude for someone with telepathy," Cassie pointed out. "People probably would find that strange even in New York."

"All right. Fine. New York City it is." But he didn't look happy. "Why do you want to be in the city anyhow?"

"Well, I know it pretty well. Mom went to live there when she got married so I hung out there some. Hey, maybe we could stay with my step-dad!"

"Cassie."

"All right, bad idea. They know everything about both of us, including where Tim lives. Besides, Tim isn't the most reliable guy in the world."

"What does he do?"

"Do? Hmmm. Do. Well, he's an artist. He doesn't sell a lot of stuff and that means he sort of drifts from job to job... He doesn't do much of anything, I guess. Doing isn't what Tim is about. Being. That's what he likes."

No, Tim Borges was not exactly the solid father figure every girl longed for. Or much of any solid figure at all.

Sounds like Ned.

"Naw. Ned is—" Cassie stopped.

He's exactly like Ned. What did that mean? Cassie'd met Ned just about the time Mom died. She was sure she could go back to the shrink with that and get hours of conversation out of her new insight.

In a way that was a relief, Cassie admitted to herself. She'd thought she stayed with Ned because of low self-esteem. But now it was Mom's fault.

"I don't know what you're talking about," Cassie finished in as dignified a manner as she could.

"Cassie, you seem to forget who you're talking to," Wynn reminded her.

"Oh. Well, shut up. And stay out of my thoughts."

Suddenly Cassie got an image of snowflakes drifting down from the sky. Millions of snow...*flakes.*

Not funny, Wynn.

Wynn began to laugh.

"It's nice to know you only hung out with Ned because your mom would have wanted you to," he said. "That's so—dutiful—of you."

That was a nicer word than any that Emily had ever come up with for Cassie and Ned's togetherness. It was better than anything Tash or her dad had said, too. But it irritated Cassie even more than Em's ruder terms or the parental lectures on poor choices.

Since he was definitely awake now, Cassie turned on the radio, pushed the volume up and then put her foot on the accelerator.

"I'm not talking to you. I'm driving." She paused for a while and then said, a little belligerently, "What's wrong with New York City?"

"Never liked the place. Besides, that means we have several hours to drive."

"And driving now bothers you?"

"Waiting several hours to get you in bed bothers me. It's starting to bother me a lot."

Hands unbuttoning her shirt. Short dark hair tickling against her body as he moved his head down from her breasts to her belly button and then to her thighs. Going further down yet with that flickering, relentless tongue of his. His teeth bit, then his mouth sucked. Then she felt his tongue reaching her pubic curls. Cassie was sweating. Wynn's hair was damp. They'd been at this for hours and hours. They'd be at this for hours more.

This time Cassie knew she did blush. There was no doubt about it. That was a wonderful fantasy but not hers. She just wouldn't—even if she hadn't felt the heat going up her face, she would have known by the satisfied smirk on Wynn's face. They were sharing his ideas this time.

Fine. Let him smirk. They were still in for a long trip. She could create plenty more sex scenarios in her head.

Cassie wondered when she had learned to switch from sharing just words in her mind to mental images. That seemed like she was getting better at linking.

Obviously Wynn was well able to see her mental images too. Only too well. Oh, God. That was embarrassing. Exciting but still embarrassing.

* * *

Wynn watched, almost asleep, as Cassie switched the radio channel. She was avoiding looking over at him.

That was all right. He hadn't been entirely kidding her when he said he didn't want to wait. If she started to look at him again like she wanted to stop the car and crawl in the back with him—or if she started with those fantasies again... It was better if she didn't look at him. But his mind started to drift back to them anyhow. Somehow Cassie and self-control didn't go together well.

"...the results of the primaries in the Super Tuesday contest are coming in. Senator Arthur Hornsby appears to hold a commanding lead and, if so, will have a virtual lock on his party's nomination..."

Cassie switched off the radio.

Wynn let out the air he had sucked in at Art's name.

He had almost forgotten his responsibility to Art.

He'd been busy, of course. Being chased all over the East Coast could make a man forget his responsibilities sometimes. But maybe that was why he was being chased—to be kept out of the way right now. What the hell did Lida and Emmanuel have planned next?

Wynn wondered how he could reassure Cassie. While he thought about what to say, Cassie broke the silence.

"I'd really hoped this was going to be over with. Well, so much for all this just going away by itself. I bet your buddies Emmanuel and Lida are really excited now," Cassie observed, her voice very even.

Chapter Ten

"Stop here."

"But we're in Harrisburg!"

"You have a problem with Harrisburg?"

"I'm sure it's a lovely city, Wynn, but the goal was New York City by nightfall, remember?"

"Later. Tomorrow. I just spotted a likely looking library. It's past time to send that message to Art."

"But—" Cassie gave up. Wynn usually had reasons for what he did. Or if they weren't reasons, they were gut instincts that he had learned to obey. He wouldn't change his mind. Besides, why should she argue? So far he'd been right.

* * *

Within minutes Wynn was in front of one of the library's public computers, tapping at the keyboard. Cassie tried not to be impressed. She could use a computer, all right, but Wynn obviously could make his computer sit up and do tricks. Just the way he sat in front of the monitor, his face looking interested and alert, told her that.

"What are you doing?" Cassie ventured.

"Getting the message to Art. Hope he pays attention. And I'm making sure it won't be traced to here or to me." Wynn spoke a little absently.

"How do you do that?" Cassie couldn't help but ask.

Wynn grunted, finished tapping the keys and then switched off. Then his attention switched back to her.

Cassie hadn't realized how strongly Wynn could focus on a person until she had felt his attention on her with only half its strength. Now his thoughts were as powerfully intent on her as they had been on the computer a moment ago.

"Do you really want to know?"

"I asked, didn't I?"

"So you did. Let me keep it simple." Wynn smiled and stood up. His message to save the free world had taken all of about ten minutes to deliver, if that. "I have a number of e-mail accounts with false names. Sometimes I use them to send messages to people. Art just got an e-mail from Horace Jones. I knew he'd be on around now so I sent him a message. Now I've deleted the account. He had best delete it on his end."

"That sounds devious."

"I'd like to think so. I also have a friend—well, an associate—who has helped me out considerably with information that most people would find difficult to obtain. We use one or another of my special accounts for that, too. He still owes me some favors if I should ever need to collect again. Yes, the Internet can be quite a help."

"Sometimes you worry me, Wynn."

"There are always ways to do things indirectly, Cassie. Da taught me that years ago."

* * *

Well, despite fuming over waiting at the appointed time for days to receive a mysterious message—while he was in the middle of a presidential campaign, no less—this message had been worth the wait. Or was that the term he should use? Art Hornsby hit the delete key without conscious thought and it vanished out of sight. He didn't need to save the message anyway. He had it permanently saved in his brain.

Lida was a serious threat to him? Using a cult to harm him? None of that made sense. But Wynn had given him amazing information before that proved to be true. And he was obviously afraid enough to keep away, even when Art needed his expertise more than ever. After all, he was starting to run background checks on potential vice-presidential candidates…

"Jeffries." Art let himself relax a little.

Sam Jeffries, his campaign manager, knew plenty. He could ask some questions of Jeffries and learn what he needed to know without Jeffries knowing why his boss was asking. And he should ask how the background check was going. Yes. Of course he should. And, of course, Lida was a potential running mate. Asking about her would be perfectly normal. And this information required some serious double-checking.

Art picked up the telephone.

"Hey, Sam. Can you come over to the office? I think it's time to pick your brain about some of the people I could be on the same ticket with."

* * *

Well it wasn't the Bide-A-Wee, but it was pretty darn close. They had a hotel near the old airport in Harrisburg and every few minutes you could hear the roar of the planes overhead.

For dinner they walked across the street to an Italian restaurant that had come straight out of the '50s, complete with red checked tablecloths and a waitress who called them both honey. The food was good, too. Well, Cassie was sure it would have been if she could actually taste anything. But her mind wasn't on linguine in tomato sauce.

It shouldn't be romantic. Cassie knew she shouldn't be feeling turned on. The two of them had barely spoken to each other all evening. She and Wynn certainly hadn't said anything about their interrupted encounter. But she could feel him thinking about it. He didn't try to conceal his thoughts. So she didn't, either.

This was worse than playing footsie under the table. Cassie tried not to squirm as she received mental images of fingers dancing down her body, staying for a long time to play with her nipples. She felt those nipples stiffen and prayed the restaurant was dark enough so no one else saw.

By the end of the meal—no, well before the end of the meal—Cassie was desperate for Wynn to pay the check so they could go back across the street to their tiny little motel room.

She figured it was more than time to put some of their thoughts into action.

Wynn looked at her and he stretched out his hand, tentatively toward her. Suddenly, for the first time that day, she was almost afraid to take it. Last time she had felt so much, too much, for what was meant to be a brief sexual encounter.

What else could it be? They hardly knew each other. The feelings couldn't be real. They were threatened and dependent on each other and so it was natural to want sex under those circumstances, right?

Don't pick it apart, Cassie. Just feel.

That's what I'm afraid of doing, Wynn.

Don't be afraid. Not of me. Not right now. Trust me on this.

* * *

"So Morris would be all right but for those debts he has been running up and mysteriously paying. He doesn't have the money for the lifestyle he has right now. Who is footing the bill?"

"Does it matter? Whoever it is, this will make him look bad once the press starts investigating."

Art nodded thoughtfully, trying to look like he gave a damn. Then he made his next question very casual.

"And Chatham? What about Lida?"

Sam Jeffries shrugged.

"She's relatively inexperienced, but she does have one real election under her belt. Listen, she's clean, boss. A real choirgirl."

Now who should he trust? Wynn or Sam?

"That's good to know. Any other tidbits I need to think about with the others?" Art kept his voice very calm.

Jeffries began to talk, eagerly, gesturing as he made his points. Art's mind drifted. Who should he trust? Who could he trust?

No one.

* * *

Wynn jiggled the lock to open the door. The musty smell of motel air conditioner blasted at them. Wynn went to switch it off. Although the room had been hot when they first arrived, the spring night had already turned cold. He hesitated, then turned the heater on instead. That was just as noisy. Maybe that was good. He'd bet the walls were thin and anyone in the room next to them could hear…well, things. Like the bed rocking hard against the wall. And was Cassie a screamer when she came? He'd like that. He'd never been good enough to make anyone scream. Moaning, yeah. He'd managed to wring out some moans from women. Moaning was fine for starters. But he wanted Cassie to scare people with her cries by the time they were done.

Wynn smiled at her. Cassie took a deep breath and all the tension—from sexual frustration, from their flight, from what they planned to do next—went away. She was filled with anticipation instead.

She looked at Wynn with sudden suspicion.

"Can you do that, too?"

Wynn looked innocent as he locked the door behind her.

"What?"

"Make people forget bad stuff. Things that make them tense."

"It's a new talent." Wynn shrugged. "I never really tried before. Maybe it only works with you, Cassidy."

He pulled off his T-shirt and waited for a moment. He didn't even look directly at her but Cassie knew he was suddenly feeling hesitant, too.

"Don't stop now, big guy."

His beautiful smile flashed once and was gone—and so were his boots, jeans, and underpants. Cassie smiled now, too.

"Wow."

He was—hung. Big and beautifully hung. She looked over all those inches of eager penis. The vein that she could almost feel throbbing. His balls, so sensitive to the touch. Oh, yes. All of his body was beautiful and she wanted to touch and look at every inch. But his cock was just the icing on the cake.

Cassie licked her lips. She wanted to get closer and more intimate with that icing.

Somewhere, in the middle of all this mess, she'd done something right. It wasn't often that a man looked like everything you had fantasized he'd be. Lady Luck had arrived this time.

"Please." Wynn looked at her. She was startled when she both felt and saw the flash of suspicion. "You don't have to say things just to swell my...ego."

Oh, God. That wasn't his ego getting bigger.

She felt another flicker of surprise. Uncertainty.

"Wynn?" Cassie began to see there was more going on than Wynn had let her realize before. "Wynn, believe me, I'm not trying to flatter you. Sincerity. Yeah, that's my middle name."

Actually, Lust might be her middle name right now. But she didn't think he believed her. There was only one good way to make him sure. She began to unbutton her shirt.

His hands were there, over hers. His mouth was very close to her own.

"Allow me." Wynn's breath sent small prickles of warmth sparking out across her skin. "It would be entirely my pleasure, Cassie."

"Not entirely yours." Cassie got the words out.

He had barely done anything and she was feeling a little weak-kneed. And wet-pantied.

Whatever fed Wynn's doubts, it couldn't be inexperience. His hands were quick and gentle and knowledgeable as they got rid of her shirt, shucked off her pants, lingered over her bra and then stroked her soaking panties off. Well, she wasn't able to hide how she felt about him any more than he could about her.

She was naked in front of him before she'd even had a chance to fully realize what he was doing.

"Wow." His word echoed hers with a remnant of a smile in the voice.

Cassie thought about being small—small on top as well as the rest of her body. There was pudge around her waist that no amount of exercise or housecleaning work had gotten rid of.

No. She didn't want to think like that. She decided she'd accept his words at face value. She wasn't going to be like Wynn and doubt. For right now and for him, she was wow.

He hooked his arm under her knees and scooped her up onto the bed. For someone that thin, he was strong. Cassie held onto his shoulders and felt sinewy muscles bunch for a moment. That was nice.

Then she felt his mouth exactly where they had both imagined it would be earlier. Her entire body felt like it was rocketing up into heaven as his tongue played with her pussy. Cassie threw her arm up over her mouth and bit hard. She hadn't expected anything quite so—

And then she could feel his thoughts pouring in. Oh, my God!

I forgot to ask. Is it OK, Cassie? Is it OK if I enter your mind now? Please tell me it's OK.

Having her own lust doubled when his combined with hers, her own desire reflected back with his, his and her need blended, melded, put together—

Oh, yes. Yes. Absolutely.

Her first climax happened so fast and so strong, she wasn't quite sure of anything but that she blanked out for a moment. She caught her breath for a moment afterward.

But then Wynn's lovely hard, huge cock was inside her and she could feel her second orgasm begin to climb upward. Lord.

What the hell were you worried about, mister?

She was pretty sure she got that thought out to him because she heard a muffled laugh. Then he pumped into her hard and she lost it again.

Wynn felt the slickness of her around him, heard the little moaning whimpers that made him want to whimper too. His body wanted this moment to last forever.

Then his body wanted more. For a second he didn't think he could ever thrust fiercely enough, fast enough to finally slide over into the physical satisfaction he knew was just almost there, waiting, beckoning, demanding. Must. Wait. If he came too fast, it would be good but not good enough.

Their ability to link came through. All her thoughts and feelings swept into his head and threatened to throw him right over the edge. He could hear them louder than he ever had heard anyone before. There was more. He could feel what was happening to her.

He'd never heard or seen or felt anything more exciting in his life. He didn't have to guess if she was excited or wanted more. He knew, just as well as he knew what he wanted and enjoyed, what she desired.

Wynn tried to keep his distance, tried to make it last, but the emotions that were tangling him up with her were overwhelming. More. He needed more. Wanted more. Damn her for making him feel like this. So much. Too much... He knew he couldn't hold on much longer.

He didn't need to wait. He could feel her quivering, feel her clenching, feel her thoughts blasting off into a multi-colored blaze of delight. And for the first time in his life, he could feel himself falling into the same blaze, burning up with the sex and the excitement and the woman. He saw what she saw, he felt what she felt and he knew she did the same.

He heard the scream begin from far back in his head, almost lost in the buzzing of his own thoughts and sensations.

No. No, he wasn't supposed to scream.

Then he heard the sound rip out of her throat. A real scream. Like the one he was hearing inside himself. He'd done that to her. He felt himself come as she convulsed around him. He could see and feel and know the mindless orgasm she was lost in.

But he was the one who was lost, totally lost in their mutual climax.

Bless her.

* * *

Emmanuel finally felt himself drifting back to the world the rest of humankind lived in. He hadn't used his special ability so intensely for years. But it hadn't failed him despite his neglect. He had found his answer.

He smiled.

"New York City." Some people might find the idea of finding two people in a place that huge intimidating. Emmanuel wasn't one of them. But then he had no particular reason to worry. After all, he had more than one ability he could use to get what he wanted.

He shifted his body upward from the chair. His time for contemplation was over. He began to pace up and down. Now he needed to act.

It was time to see whether he could still make another telepath do what he wanted him to do.

* * *

What were you worried about?

She repeated herself when she saw Wynn sitting there at the edge of the bed, holding out a mug of coffee for her. He was the perfect man—great in bed and knew what to give a woman once he was out of it.

"Although the coffee could taste better," Cassie remarked, knowing perfectly well that he knew what she had been thinking. "Maybe it's because you drink tea. You do drink tea, right? This doesn't taste all that good."

"That would be the only thing that didn't taste good," Wynn used his blandest tone.

Cassie gulped down some coffee a little too quickly at that.

"Felt great, looked good, tasted right. What did you think was going to go wrong?" Cassie kept her voice as bland as his. "Wynn. What the hell were you worried about? Tell me."

"Nothing."

There was a long silence. Cassie kept her gaze on him while he avoided returning the look.

Then he sighed. Finally he looked up and back at her. His mouth lifted in a half smile that appeared almost pained.

"Ah, Cassie. I call it my gift but sometimes it's less a gift than a curse. I'm different. When I'm with a woman I try to be careful because I don't want her to think I'm some kind of freak."

"Right." Cassie wanted to scoff and then she thought about what he'd said and the way he had said it. He was serious. "Then you're an idiot, Wynn."

"Maybe with you that worry is idiotic." Wynn slid closer to her on the bed.

"Seeing as we're freaks together."

"Seeing as I don't feel worried or closed off from you. I've had women say they couldn't deal with me because I just didn't try to understand them."

Cassie laughed. She put the cup down and slid her finger down that clenched jaw of his. He was so delightful when he was nervous.

"No, really. They were right. I couldn't afford to get too close in case they realized—I couldn't let them know what I was. That probably makes me really bad in bed." His finger traced a vein on her breast as she sat, propped against the pillow. Her breath caught as his finger slowly, slowly made its way along her skin. "But you understand. You let me in. There's nothing to worry about with you. Not this time. Right?"

He bent his head to tease her nipple with his lips. Cassie's mouth went dry. He had one hell of a tongue on him. She tangled her hands in that newly spiky, ticklish dark hair, inviting him to keep going.

"Well, I don't think you have to ask if it was good for me, since you can tell from what I've been thinking that it was...all right." Cassie smiled down at his bent head although for a moment she almost wanted to cry. There was no reason he should be so unsure of himself. "Know what? I think you underestimate your abilities in the sack, Harmon."

That was you, Cassie. You thought about what you wanted and I did it.

And that's a bad thing, Wynn?

"Well, sex with you was fairly tolerable for me, too."

Cassie nipped at his ear and then flicked her tongue against an earlobe. He shivered.

"Tolerable. Yes." Cassie slid her body against his. She could feel his physical response to that. He wasn't trying to hide anything from her in that department. That cock was ready for a lot more than a little tongue tangling and breast play. "Maybe we just need to work on it a little more to make it a little more…tolerable. You think?"

Wynn bit his tongue hard. He'd done things tonight that he'd never done with any other woman. He'd done things he had been sure he'd never wanted to do with any woman. Cassie'd put her hands and mouth on places that—well, he'd always been wary of having anyone get that close. It had seemed too intimate to allow someone to do that to him, to make him lose control that way. That was before Cassie, though.

She'd say control wasn't everything.

"We haven't gotten any sleep to speak of and it's going to be a long trip—oh, hell." Wynn knew his voice was slurring a little. He could barely get the words out, he was so focused on what he wanted to do next. And it wasn't sleep. "I suppose we could try."

Chapter Eleven

"Well, we've made it into New York City. Satisfied?" Cassie heard Wynn grumbling as she unpacked. She decided to ignore him. He didn't make that easy. "Expensive bloody place—you know I don't have an unlimited amount of money here. In fact if we stay a day or two in this spot we'll be out..."

Wynn might have a thing against New York City but she'd always enjoyed it. And she had a feeling she was really going to enjoy the apartment Wynn had dug up through a bed and breakfast registry service.

"You're so smart, Mr. Harmon. I had no idea you could rent out people's empty apartments. And this one is amazing!" Cassie kept her tone deliberately cheerful but just short of saccharine as she peered down from the window. She knew cheerfulness would drive him crazy at the moment. "We're in the Village. I love the Village."

Wynn grunted.

Cassie knew he was in a bad mood. So, as long as he was going to be that way, Cassie decided she would do what she had wanted since she first walked in.

She walked to a writing desk and opened it.

"Hey!" Wynn said. "What are you doing?"

"I like to find out things about people," Cassie said. "Ever since I started cleaning houses it's become a thing with me. What people have around says so much about them. And—well, I suppose I don't see or talk to enough people. I don't socialize much. This is my way of connecting with others."

"But Cassie! That's—that's snooping!"

"Oh, Mr. Walk on Into Someone's Mind and Stay, you have a lot of room to talk. Now this guy is in politics." Cassie virtuously only looked at the open correspondence. "He sounds pretty important, too. I'll bet you've probably heard of him even if I haven't."

"Cassie, I can't believe you would do something like this. Wait. What?" Wynn's voice changed from one of horror to one of suspicion. "Who is he?"

"Oh, now you want to kn—oh-oh." Cassie's laugh stopped. "Is he someone you think you know? Or Lida knows?"

"Who the hell is he?" He spoke through clenched teeth.

"His name is Jeffries. Samuel Joseph Jeffries..."

"Junior." The two of them said it together.

He'd always thought Jeffries was something of a little prick, but that was just the nature of being a campaign manager. You didn't hire anyone but little pricks for that job. Wynn had always thought Jeffries was loyal, too.

Hell, he'd never bothered to give Jeffries more than a passing thought or two.

But it was too much of a coincidence to have them suddenly using Jeffries's apartment. With a detached astonishment, Wynn realized he'd had no idea he was being used when he picked this place. Bloody hell, but Emmanuel was good.

"Listen, Cassie—" Wynn knew he was running low on cash but it was time to run. They'd work out what they did and how they did it later.

The door clicked open. He had specifically requested an apartment with good security. But the security system didn't mean a thing if someone else had the key and the code to the alarm. Wynn turned quickly, ready to do something, but paused.

Too late. Trouble had arrived.

That Glock looked pretty threatening. And, unfortunately, it also looked as though Emmanuel had finally stopped underestimating Wynn. The same goons he'd last seen trashing his home were in front of him. But this time there weren't just two goons. There were the same two goons and a very experienced thug.

Jock Stuart had done Art's security forever. Wynn had never given him much thought either. Jock knew how to do his job and Wynn had let it go at that. But who better to know Art's security than the man in charge? Who better to know how Art's campaign was going to be run and who would be involved in it than his campaign manager?

Wynn looked at the cold eyes of the security chief and knew they were in big trouble.

Damn it. Emmanuel or Lida or both had managed to pretty much get to all the people Art trusted. Wynn wasn't sure why he had been careless enough to trust them as well.

He wasn't going to be careless now. He didn't know about the other two, but Jock was going to notice anything that most people could do to escape him.

Wynn? How much trouble are we in?

But he wasn't most people. Neither was Cassie. Somehow they would get out of this.

Trouble enough. We'll be all right, though.

"I won't get problems from you, Wynn, will I?" Jock asked. "Because that would be useless, you know."

"No problems, Jock."

"Then don't talk. Just follow me."

Wynn kept his thoughts calm while he and Cassie were hastily moved down the stairs and into the underground parking garage. This was supposed to be a safe, guarded building but no one stopped them. No one was around to stop them. Where was the security in this bloody so-called safe building?

The one goon kept the gun on Cassie, the gun concealed under a carelessly rolled up sweatshirt. Otherwise Wynn might have tried—oh, hell, he wasn't sure if he would have tried anything on his own. But they knew he wasn't going to get Cassie hurt.

He was pretty sure they didn't once point that gun at him, but they didn't need to. All they needed was to threaten Cassie. How the hell did they know that would be all it ever took to get him to obey when he had pretty much just figured that out himself?

Whatever happened, this time he wasn't going to run. Or at least not without her.

When they reached a large, nondescript car, one of them opened the trunk and looked at Wynn. Wynn climbed into the trunk. Seemed like some outsider ought to see that. Wynn wondered, even if someone did, if that someone would bother to report the occurrence. Bloody blasé New Yorkers.

"You. Get in here." One of them gestured to Cassie as he opened the back door.

The trunk slammed shut. Wynn squinted. It wasn't as dark as you might expect. Once his eyes adjusted, he could see the signal lights in the car.

Things could be worse. His head knew that. His body was the one that didn't understand.

Wynn!

I'm here, sweetheart. You all right?

Yes, except that I'm scared spitless.

I never did much to show you how to use those mind-reading abilities, like how to block out other people. Strikes me that this would be the perfect time to give you a few pointers. Just remember that Emmanuel may have slightly different skills or strengths than me, so watch out.

We're going to meet him?

I'm sure of it. Now listen to me.

A few instructions in a dark, locked trunk weren't much help, but that was all he could manage. He hoped that she would pay attention and not panic. He hoped he could tell her everything she needed to know.

Damn him for not taking more time to help her defend herself before this. What had been wrong with him? Sloppy idiot. Bloody fool. He'd spent more time thinking about her butt and how she'd be in bed than what might happen to her if he was unable to stand between her and Emmanuel.

Wynn?

Yes?

Stop beating yourself up. We'll manage. We will.

Of course, Cassie.

* * *

The car reversed quickly and Wynn banged his head against the side of the trunk. He pushed himself away. He needed to be more careful.

If he was careful, he could handle this.

Wynn was glad Cassie couldn't see as well as hear him. He could feel the sweat starting to pour down his face. He hoped his hands weren't shaking. This was a little too much like one of the experiments they'd tried at the Institute.

No. No, he was going to handle this.

But knowing he wasn't going to run wasn't the same as not wanting to.

* * *

Cassie wondered how Wynn was. They'd left the guarded gate without anyone questioning them. Why not? People left garages all the time. Cassie wasn't about to say anything to anyone with a cold, metallic gun pressed against her side.

Trunks were dark. Was there air in there? Was he all right?

I am in control. I am in control.

The anxiety behind the monotone repetition of his words answered her question.

The car hit a huge pothole and Cassie winced for Wynn.

She heard some words in Welsh. It was probably just as well she didn't know what they meant.

Wynn? It's me.

For a moment she could hear nothing.

That was a very long, very bad moment.

I forgot. Sorry. Forgot you were even there for a minute.

Cassie could feel how Wynn hated the closed, trapped feeling of the trunk. She could feel the waves of fear being firmly beaten back, only to creep in again.

Wonderful. He was only reinforcing her own fear.

Wynn, I've been trying, but I can't figure out where we are.

And you think I can figure it out?

Cassie bit her lip at the faint annoyance in the thought. That was good. Wynn was thinking about something else besides his confinement.

Hey, I'm the ally, not the enemy, Harmon. Remember?

Right. Listen, Cassie. I suspect we don't have much time. Let me explain about blocking. I have to teach you fast.

He was all right, then. He sounded coherent. He did sound in control.

Cassie knew neither of them were at their best as Wynn instructed her while he rolled and bumped with each turn and pothole. But she tried to learn.

Wynn had been right, though. There wasn't much time. The car braked soon afterwards.

They'd arrived.

* * *

Cassie watched Wynn when he was roughly pulled out of the trunk. She was pretty sure he wasn't watching her. Wynn stared straight ahead as if she wasn't even there. Or maybe as if he wasn't.

This was not the guy she had come to know. This was the original Wynn—the remote, detached one. The one you couldn't read.

Wynn knew he was with the enemy. Becoming an ice man might be Wynn's way of dealing with danger. Cassie knew she dealt with it differently. She got mad. She hated being pushed around. Always had. It might not be smart, but she could feel the anger snapping at her.

"Be gentle with her." Wynn's voice was as remote as his expression, but Cassie realized he had been watching while they tugged her by the arm to get her out.

"Worry about yourself, Harmon."

That is—was—Art's security chief.

Damn! How many of Art's employees are really working for the other side?

I wish I knew for sure.

"Why don't you worry about your next job, Stuart?" Wynn's voice was almost pleasant. "I figure Art won't be giving you much of a reference. Why'd you sell him out?"

"Hornsby wasn't going to do anything more for me. He's already let those damn Secret Service agents take over everything. I'm going to have more power and more money if I go against him than if I stay with him. To hell with him. To hell with you, too."

Cassie wasn't crazy about the conversation, but as the man spoke, his crushing grip on her arm eased. She had to figure that was what Wynn had had in mind when he bothered to talk to the scum in the first place.

Or was Wynn using some kind of mind command on the person who held her? She couldn't tell.

She looked around. They were in a warehouse. Not much was there that Cassie could tell. Nothing to identify the place at all. She almost wanted to giggle. This was just like the movies— a huge, half-lit, scary warehouse.

But the other people didn't seem to appreciate the cliché. She and Wynn were marched briskly along until they reached a brightly illuminated area where a man sat on a packing box.

The two goons shoved them forward. Cassie caught her balance before she sprawled in front of the seated man. The anger got just a little hotter inside. Then she looked up.

"We got them, sir." One of the men finally spoke.

Cassie heard the respect in the goon's tone and knew who they had to be looking at.

Cassie hadn't expected Emmanuel to look the way he did. He looked his name. Wynn might look tall and dark and spooky. This man didn't. Emmanuel was almost Wynn's height but he was golden. He was blond and golden tan and smiling. He had a beautiful smile. She'd never seen eyes that blue.

She'd never seen eyes that cold.

"Wow. We finally get to meet. I've heard so much about you, Godfrey." Cassie's voice was mild.

"Emmanuel."

"Godfrey—Emmanuel. Oh, yeah. One of those Savior-sounding names. I got confused."

For just a moment Wynn felt a huge desire to laugh. Damn that Cassie. She knew how to make something funny and have it sting at the same time. But Emmanuel didn't like either at his expense. The laugh inside Wynn died.

Bastard. Thought that would hurt his ego.

No, Cassie. Block your thoughts.

Like a light snuffed out, the thought was gone.

He couldn't read her mind anymore. He knew she couldn't read his. He'd retreated far into his brain. Nothing could reach there. He hoped. But he missed hearing Cassie's voice.

He hadn't realized how used he had gotten to having it pop in his mind at unexpected times. Her voice had almost become as familiar to him as his own thoughts. Bloody hell. He stopped thinking about that.

He tried to shut off thinking at all. That was safest for now.

Emmanuel had learned the same tricks he had at the Institute. He must have.

For a moment Wynn thought he felt a faint tug, almost a burrowing at his thoughts. That was probably going to be his only warning. Wynn retreated further.

"What have you been telling Art then, my man?" Wynn wasn't sure if Emmanuel said the words aloud or in his thoughts.

"I haven't been around to tell him much." Wynn spoke out loud, very evenly, all emotion out of his voice.

Emmanuel beamed at him. He looked like a saint out of heaven when he gave that smile. Wynn forced himself not to clench his hands or his teeth. No sign of emotion was better.

But he acknowledged that Emmanuel was soon going to be able to scare the hell out of him. Maybe he was already.

"You and I don't need to be around, as you say, to tell people whatever we choose."

Wynn suddenly realized something and hastily forced it out of his mind. Emmanuel didn't know about what Cassie could do. He wondered if Cassie had realized that, too.

"Handcuff him, Ullmann. We can't be too careful. Especially after your carelessness with him previously." Emmanuel's tone was cheerful, with just a slight sting to it in the last sentence.

Ullmann cuffed Wynn. Wynn still seemed impassive, but Cassie knew she couldn't help showing a little of the anger and fear she had.

She tried to smooth her face out. She couldn't afford to have anyone else see her react. They didn't care about her right now. That was good. That could give her an advantage.

Cassie knew she couldn't do anything stupid or impulsive. That might hurt Wynn. She wondered if she was really catching all of Rauss's thoughts or just imagining she heard him.

Suddenly she realized something. Rauss didn't know about her. How could he?

Don't think it.

The voice flashed in and out again. Wynn was looking at Emmanuel, not her. But she thought the voice was from Wynn.

Unless it was Emmanuel at his slyest.

At any rate, she carefully blocked out her thoughts again. To do so was a struggle, sort of like when she first learned to ride a bicycle. With practice she thought she could do her blocking as easily as she now could pedal a bike, but she hadn't had time to practice. Damn, she wasn't prepared enough for any of this!

She saw Wynn give a half-gasp, then his lips set firmly. He looked almost in pain. Lord, maybe even practice didn't help right now.

No. No, no, no.

Cassie heard the voice's protest. This time she was sure it was Wynn.

They always made you tell at the Institute, didn't they? No matter how much you wanted them to go away. I know. I know everything they did to make you tell, too. I made it easy. I always told them. Even when it wasn't true, I told them whatever it was they wanted to know. I heard you fought sometimes. I'll bet that hurt. And I know they always won.

That was Rauss.

Cassie knew she couldn't say anything, do anything. She wasn't supposed to know. Emmanuel didn't know what she could do. Wynn didn't want her to be found out. But she hadn't counted on having to hear this and pretend nothing was going on. She looked at the other men around the warehouse. They didn't react. They didn't know. She tried to act the way they were.

"I could find out what you know and what you told Art by several methods. I'll take the quickest way," Emmanuel said aloud.

He gestured and one of the men took out a small black bag. Emmanuel smiled, winningly, once again.

"I'm sure with your powers you can tell what's inside."

They tried this on you, didn't they? They would've done it to me but I was warned and got out in time. I bet it isn't much fun. You must have cried with joy when the Institute ran out of funding. Using drugs could destroy your abilities, don't you think? Or did it? You don't seem to be able to do much.

Cassie wasn't sure but she thought Wynn didn't respond. She didn't hear anything.

Maybe they were wrong about you at the Institute. After all, what are you anyhow? I own these people around me. I'm going to rule more when my plans are completed. What have you done with your life in comparison? I suppose you're proud that you're Art Hornsby's little pet. That's probably the highest achievement you could imagine.

What could she do for Wynn? She had to do something. For a moment Wynn looked at her then looked away. She couldn't see any expression in his eyes.

But then you were nothing before the Institute, too.

Suddenly, just faintly, so faintly she wasn't sure she heard it at all, she caught two words. Her breath caught. Even if she was wrong, she wanted to believe she had heard them.

Love you.

She didn't want to ponder why she wanted to hear those words. She wasn't sure whether or not Wynn heard Emmanuel's thoughts, but she knew Emmanuel was doing something—something terrible to Wynn. Wynn must find it difficult to respond only with silence.

Yet Wynn had risked saying that to her.

She shut her eyes for a moment. He'd better not believe that was his last chance to say anything like that to her again.

Cassie had never really thought of herself as some kind of female version of those ridiculous television heroes who came in and saved the day when everything was about to blow up. But she didn't see anyone else around to volunteer.

This might be the right time to act. Right now everyone else was concentrating on what was going to happen to Wynn. She could feel the energy surging up in her as she got ready to move.

There was only one problem.

What was she supposed to do?

Chapter Twelve

"Arthur." Lida stepped forward to give him a brief embrace and kissed his cheek.

That was her public greeting. After all, they'd known each other ever since she was in grade school.

Art smiled at her, but he still wasn't sure. Had he been a fool? Why would someone more than two decades younger than he really be so interested in him? He'd been a senator, an important man, ever since she was in puberty. And she had learned to value important men from her family. That education had begun long before he had ever met her.

"Sam."

Laura gave Jeffries's hand a shake while she smiled at him warmly. That was the correct greeting to give to a colleague you knew well if not too well.

Lida was so perfect. Too perfect?

"I asked you and Sam to come over tonight so that you could hear a decision I've come to about my campaign. I didn't make it lightly."

Both of them looked at him expectantly. He felt like he was on a podium. Art tried to make the words sound less like a speech and more spontaneous. But he had rehearsed the words and their alternatives, many times over.

"Both of you are very close to me so I wanted you two to be the first to know my decision about a running mate." Art hesitated. "I'm making my decision now because I expect that choice to be thoroughly checked out before I do the nomination. I don't want a nasty surprise."

"Yeah? Who is it?" Jeffries didn't waste a second.

"Glendon."

There was no sound at all in the room.

"Matt Glendon?" Jeffries sounded stunned. "I mean, he's a good man and all—"

"But what about me?"

For the first time, Art saw Lida's composure crack.

She was hurt and she was furious. He went to hold her and she stepped back.

Then she erased all those incorrect emotions and all he saw was an icy, well-mannered woman.

"My dear, I'm afraid I can't consider you." Art waited to see what would happen.

"Why not?" Her composed façade almost crumbled again, but then her training kicked in and she held steady.

Barely.

"First of all, our relationship—between your family and mine—is so close that the press would have a field day. They'd call it cronyism or pay back for all the help you and yours have given me. And second, well—"

"Yes?"

"You're a woman. This is going to be a hard-fought election. Not enough voters are ready to vote for you as a presidential candidate. I don't think enough would vote for you if I put you on my ticket. I just plain don't think the nation is ready for a female vice president."

There was no sound at all in the room again.

"Sam, may I talk to Art privately?"

Lida gave her sweetest smile to the campaign manager.

Art gave a brief thought to the security detail he had outside. He'd told them they needn't be present. Of course it would be all right.

"Go ahead, Sam." Art nodded to him.

This was Lida. If she wanted to yell at him in private, well, he supposed she had the right. He'd been yelled at plenty during this election year.

But after Sam left, she didn't yell.

She walked to him and held him. For a moment he thought everything really would be all right. His most reliable informant had been wrong at last.

Then she murmured, "Fine, darling. Was this a test? A joke? You aren't serious. After all, I deserve this chance. Wasn't I supportive and cooperative for you? In everything? Didn't you appreciate how nicely I stepped out, even though I was doing better than all the other candidates except you? I came in second, Art. Why can't I be second in command?"

The pain in his gut came back.

"I'm very serious, Lida."

That was when she looked at him. It was a cool, appraising look that made him uncomfortable.

"I'm sorry that you said that in front of Sam." Her voice was cool, too.

"I didn't mean to embarrass you, Lida—"

"I see you meant to make the decision final. But you'll just have to tell Sam that you've reconsidered."

"Oh?"

"Or you can tell Sam he better start damage control. Fast."

"What do you mean?"

"I can call about four journalists in less than five minutes and give them enough details about our affair to get the whole press corps buzzing. Your reputation will be gone in less than a half hour."

"You're threatening me?"

"No. I'm telling you. And don't try to bullshit me about how other men have weathered worse scandals. That wasn't during an election year and it wasn't with the woman talking. I can tell them we didn't just have sex. We talked policy, I helped you make decisions. I'll kiss and tell all right. You'll be dead meat."

Art looked at her. His Lida had disappeared. The woman he saw now was—someone else.

No. This must be Lida. The one who had managed to get to where she was in such a short period of time. The one who was her father's daughter. Jack Chatham was a good friend—mostly—but only when it was worth his while. Otherwise, as Art had learned to his cost long ago, he was a ruthless son-of-a-bitch.

That was it. She looked like a younger, female version of Jack Chatham at his meanest.

He'd handled Jack before. He could handle his daughter.

"Go ahead."

She stared at him.

"You're bluffing!" Lida breathed it out.

"Do it now. If you're going to try that as a threat, you'll use it later, too. Blow things open now."

"You'll never be able to do anything in politics again. Your party will disown you."

"Neither will you, Lida. I've had decades doing this. Being president would be an—achievement—but I don't need it anymore. You've just started. You'll go down with me and never get anywhere near what you want. Remember, should I win, we still have many options together. There are Cabinet positions available. I had been considering—But never mind. As president I can help you. As your discredited ex-lover, I can't do anything for you at all."

"Bastard."

She turned to walk out.

Art wondered, with a certain detachment, which way she would go. Would she take his advice or not? She was furious, but she wasn't stupid.

"Lida, my dear—"

She swung back, looking ready to kill.

"What?"

"Do you know someone named Rauss? Emmanuel Rauss?"

Complete, stunned dismay showed on her face for a moment. Then nothing at all. Art realized she really was still a little inexperienced. A few more years and she wouldn't crack at any question. She had recovered well. There was hope for her yet.

If you hoped for her to become an accomplished politician, that is. An accomplished politician who was associated with a crazy cult leader.

Then she left. She handled that with a certain polite perfection, too. She didn't even slam the door. It shut with a firm click as she marched out.

And there went his perfect woman. She was undoubtedly running off to call this Emmanuel and tell him how their plans were ruined. Art imagined the phone call Lida was about to make. She was going to be outraged and unhappy and look for sympathy.

Well, his plans for a refuge from the world with a woman had been ruined, too, but he doubted there was anyone in the world who wanted to give him any pity. He knew there wasn't anyone he could ask to give any.

Who the hell could he call for help right now? No one.

* * *

Emmanuel's cell phone gave a shrill beep. Everyone jumped. Cassie just jumped the right way. She went toward Ullmann and tried using her gift the way Wynn or Emmanuel might. She mentally snapped her command out.

Drop the gun!

She could feel the man's hand forcing itself open. That felt odd—like making a toy car move with a remote control. Cassie concentrated.

Then, to her stunned amazement, she realized she had done it. Looking bewildered, the one goon dropped the weapon and then hastily bent to retrieve it. But Cassie got there first.

She couldn't quite figure out why her reflexes were going quicker than anyone else's. Maybe the adrenaline was going so hard now that she was moving faster. She could see other people move, but they looked like they were almost in slow motion. She was in fast forward. Weird.

She didn't have time to think about why. She just had time to use it.

She scooped the gun up and cradled it against her.

"Free Wynn." She motioned to Ullmann.

As the man grudgingly undid what he had done a few moments before, she saw Wynn seem to come to with a start and move toward her.

"Can you use this?" she asked.

He grabbed the gun without a response. Yeah, well she was no expert but he looked like he could.

The three underlings began to move and then stopped when they saw what Wynn was doing. They seemed to think he could manage a weapon, too. Good.

But Emmanuel had disappeared. Not good.

"Cassie, get out." As he said it, Wynn shot the lights out overhead.

Cassie ran. But she didn't know the way out, especially now that it was really dark.

Wynn?

Then it occurred to her that Emmanuel could trick her, especially in the dark. What if he answered her?

She imagined running toward Emmanuel, all unknowing, and him grabbing her out of the dark. That would be just like the bogeyman in nightmares or horror movies.

She tried to laugh but couldn't. Emmanuel was the bogeyman. Her adrenaline was running down or at least she was suddenly aware that she was breathing hard from her running. She hadn't noticed that before.

She paused in a dark corner and tried to reassess. She could hear crashes in the back, away from her. But maybe that was where the exit was and they figured she would be there. Oh, damn. What next?

Suddenly she thought of snowflakes.

"Wynn?" she whispered it.

A hand touched her shoulder. She almost jumped and then she almost cried. Wynn.

"You OK?" His hand brushed over her to assess rather than comfort.

His touch was comforting all the same. Yeah, the adrenaline was definitely running out. Cassie clenched her teeth to try to keep them from chattering.

"Sure. Never better." She managed. "You?"

"I've been worse. Would have been worse, except for your insane trick back there." His whisper was barely audible, but she heard the exasperation clearly nonetheless. "You could've been killed."

"You would've been if I hadn't done something. Or worse."

"A fate worse than death? Ah, maybe. Probably. But hush. I'll get you out. Follow me." He gave her the lightest of kisses and then moved out.

Edging from shadow to shadow, listening for the sounds of others, took up a good bit of Cassie's time. Still she had time to think about what that *I'll get you out* meant. He better have meant *I'll get us out.*

She really didn't like the way she was interpreting Wynn's brief statements at the moment.

Cassie tried not to stumble over things in the dark but she was getting tired and increasingly afraid. Wynn would move closer to guide her when she needed it, but otherwise he was just a shadow in front of her.

He seemed very far away and, despite spending most of her life without using telepathy, she suddenly felt lost without using it with Wynn. She had never been overly trusting before, but she trusted him. Considering that they had been in nothing but danger recently, that implied a lot of faith or stupidity on her part.

She didn't care. Wherever he was going, she knew he was going to do his best to keep her safe. She decided that she would concentrate on keeping as hidden as possible and leave the rest to Wynn for now.

* * *

Wynn wasn't feeling at all sure about what he was going to do. He was almost glad that he and Cassie couldn't communicate with just their thoughts right now. He didn't want her to realize just how worried he was.

The panic wasn't there for him—or at least not as much. Not anymore. If all Emmanuel could do was shoot him with bullets or sodium pentothal...well, Wynn had lived through both once before. He could deal with what he knew.

When Emmanuel began probing his mind, Wynn figured that would be the end. If Emmanuel could destroy or cripple his gift, Wynn wasn't sure that he could go on. But he had managed to resist most of Emmanuel's telepathic linking attempts. The time Emmanuel had forced him to his knees, humiliating him, he'd been young and unprepared. Nothing like that had happened now.

So that must mean he could deal with whatever Emmanuel could try to do.

What he couldn't deal with was what Cassie would do or what others might do to her. He'd never expected to be so scared for anyone else, but he'd thought he'd have a stroke when he saw her waltz over and take the gun away. He supposed she'd gotten away with it because no one had expected her to do it. She couldn't do anything like that so easily a second time.

A second time and she'd be dead. But he knew she'd try if she thought she could manage it. She might try it even if she thought she couldn't.

Good. He could tell they were close to the door leading out. He heard nothing, but his neck was prickling again. There was danger nearby. Not just his gut but his head told him that. This would be a logical place for someone to wait. After all, he and Cassie would have to come out some time.

But he had the gun. If anyone else had a gun, wouldn't they have used it long before this? If so, the worst that could happen was that someone would follow Cassie and him—at least until they could get their hands on another weapon.

Wynn knew he needed to act fast, before that other weapon arrived.

"Cassie, when we get out, I want you to take off. Anywhere. I don't want to know where and I don't want to know how. They may try to follow you. I don't think so, but they might. Confuse them. We've thrown people off track together. You can do it alone."

"Where the hell will you be while I do this?" Cassie could feel a distinct need to wrap her hands around his neck—or his shoulders.

"I don't know. Wouldn't tell you if I did. I'm the one they want. I figure most or all of 'em will follow me. They don't think you're important. If we can keep things that way, you should be much safer."

"Wynn—"

"Hey, I'm the one who grew up with the con artist, remember? I'm fine. I'm more worried about you."

Cassie'd had enough. "Well, great. That makes everything OK. I don't need to give you a second thought then."

Wynn looked a little stunned and puzzled at her raised voice. Then he gave her a sudden, much harder, kiss than the last one.

"Thanks. Thanks for worrying." His expression closed up again.

Cassie wanted to yell at him some more. But she found she couldn't. Why wouldn't he expect her to worry, for heaven's sake? Even if no one had ever worried about him before, she was different. She was in l—

Oh. That.

Cassie stared at him, wondering if he had picked up on the thoughts she had grown too upset to remember to block.

If he did, he didn't show it. But then he could hide feelings really well. Instead he twisted open the door to the outside.

"I'll go first. Wait a bit. Then take off, sweetheart. Fast. Be tricky."

He hesitated a long moment then went on, more reluctantly. "If you get thoroughly stuck, use this phone number. An—ally of mine will answer. You call him Squint and he'll know I sent you. I believe he'll help you. We have a—a mutually advantageous relationship. Squint gives me information and I help him discover things he can't get from his damned computers and agency job."

He muttered a phone number and Cassie gaped at him. Impatiently he gestured and she repeated the number. He nodded.

"Don't use that unless you must. You hear me? I've never given anyone else Squint's number. I never thought I ever would."

Cassie nodded. He handed her the gun.

Oh, right. Like she knew what to do with it.

He hesitated a half second more before, without a kiss or wave, he walked out into the open.

Then he was moving down the alley without any more hesitation. He didn't try to hide. Cassie waited for a gunshot. There was nothing. In this case the silence was a good thing. She hoped.

After a moment or two she realized he was gone. Somewhere.

She was on her own.

And she had no money.

Wynn had said he was running low, but she'd left with nothing at all. Alone, chased by the bad guys and with no money, somewhere in New York City. Every woman's nightmare.

Damn that Wynn.

Looking for change, anything, she stuck her hands in her jean pockets. She could feel paper. She pulled the paper out. Amazingly, she now had several twenties and a fifty. How... Wynn. She hadn't even felt him do it.

She tried not to cry. He better not have given her all his money.

Before she let herself get too worked up, a glimmer of sense returned. If he was that slick at putting money in pockets, he could probably lift more out of someone else's. Before long he'd probably be rolling in money and then he'd find her again. If he could.

In the meantime she had to think for herself. Cassie told herself that she would come up with something on her own. She hadn't had any problems doing that—well, not too many— before she met Wynn. He seemed to believe she could manage a few thoughts, too. He'd told her to be tricky.

How tricky could she be? Cassie took a deep breath and began to make some plans. The only one she could come up with wasn't incredibly devious, but it was at least more of a plan than she'd had five minutes ago.

Very well then. She'd waited a few minutes. If Wynn could do it, so could she.

She took off in a quick walk down the alley.

Chapter Thirteen

Cassie sat up in the bed, her mouth unable to make a sound. The scream was frozen somewhere around her tonsils. The noise of someone opening the window was faint but she knew what it had to be. Someone was coming in.

She edged her hand out very slowly to find something heavy or sharp or any kind of weapon. Her hand fumbled in the dark. She wasn't familiar with the bedside stand and couldn't even figure out in her panic just what she was feeling.

"Cassie."

She almost hit him with the drinking glass anyhow, just on general principles.

She turned on the light instead. The light was a little dim but he looked fine. He didn't have any bullet holes. At the moment he was probably feeling better than she did. Her heart was still pounding.

"Damn, Wynn, you scared me. How did you find me anyhow?"

"A little telepathy—thanks for sending out the message—and a lot of common sense. You'd mentioned your stepfather."

"Oh, yeah. There must only be three or four million Tims in the city. Maybe more."

"Tim Borges, an artist, is a little easier. I had a friend of mine find his address—"

"Squint?" Cassie asked.

Wynn shrugged. "Yeah. I had Squint find his address. You thought of his last name when you talked about him to me."

"That still couldn't have been easy. He's changed addresses at least three times in the last year. And this loft is his—um—lady friend's. She's staying with him for the night. I thought I'd be safer here. But you found me anyhow."

She had hated the waiting. She had hated the uncertainty. She had especially hated seeing Tim again—or at least seeing Tim just the same as he ever was, except with a new woman to fuss over him. Maya was a nice enough person, but she wasn't Cassie's mom. That didn't matter to her stepfather. Tim had apparently found a perfectly good replacement for her mother in someone else.

Cassie didn't like to think anyone could ever replace her mother in any way. Maybe Tim was self-centered and shallow, but he shouldn't have found anyone else that could suit him the way her mother had.

Cassie almost wished she could find people to love that easily. For Tim, anyone who would take care of him would do. That meant her mother hadn't been that special at all to him. Not special in the way Cassie thought her mother had always been. Not special in the way Cassie found the few people she did love were special. She could never replace any of them.

Take Wynn, for example. She didn't think she'd ever even try. She couldn't.

Then Cassie determinedly shoved those nasty little thoughts aside and concentrated on Wynn. With him here she wouldn't have to stay much longer.

Wynn scrunched a little further down in the loft bed that reached almost, but not quite to the ceiling. Cassie could sit up, and Maya could. Wynn, however, was definitely cramped.

"That's because you went to Tim's first. I was waiting. Not quite as tricky as you could be, Cassie."

"Fine. Next time I'm being shadowed, I'll know better. No, no I won't. I had to get Tim's help. What else could I do besides take the next train back home? I don't have enough money to do much. Shoot, I was worried about buying a change of underwear. Even with Tim's help it hasn't been exactly fun. I've been sitting here for the last day and a half wondering what to do."

"I have some more money." Wynn didn't elaborate as to how. "And taking the next train back to D.C. isn't an altogether bad idea."

"What?"

"Getting back to D.C. isn't a bad plan. I'm feeling like Art needs some reinforcements."

"Sorry to repeat myself but—what?"

"Don't you read the paper?" Wynn tossed the *Times* down. The headline read: *Hornsby Pondering Vice Presidential*

Candidate Choices. "He must be making some decisions about now that could get him into trouble."

"Forget Emmanuel. I'm going to kill you instead. If we could've gone back to D.C. before, why have we been hiding and running?"

"Because they were afraid of what I would tell Art. I've told him. Now they know I have."

"I don't think Emmanuel is going to like you for doing that. Why wouldn't he kill you just because he doesn't like you?"

"Oh, he might. That's why Art has to be made aware that his Secret Service agents should be extra alert. That ought to help take care of his security. Old Jock may be one of the bad guys but I don't think Emmanuel's got all the Secret Service under his control. Really, once Art announces his pick, I think we're all safe. What can Emmanuel do? I'll just need to make sure Art doesn't take any risks before then. There are dangers out there no one else knows about except me. He needs my abilities right now."

"You're making my head hurt." Cassie gave her best moan. "And you make it sound too easy. How can we not be in danger? We could get Emmanuel arrested. Why wouldn't he want us out of the way just for that?"

Wynn shrugged.

"There's nothing we can say without making us—and Art—sound mighty foolish. We have no reason to talk. Emmanuel will think of that soon, too, if he hasn't already."

"Some megalomaniac is trying to kill us in order to run the country and we don't need to say anything?"

The worst part was that Cassie wasn't sure who was the bigger megalomaniac any more—Lida or Emmanuel. She had a feeling Lida must have taken on more than she could handle when she hired Emmanuel on.

Briefly Cassie wondered what Lida would do with Emmanuel afterward. She could almost feel sorry for her. Which would be harder? Dealing with him if you were president or if you weren't?

"If Art is president, he can take on that problem with the FBI or CIA or whoever."

"Won't Emmanuel think of that too? That no one is going to just let it drop?"

"Cassie—I can't sort it all out right now. I'm just feeling we need to get back. Soon. Will you trust me?" He looked hopeful. She could hear the unspoken: *Again?*

I trust you still, Wynn.

"I hoped you'd say that." Wynn slid himself next to her. "Now. This should prove interesting, given how close I'll be to the ceiling, but what do you say we go to bed together? I missed you."

Cassie could hardly believe he'd actually said that. The missing her part, that is.

He even sounded serious.

"Me, too, Wynn."

"I particularly missed certain parts of you—" The amused note was back in his voice.

"My mind was the first thing on your list, I'm sure." Cassie was relieved. That sounded much more like Wynn.

"Darling, I do love your convoluted, flaky mind. Your convoluted, flaky, sometimes missing mind."

When she laughed, Wynn relaxed. He had almost gotten too serious there. What if she believed him? What if he believed him?

But he had missed her. He was afraid that he had missed everything about her. Certainly he had missed her body—the one she was moving up against him now in a very interesting way—but he'd missed her mind, too. He'd missed her, damn it. All of her.

That was a problem if you were used to living your life on your own. If you were a person who needed to live your life on your own.

Attachments got entangling. You had to explain too much or too little. When you had to move on for a different job, other people didn't understand. If you sensed there was a problem and couldn't explain why, other people couldn't figure it out.

Of course, if anyone would understand, it would be Cassie.

Bloody hell, he had to stop thinking like that.

Besides she didn't always clue in. She didn't understand his need to get back to Washington. He couldn't explain that rationally and clearly. There was a tug pulling him there though, and he had learned to obey what his gift told him to do.

Cassie'd seemed to understand before but if she couldn't now—too bad. He could still learn to live without someone he had also learned to miss.

But when Cassie opened her mouth and moved it down his chest, he very happily forgot to think about anything.

* * *

Something wasn't right. Cassie couldn't quite put her finger on what was different about Wynn, although she was happily putting her fingers on other parts of Wynn that were starting to feel very familiar.

He was a little...off. A little too manic where he never had been. A little too ready to joke where he had been reserved. Maybe it was the tension. Or maybe it was because he felt a release from the tension after they got away from Emmanuel and his goons.

But he hadn't been that way before. Where before he had been almost too wary, too ready to run, now he seemed almost careless.

Suddenly she could feel a warmth both inside her body and her mind. That was Wynn's doing. The Wynn she knew.

Her intuition had been right. There were advantages to making love with someone who could enter your mind—she'd never had anything like sex while mind-linking before. She probably never would with anyone else.

There won't be anyone else.

Cassie almost stopped her exploration of his stomach at that thought. Had she thought it? Had he? She'd like to believe that there wouldn't ever be anyone else, now that she knew she loved him. But love had been around for her and then left before. Realistically—

No one else. Ever.

Her hands tightened on his thighs. She felt the muscles in his stomach quivering and smiled. She could feel her own response to his.

Tentative licks made him groan. She wanted to smile some more but became too involved in their mutual pleasure. His hands were on her and then clenched in her hair when her touch became more intimate still. Her lips fastened around his hard cock and she heard his sigh of pleasure.

She could feel the power in him bursting up higher, like sparks crackling in a fireplace. She began to get flickers of images, of her straddling him, of her moaning with pleasure. She sank down and then stroked herself back up that eager cock. She could feel the heat shooting through his erection, almost sizzling. This must be Wynn's fantasy she was entering. And it was kind of sexy and kinky, almost like seeing herself in a mirror while making love. Her excitement began to mount as the flickers became more intense, more erotic, more powerful.

Then she saw something completely puzzling. A sudden image flashed in her mind of a huge room of screaming, cheering people. And a man crumpling up in front of them. The cheering stopped. There was nothing but silence from the crowd.

A sudden wave of panic and fear swept through her. What was Wynn thinking now? If he thought that picture was romantic, he was terribly mistaken.

"What—" Cassie began and then his hands pulled her over him and she forgot the last image in the reality of what they were doing.

Cassie was straddling him, just the way he wanted. His cock slid into her. His body arched up into her. He withdrew and thrust up again. So beautiful. So urgent.

She looked down at him, watching him, watching his images of her in his mind and she could feel her vaginal muscles start to clench. Not much foreplay seemed to be required when she and Wynn were involved. Maybe the mental foreplay was more than enough. She was going to burn up with the heat they were generating.

Oh, yes, she was. Cassie moaned as her orgasmic spasms began. She saw Wynn's face tensing while he stared into her face. God, he was as close to the big finale as she was. Looking at him, at his excitement, she took off. She couldn't help herself. She knew he wouldn't be far behind.

But then he did something that, even in the midst of her final moments of pleasure, dismayed her. He pulled away from her just before he climaxed. His sperm, wet and plentiful, drenched her pubic hair as it spurted. Once. Twice. Three times.

"That was close."

"What?" she gasped, still shivering from aftershocks and just plain shock.

"No condoms, baby." His voice was rough. "We gotta get some. Don't want to have—to do that again."

She was a little comforted from the unevenness in his voice, especially as he pulled her closer to him. As he held her, she nestled next to him. Strange. She wasn't a nestler. Neither was he. And she didn't usually forget about things like protection. And she never liked being called baby. Not usually. But despite a niggling worry in the back of her thoughts, she liked all of those things right now.

"Cassie...always so good..." She thought she heard Wynn mutter that, with sleepy satisfaction, as he began to doze. He mustn't think anything was too wrong. Cassie wanted to smile but she was too tired to make the effort.

She'd figure out what was going on, what was going wrong, later. Not now. Not now. She felt so peaceful like this. Maybe this warm feeling was temporary, but for just this second, with Wynn's breath tickling near her ear, listening to his sigh as he gradually completely fell asleep, everything felt right.

As her body relaxed next to his, as she felt the heaviness of the arm that he threw over her body, she didn't feel trapped or isolated or worried or anything bad. She felt like—she groped for the word as she began to slide into sleep herself. There, she had it.

She felt like she was home.

Chapter Fourteen

"It's all here. They didn't destroy anything." Cassie couldn't keep the happiness out of her voice. "And Ned parked the car out front. Just like I was never gone."

She crawled out of the battered Ford compact. When Wynn had calmly walked to that car on the city street, opened the hood and, using a screwdriver and wire, hot-wired the car within minutes, she almost died. She was with a petty criminal.

A very quick, adept petty criminal who drove them all the way back to metropolitan D.C. in their stolen car. Somehow she was going to have to get the car back to its owner. Later. She'd think about that problem later.

She moved for the door. She was ecstatic about getting home for many reasons.

One of those reasons was moving the car away from the front of her house right now. All during the ride back, Cassie kept trying to not think people were after them and trying to figure out why Wynn was becoming more and more distant.

She wasn't getting any thought messages anymore. She was barely getting any words out of his mouth. Wynn was leaving her behind mentally, if not physically.

Although she was starting to wonder about the physical part, too.

She knew for a fact he hadn't stopped anywhere to buy condoms. That wasn't the Wynn she had come to know. Actually, forget Wynn. She had more than indicated she was ready and willing and he had seemed interested more than once. If he wasn't planning to have sex, then that wasn't any man she knew.

As they walked in, Cassie saw the blinking lights on her voice message unit. She winced when she thought about what those messages would be about. Lord, she was going to have to fast-talk so many outraged clients…

She looked around. Nothing was damaged, nothing was even out of place. Things were just as always, normal and expected. She could believe nothing had ever happened.

Then she saw Ned, head cradled in his arms, sitting at the kitchen table. She went toward him and he lifted his head up as Wynn came through the door behind her.

"Ned, what—oh."

She assessed the black eye and the very uncharacteristic expression on Ned's face. Ned wasn't Mr. Laid Back right now. He was unhappy. Very unhappy. Cassie realized she'd finally seen Ned truly upset at last.

"What the hell have you been getting into, Cass?" Ned's tone was edgy, too. "And why didn't you warn me?"

"Oh, God. Ned. I never thought about anyone hurting you!" She hadn't. People didn't get mad at Ned. Not beating up mad. What would be the point of doing that?

"You know, Cassie, you need to think about stuff more often before you get into it." He delivered that bit of wisdom as if he had lived it himself. "Like, those guys you've been hanging with are dangerous. There's been nothing but strange stuff going on here. Ever since him." He nodded at Wynn.

Suddenly she remembered the last time she'd seen Ned. He'd been boring and her life had become a numbing routine. Well, she'd gotten the something different she had wanted when Wynn first asked her to join him in this craziness. And she was certainly doing something new. Now even Ned was doing unfamiliar things.

"Oh, Ned. I understand. I'm so sorry. Really."

"Well, Cass, y'know, now that you're here I think I'm gonna take off. Y'know like really take off. Emily told me I should. But they said I had to stay until you showed up. Now you're here and I'm gone." Ned got up, looked a little blankly around, then focused on the door and moved toward it.

He paused and looked back at Cassie. "Maybe you better, too, Cass. You know?"

"Oh, Ned—" Cassie took a deep breath.

She had to tell him. Even Ned had feelings. No. She wasn't going to disparage Ned this time. Of course Ned had feelings. "Ned, I can't. I'm going to stay with Wynn. I have to. He's too important to me for me to leave."

Ned looked like he was going to say something more, but he didn't. Instead he touched her cheek the way he used to, once, long ago, when he'd mattered more to her.

And Ned was gone. He was going to, like, really take off and she hadn't said a real good-bye to him. Or had she? What more did she need to say? She turned to Wynn, who was standing near her. To keep her from leaving?

She'd like to think so but he'd shoved her away a lot lately. For her own good, of course. That's what he would say, anyhow. It didn't feel good, though.

"I hate to say Ned has a point. But he does. Why are we back here, Wynn? These guys are dangerous."

He didn't say anything. Cassie had a sudden urge to shake him, almost the way she used to want to shake Ned.

"Wynn!"

He was looking confused. Cassie refused to compare him to Ned again, but she was tempted.

Wynn might be confused, but he knew he was heading for trouble. He also knew he needed to make something clear.

"I'm not important to you. You don't love me." Wynn waited for the hysterics. He hadn't had to say that often to anyone but he'd never liked what happened after he did.

"Oh? Why not?" Cassie looked amused rather than shattered.

"Because I'm not the type of person people love. Because I don't know what to do with love."

"What do you have to do? I love you. You like being around me. We can stay around each other until things don't work.

Maybe that will never happen. Maybe that will happen tomorrow. But you can just go on being you."

"But you'll want something more than that someday." Wynn groped for the right thing to say to Cassie.

"What?"

"Well, marriage, I suppose."

She looked at him and shrugged, deliberately saying nothing more.

"Don't do that." Wynn didn't like the feeling of being shut out. He wasn't used to having Cassie do such a thing to him. "What's going on?"

"I don't want to get married. I've never wanted to get married. I didn't want to fall in love either, of course, but at least I've got some more control over the 'til-death-do-us-part thing."

"Why don't you want to get married?" Wynn almost added "To me?" and decided that would show too clearly how strangely insulted he felt.

"Wynn, I grew up in a commune, remember? My mom and dad had split up long ago. I hardly ever saw my dad. Then Mom met Tim. Bam! I may not have been crazy about growing up like a '60s flower child when the '60s were over, but I sure didn't like how everything changed once Tim showed up." Wynn watched her scowl, try to smooth out her face and then give up and scowl some more.

"Tim changed things? He doesn't seem like much of a mover and shaker."

"Well, he did. All of a sudden my mom, the original free spirit, was dying to get married. And Tim didn't want to be in the commune. He didn't want me, either."

"And—"

"And I was sent to my dad. To my dad and stepmother and baby brother. Believe me, if I barely knew Dad up until then, I had no idea who Tash or Hank were. Not that I had a chance to really settle in and get to know them."

"You said you went to boarding school." Wynn suddenly remembered. The words hadn't seemed important when she first said them.

"Yeah. The commune didn't prepare me to be upwardly mobile the way Dad and family were. The commune didn't prepare me for anything I hit with my new family. Tash and I lasted about a month together before she announced it was time for me to go to school. Somewhere else."

"I don't really see you in boarding school." Wynn tried to imagine it and came up with a disturbing picture of Cassie trapped at a place rather like the Institute.

"No one really saw me in boarding school except Tash, but Dad always let her do whatever she wanted about me. To give him credit, I suppose he didn't change all his opinions just for his spouse like Mom did. I don't think Dad ever had any opinions on what his children should do. Dad runs his family like his corporation. He delegates the stuff he doesn't think is important to other people who're willing to do the work." Cassie's scowl was ferocious now.

"And all this made you decide marriage was the wrong thing?" Wynn wished he knew how to make the scowl go away.

"Marriage sucks. Mom turned into someone else just because she married a jerk. My dad and Tash just reinforce each other's own prejudices. Now even Emily is getting a divorce. I don't want any of that. Marriage makes you into someone else. Marriage makes you do things you wouldn't do otherwise."

"Maybe that wasn't marriage. Maybe that was just your parents."

"What about Emily? If ever anyone could hold a marriage together, it ought to've been her. And then there was David. Everyone but Em thought we were perfect. What a mistake that turned out to be. No. I just haven't seen anything about marriage that's ever made me change my opinion."

Wynn wanted to say she was being childish, that she was holding on to opinions from problems that had happened to her long ago. Then he rethought.

Was he doing that, too?

Not knowing what to do with that idea, he concentrated on Cassie instead. Then he backed up a few sentences.

"Wait a minute. Who is David?"

"My ex."

"You were married before?" Wynn dimly remembered Cassie saying something about this long ago when he hadn't thought any of it mattered. Back when this guy didn't have a name and Cassie's feelings on love and marriage weren't vitally important.

Not that they should be important now, he supposed.

"Engaged. I told you this before, didn't I? Back in my lawyer days. We were going to be upwardly mobile together. He was an associate, too."

"He dumped you when you quit the firm?" Wynn felt a sudden urge to hit a guy he didn't know.

"I dumped him, thanks. He was just another problem I didn't want to deal with. After I decided that, Tash was sure I had cracked up. But I knew I was heading back to sanity with that decision. Marriage is all wrong for me. To be honest, love sort of stinks, too. But I'm willing to make an exception in your case."

Cassie waited while Wynn seemed to stand, immobile, for an amazingly long time. She figured he would ask more about David. She'd wondered why he'd let it slide for so long.

Funny. David had been smart and ambitious and seemed like a good match. But he had never meant nearly enough to her. She'd really almost forgotten him until now. Maybe Wynn had figured that out before.

At last Wynn responded, but not the way she expected. He looked at her and held out her hand.

"C'mon, Cassie. We're alone now. Let's go upstairs and go to bed."

She hesitated and he smiled at her.

"It will help, Cass. Trust me."

She trusted Wynn, all right. The problem was that she wasn't sure she was talking to Wynn anymore. Or not the Wynn she'd come to know. He'd been there for a few minutes but he was gone again. Then he grasped her hand and tugged it gently. She thought about refusing but she moved forward anyhow.

* * *

"Oh. You're here!" Lida ran to him, reaching both hands out. "I didn't expect you but I'm so glad."

She paused as she got closer, looking at him, and her face crumpled.

"You're angry."

"Disappointed, Lida."

"I did what I could. Art wasn't the way he usually is. He acted—he acted the way he would act toward anyone he thought might harm him. He told me what he planned to do and I didn't know how to react."

"Well, Lida, don't be too upset. I think he was warned about you."

She began to cry. He disliked crying in women.

"I'm sorry. So sorry, Emmanuel."

"Yes. Well. I've been thinking of alternatives to our original plan, my dear. I've come up with one. It isn't quite as good as the first, but we need to work with what we have."

She still was crying. Had he thought her remarkably composed for a woman? Apparently she could only manage that when things were going as she planned.

He gave an inward sigh.

"You still trust me, Emmanuel?"

"As much as ever, my dear. Here. Let me show you."

She gasped when he smoothed his hand under her skirt. But he could tell it wasn't a displeased gasp. Such things reassured women. Foolish creatures. Doing this meant nothing to him.

But she was one of his chosen few, the one he had picked to help him command. Even more importantly, Lida was his tool.

His very useful tool to getting him that much closer to ruling the masses who needed to serve him. He needed her to stay obedient.

"Bend over the desk, my dear," he whispered to her.

"Ohhh." Her mouth quivered. "Are you—? You know that I've never let any other man do this but you."

"Of course not." Emmanuel almost laughed. How could she?

She bent over, obediently, almost quivering with lust and anticipation and fear. The fear was what added enough spice to the game to make his penis stiffen.

"Lift your skirt. Slowly."

The trembling in her hands as she did it combined with the sight of her ass bent submissively over was enough. Emmanuel stepped forward and prepared himself. Then he began to press carefully, gently, into that tiny hole between her round cheeks.

"Ohhh." Her voice was almost a wail.

"Hush. Remember people could hear us," Emmanuel kept his own voice low.

He put his hands over her mouth.

She was tight. Not as tight as some but tight enough through the initial resistance. Her legs began to tremble, too, as he pressed home. He could feel her hand begin to diddle herself, slowly. He slid out, just as slowly, and waited a moment before thrusting forward again.

"Faster. Go faster," he ordered.

He lifted his hand off her mouth. She knew what was expected of her now. No outcry. Instead he put both hands on her shoulders, pinning her down so she would find it hard to move.

"Yes, Emmanuel." Lida sighed out the words softly. They both knew what happened next.

He pushed in more forcefully. "Now *come.*"

She gave out what sounded like a muted but pained cry as she obeyed him.

* * *

Wynn was tender. He was attentive. He took her clothes off slowly, bestowing kisses on her skin as he did so. Cassie began to enjoy herself. She couldn't help it.

"Cassie, you're so beautiful."

"You've never said that before."

"I've thought it before."

Not in front of me. You thought I was flaky, sexy, attractive, annoying—Wynn?

But Wynn didn't answer. He was kissing her breasts instead. If he was too busy to mind-talk with her, how could she complain?

He was concentrating on her, after all, and he was doing a very nice job of it. He was so gentle. So attentive. Every part of her body was being tasted and enjoyed and cared for. She sighed as his mouth turned to her needy wet pussy.

But with his silence, her doubts were coming back.

* * *

She was crying again. This time he knew it was from satisfaction, not unhappiness. He lifted his head and gave her a smile. She smiled back, with tears still in her eyes.

"That was amazing."

The praise was flattering, but women had told him that before. He didn't understand why they enjoyed what cost so little to him, but he didn't need to.

"Now you see how much I trust and need you, my dear?" He kept his tone soothing. "As long as you keep doing what I want, we'll be fine."

"Yes. Thank you." She kissed his hand.

"No need for thanks at all. And you understand my plan?"

"Oh, yes. I'm sure I can follow what you want me to do."

"I'm sure that you can, too, my dear. You've managed quite well so far. I need to leave now. We don't want people to see us together."

"Yes."

"And, Lida?"

"What?"

"Pull your skirt down, my dear." He remembered to smile charmingly.

He had been careful to cause a minimum of rumpling to her clothing since they were in her office. But she really needed to smooth the skirt down.

As he moved toward the door he felt a quick flicker of desire. He rarely indulged in sexual gratification. He rarely had a need. But that silly encounter with that woman had actually brought some physical urges on him.

He wondered what he might be able to get. Young boys were sometimes a problem to get discreetly. Especially when you wanted them to be restrained. That particular desire had come from his days at the Institute. Heaven knew he had been restrained often enough there as a boy. Usually that was for the testing but once or twice he had known there was a sexual component there with his testers—Emmanuel frowned. He didn't like to think of a time when he was alone, vulnerable and helpless.

But finding a young boy in that condition now might be pleasurable.

* * *

Cassie could feel herself coming. She didn't even want to, exactly, but Wynn knew what he was doing. She couldn't help herself. He knew where to touch, where to nibble, where to suck—

Stupid bitch. They always think it means something.

Cassie heard that thought loud and clear. She stared up at Wynn in amazement. That wasn't Wynn's voice. That couldn't be Wynn's voice.

And then she realized something else. Wynn was pulling back from her. He still had his pants on, for God's sake! Wasn't he interested in—in his own pleasure?

No. Apparently not. What was going on?

Emmanuel.

She felt like an idiot. Obviously something was wrong. She should have realized what that something was before this. Wynn had warned her. Back when he was himself.

Emmanuel didn't know she could read thoughts. That was why she wasn't getting many from Wynn. She was receiving ones from what had to be Emmanuel. And now she knew she could read all kinds of thoughts in Wynn's head—apparently whether Wynn thought them himself or whether they were transmitted to Wynn.

"Darling?" Wynn murmured the endearment to her.

He never called her that.

Keep her quiet and satisfied and she'll be no trouble. She's caused enough already.

"Just a minute, sweetie. Just lie here and I'll be back for round two," she said.

Oh, God. She wants more?

Wynn stretched out on her bed obediently. She looked at him as he lay there, docile and complacent, and knew what she had to do. Docile and complacent wasn't Wynn. She wanted Wynn back.

Rapidly she went to the closet and moved quickly. Wynn stared up at her in shock, complacency gone, when she tied him to the bed posts with her scarves. She wished they'd brought along the handcuffs.

"What? What?"

"We're doing things my way." Cassie finished knotting the last one. "This is for your own good."

Don't tie me up! They did that to me before!

And Cassie wasn't sure if that was Emmanuel or Wynn talking to her. Wynn looked terrified, but she definitely had his attention. He was focused entirely on her, not his thought transmittals. But she could feel the fear.

Now she wasn't sure she could do this. Not even for his own good.

But there was another way. Maybe. A better way? Maybe.

Cassie untied him. He swallowed, his hands still braced against the bedposts.

Don't move, Wynn.

"Cassie—" He swallowed again. But he didn't move. Cassie wasn't sure he could. Maybe she really could use her mind to control him this way.

"Trust me, Wynn. This will help you. Wynn, do you trust me?"

He said nothing for a long time. Cassie kept near him, kept stroking his face.

"Yes." The answer wasn't much more than a gasp, but she heard the response.

That was Wynn.

"Good. Now I can work with you." Cassie leaned over and kissed him, long and tenderly. "Keep trusting me. I won't hurt you."

* * *

Security had been tightened as the campaign started to move from winning the nomination to winning the presidency. Art was used to security, but not this much. Sometimes he felt like he couldn't breathe, he was so crowded by people protecting him.

Art glanced at the photograph on his desk. His wife was smiling. They'd never had children. Never been able to. He wondered if he would have felt quite so alone if he'd been able to have a son or daughter.

Hell, probably nothing would make a difference. He was simply becoming more and more aware of how isolated he was. If he won the election, things would only get worse.

He glanced over at the multitude of photographs on his wall. One of them showed Lida at a political fund-raiser with him. He had many photographs of him with various political figures. That had been his secret favorite.

He'd always been isolated. He had thought Lida was with him. That had been a lie. But now he knew he was alone. Crowded by people but absolutely alone. His awareness was the only difference.

Where the hell was Wynn? Wynn had started this whole thing and then ducked out of the aftermath. He'd been gone for weeks now, critical weeks for the campaign.

Perhaps Art had grown to depend on Harmon's information too much. There was no reason to trust the man, really, but Art had relied on the other man's insights because he'd known Wynn was another loner who distrusted others. He'd known Wynn was one of the few people left in the world who could give him new insights on being wary of others. And if Wynn said someone checked out, Art knew he was safe.

Art went back to pondering what he had tried not to think about ever since the Secret Service had told him the news. Security had seen Emmanuel Rauss entering Lida's office and leaving again shortly afterward. Damn. Wynn had been dead-on right.

He was going to have to find Wynn. If he could trust anyone, he could trust Wynn.

* * *

Wynn felt confused, turned on, turned off, terrified and ecstatic. Damn Cassie. Damn his body. Damn his mind. He'd never felt so hard in his life as with Cassie moving against him, sinuously, slowly, not letting up. He strained against the nonexistent bindings. He also hadn't felt this kind of fear in years. Not since the Institute.

And his thoughts—they kept veering all over the place. He could hear Cassie pouring in tender words, sexy words, comforting words. And he could hear an unfamiliar voice—he didn't know what it was—telling him that she was just a woman and all women were fools... And he knew there was something in him telling him to get away, not to let himself be trapped. He knew that thought wasn't a new one. He'd thought that plenty of times before.

And he heard something else, deeper in him, reminding him he could trust this woman because this was Cassie. God, he wanted to trust that idea, but there were so many other things telling him not to.

Then Cassie stopped moving. He steadied himself, wondering what she had planned.

I can't do this to you, Wynn. It's too much. I can feel that. I'll let you go.

"Yes." He paused, trying to sound reasonable. "No. Don't. Too out of control. Might hurt myself. You."

For a moment he felt rational. He felt in control of his brain. He'd promised to think of Cassie first. Protect her. This was the right thing.

"Go ahead." He forced the words out.

Cassie had a plan. He needed to go along with it.

She hesitated, then began to move again.

And then the clarity he had felt for that brief moment was gone. He wasn't rational anymore. He was afraid he was going out his mind instead. He just wasn't sure if it was going to be from lust, as her mouth closed over his cock, or from fear or from the contradictory thoughts clashing in his head.

He'd always been afraid he might lose his mind. His mother had, years ago, back when he was too young to remember. Da had finally told him she jumped out of a window. Her voice had been too much for her. Wynn had never wanted to follow—

Trust me, Wynn. Let go and trust me.

"Cassidy?" He wanted to tell her to stop. But he didn't want her to stop.

Then he gave in. He might go crazy if he did that. But he would go crazy if he didn't. He had to choose. At least he was going to get some pleasure this way.

I trust you.

This was Cassie, after all. And as he told her that, he could feel his whole body begin to knot up fiercely. He convulsed with pleasure, with pleasure close to pain, and he felt himself climaxing, coming into Cassie, who had climbed on top of him and was gripping him tightly.

He had no protection; he had nothing to shield himself from what she was doing to him, what she had done—

He screamed. He thought he might have yelled Cassie's name. But he knew he'd screamed so loudly his throat hurt. He lay there, shuddering, and felt Cassie's hands caressing where he had felt knots around his wrists and ankles.

He felt her smoothing away the imaginary marks they left, kissing his wrists and ankles. But now, imaginary bonds or not, he knew he could move again.

Well, he should be able to move. If his muscles would just come back. He was pretty sure he'd lost consciousness for a minute. He felt the sweat on his body. Then he opened his eyes.

Cassie was smiling at him.

Hello, Wynn. Welcome back. I missed you.

"That," Wynn managed to say one word, very carefully, and had to stop a moment. He was very proud that his voice didn't shake. "Was quite an experience."

And his arms managed to move. He held her tightly. Wynn was almost afraid he would hurt her, but he needed to keep her that close.

She was holding him just as tightly right back. For a moment he thought of just staying this way for the rest of his life. He liked that idea.

He had never felt this close to anyone, literally or figuratively, in his life.

"You do love me, you know," Cassie was telling him. "Just as much as I love you."

"Yes. I know." Wynn gave in again. After all, he'd said it once before, when he thought one of them was going to die. What was the harm in saying it now, when he felt so very alive?

I love you, Cassie.

After all, when he gave in to Cassie last time, things had felt pretty damn good.

Telling her made him feel pretty damn good too.

"Now what?" Cassie asked him.

"What d'you mean what?"

"You know what happened, don't you?"

"I might be a little naïve now and then, Cassidy, but I think I figured that much out. You aren't going to get pregnant, are you?"

"Jerk." Cassie slapped him lightly on the shoulder. "I meant you know why we're here and you were acting so strangely, don't you?"

His euphoria faded a little as he began to think again. Really think.

Emmanuel.

Emmanuel had done it to him again. He'd slipped right into his mind and had him doing things he never should have. Wynn looked around Cassie's bedroom. Like take Cassie back here. Back to where she could be easily found. Back into even more danger than before.

Emmanuel had helped make him act like an idiot again. Going to Jeffries's apartment had been bad enough, but he hadn't let Emmanuel sneak up on him in a very long time so perhaps he could be forgiven that lapse. Becoming overconfident a second time, however, and, even worse, letting Cassie come back into danger because of that overconfidence was sheer stupidity. Maybe Wynn could bear that for himself, but he wasn't going to let Cassie down because of his weakness.

"Cassie, I sent you away before for your own good. Without me, I'm pretty sure you're not in danger. All you need to do is go hide for a while, just until things get resolved—" Wynn stopped at the look on her face.

"I don't think so, Wynn."

Her words were gentle. She smiled at him, too, but he knew she was serious. She trailed her fingers against his neck and he shivered.

"But Cassidy—" He began to protest, unsure he even wanted to protest. Not sending her away sounded so seductive. Not being alone sounded so good.

"We're a team now, mister. And I don't know that I would be safer anywhere else. I wouldn't feel safer, I know that."

He wanted to argue. But he wasn't sure that he was right. He wasn't entirely sure of anything right now except that he was never going to let Emmanuel get to him again. Somehow.

Then Wynn remembered that Cassie had stopped Emmanuel last time. Maybe Wynn needed her around for his protection. Or he needed her to protect him so he could protect her. Like a team.

He'd never worked as part of a team.

"Oh, forget it." Wynn growled the words.

Arguing with a woman after having the most intense sexual experience of his life with her was too exhausting. He'd have to try again later.

But she always confused him.

Like now. Cassie didn't say anything more to him. No smart remarks, no loving ones.

She just smiled at him again with the welcoming, tremulous smile she'd given him after their sexual bout. Then she curled up against him and fell asleep.

He listened to her breathing and realized he should try to figure out what was going on.

Instead, Wynn went back to feeling confused. But this time he was feeling a good confusion. How the hell had Cassie managed to do that?

Chapter Fifteen

"This isn't exactly my kind of place." Wynn was careful to say the words mildly, reasonably. He was proud of the calm tone he achieved.

But Cassie giggled anyhow.

"No. I'm sure it isn't. But Joe is going to be in Amsterdam for the next few weeks. No one will think of connecting us to his house. Not even him."

Wynn looked at the *trompe l'oeil* painting on the wall and the fussy wallpaper and swallowed. He forgot about the calm reasonable approach.

"God, I hope not."

"C'mon, Wynn. Admit that there is some advantage to hanging out with a cleaning lady. I have keys to a lot of empty houses." Cassie grinned. "And I accidentally took this set with me when we left, so I'm pretty sure Emmanuel and crew won't know about Joe's house."

"Fine. If we have to stay here, we'll stay here. But don't try to make me agree I'll like it."

"Wouldn't dream of it. So do you want the burgundy bedroom or the lavender one?"

Wynn shut his eyes and took a deep breath. He could imagine both rooms right now. No. He couldn't. He really hoped he couldn't.

"Lavender would pretty much put me off my stride in the bedroom. For your sake, I think burgundy has to be a better choice."

Cassie laughed again. Then she sobered.

She wandered to the telephone, punched in numbers and then began to listen. Wynn decided she was checking in with her answering service.

When he heard her mutter ugly things softly and begin to scribble things down, he was sure of it.

"I can't believe Mrs. Land wants me to do another emergency cleaning job! And Emily is threatening to kill me if I don't call," Cassie moaned. Then she looked up. "Listen, Wynn. As long as we've settled the bedroom arrangement, I think it's time for us to talk."

The half-amused annoyance he had felt vanished into complete panic. Talk? What about? When women said those words that always meant trouble. Cassie was getting serious.

Whatever she was serious about, he didn't want to deal with it. He hadn't wanted to think about much of anything lately—he was starting to be afraid to plan things in case Emmanuel checked out his brain again.

Even more, he had wanted to drift for a while, to just enjoy being with Cassie. In the middle of one of the worst crises in his life and, hell, maybe the country's, for that matter, he just wanted to be with a woman and forget the rest. Maybe what was left of his brain had begun to rot.

"I bet Ned was an intellectual giant before he met you," Wynn mumbled. "Something about you destroys a man's brain cells."

Cassie stiffened, then paused.

You're not really mad. Or not at me. You're worried. Me, too, Wynn.

"All right, yes, I'm worried."

"And I think that was almost a compliment anyhow." Cassie finished the thought aloud.

"Almost."

"Anyhow. Wynn, I could hear and see Emmanuel's thoughts through you. Do you remember them?"

Wynn almost laughed. Cassie just wanted to talk about the danger they were in. He was less worried about that kind of problem than—well, whatever else Cassie might have brought up.

"Some of them. Not all. Emmanuel can erase a person's memory."

"Not mine. Perhaps that's because he didn't know he had to. But this is what I caught from you. Besides some really ugly thoughts about women which, despite your surly general attitude, I don't think you really think, I also got an image of someone shot and falling in front of a crowd. That must mean Emmanuel has thought up another plan."

Wynn rubbed his forehead. "That doesn't surprise me. Emmanuel never stops until he gets what he wants. Violence wouldn't surprise me, either. But can you figure out any more? Who is the man? Where is the crowd?"

"Art, I suppose. I can't place where the crowd is. But why shoot him before he becomes president?"

"Is that what you think Emmanuel wants to do?"

"I don't know. Yes. I think he does. I don't know why."

"Works for me. Why would he shoot Art now? Or at least soon?"

"If Lida doesn't get the vice president's slot?" Cassie asked. "Emmanuel hates women. All of us. But he seemed particularly angry about some woman—maybe he's mad at her in particular."

"And shooting Art would... Oh." He stopped but he'd already thought it. She'd know.

Wynn looked at her and waited.

"You said once that there would be no reason to hurt Art once he made his vice presidential selection. But what about before that?" Cassie echoed Wynn's thoughts.

"She withdrew from the primaries, but she still has delegate votes. A few. More than a few. More than anyone else except Art."

"If he was shot after the primaries and they couldn't hold any more, what happens?" Cassie asked. "I never was much good at political science."

"I don't know. But she might have a decent chance at getting the presidential nomination."

"You need to get to Art."

Wynn stood up.

"Right." He paused. "Alone. But if I go, will you be safe?"

"Sure. I might even be able to do my job."

"Cleaning by yourself in an empty house…"

"I'll call you if there's a problem." Cassie smiled. "By cell phone, not brain wave."

They both hesitated.

"Wynn—"

"Yes?"

Damned if he wanted to leave her. He couldn't figure out if that was because there was real danger or just that he didn't want to. Coward or totally unable to leave her alone? He didn't like either choice. Not long ago he had let her go off on her own right into danger. He couldn't do that to her now. Stupid or not, he was afraid to let her go on her own.

Meanwhile Cassie was looking nervous and then she began talking fast. "I did want to talk about something else, you know. About yesterday."

The tension came back again. He wasn't going to get away that easily after all.

"Yes?"

"You know why I did that to you, don't you? I don't get my jollies from doing things like that. I'm not into bondage."

"I know. You did it because it was going to get me back. But I don't understand how you knew."

"I don't either. But you were withdrawing in every way from me and from what you are. I couldn't let you leave. And— and that was what I needed to do."

"It worked." Wynn hesitated again. But she had started all this talking. He needed to know. "Cassie—"

"What?"

"I asked you before. Could you be pregnant?"

"I have contraceptives."

"Could you?"

"Probably not."

Maybe.

"Well then." Wynn swallowed. "Well. Then. I'll be back. Once I figure out how to get to Art before Jock sees me. Maybe it's time for Art to go take a walk. You can meet lots of old friends on walks."

"How do you know when he'll decide to go take a stroll? And the Secret Service agents won't let you near him—"

"I'll e-mail him first and hope he checks his messages."

This was ridiculous. Wynn had taken care of himself most of his life. He was taller and stronger than she was.

She was still afraid to let him go out on his own.

She tried to reason with herself. He might not be quite as old as she was—she had a feeling he wasn't even close to her twenty-nine—but he was plenty old enough to be allowed to make his own decisions. And she was terrified for him.

"You're making me crazy. I don't know what to do with you or about being in love."

"Guess I'm good at making you crazy." Wynn shoved his hands in his back jeans pockets. "But all this other stuff—"

Like love? Like worrying over you?

"Right. You know. Stuff. Same goes for me. For you."

Wynn was usually a lot more articulate than that. But he didn't say any more although he looked for a moment like he wanted to. Instead he just swallowed, then turned and walked out the door.

Cassie glared at the closed door. This was the first time he had said anything out loud about how much he cared and all he could manage was to mutter something about "stuff" and "same goes."

"Men. Why do we bother?"

Because I'd die for you, Cassie. You know that.

Cassie swallowed this time.

"Same goes, Harmon. Of course."

She scowled. Now she was supposed to be the one who stayed at home while he risked his life. She had never expected any of this. Never asked for it. Never wan—OK. She'd wanted love. Didn't everyone? But she hadn't wanted everything that came along with loving Wynn. Who could?

She couldn't return the bad stuff and keep the good, though. She knew she was stuck with the whole package.

He was quite a package, all in all. Sometimes it was better when she didn't think about who she was involved with. She loved a telepathic, way too young advisor to a presidential candidate. A candidate that was going to be shot unless she and Wynn could stop the bad guys. And she had thought Ned was a problem!

"I cannot think about this. I need to clean houses." For the first time in a long time Cassie resented having to deal with her job.

On the other hand she couldn't sit here in Joe's house, biting her nails and hoping everything was going to be all right.

Cassie automatically looked down at the list of cancellations and changes she had from the answering service. She went downstairs to start collecting mops and cleaning solutions. Between doing her job and placating the people she hadn't done work for, she would have a plenty busy enough day.

It was the last message that disturbed her most. Tash had called. Tash never called her at work. She hardly called her at all.

What new kind of trouble was Cassie in now?

The image of the man crumpling down flickered once again in her mind. Didn't she have enough trouble without her family butting in? Somehow she had a feeling that everything wasn't going to be wrapped up with Wynn trotting over to Art and telling him to watch out for stray bullets.

* * *

Art smiled when he saw him. The smile was warm and wide. Wynn had always liked it. He didn't flatter himself that Art couldn't turn that smile on for effect to anyone he chose, but Wynn liked to think Art meant it for him.

"Good to get some fresh air, Harmon, don't you think? Glad I happened to see you—no, no, he's all right. Friend of mine," Art tossed those words off to the intent-looking men surrounding him.

Wynn would like to think that, too. He knew Art had many friends, some useful, some political, some in name in only.

Wynn wasn't sure where Art classified him, but he supposed Art might be the only one who knew for sure.

"Glad we could meet." Wynn kept it brief.

Part of Wynn, the part that wasn't worried to death, said he should be proud of himself. He'd come a long way since the Institute—since before the Institute. After he got out, he'd sworn there was going to be nothing left of that scared kid who had to either please or trick people to survive. He'd done his best. He'd left his homeland. He'd worked to get rid of his old image and make himself into a powerful person, the man people turned to for help. He'd studied, worked, made plans.

Now he had a presidential candidate next to him, willing to listen to anything Wynn might have to say. He'd done what he set out to do.

"Hard to find any time to talk about anything but the campaign anymore." Art looked up at the sky. "What month is it now? Almost May? God, I'm already getting tired of the campaign."

"I know. Unfortunately this meeting is also about the campaign."

Art's gaze returned to earth and Wynn saw the other man was completely alert and focused on him. Art wasn't tired of the campaign just yet.

"Go ahead then." He moved up to just out of earshot of the Secret Service detail.

"I believe someone is going to make an attempt to silence you before you can announce your pick for the vice president." Wynn wanted to get the most important piece of the problem over with first.

"Ah."

Wynn began to talk, as urgently but succinctly as he could. Art said nothing. He listened but was silent. Wynn felt the prickle begin at the back of his neck.

Something's wrong.

Art wasn't reacting. His smile was pleasant, he was obviously taking Wynn's words in, but Wynn wasn't getting any real response from Art. There was no fear, no anger, no surprise. Even the most seasoned politician must have some reaction to hearing a determinedly evil man was planning to kill him.

Art wasn't really listening to him.

"So. What do you want to do?" Wynn prodded.

"Tell security. Let them do their job."

"Not Jock."

"Jock disappeared a few days ago. He hasn't come back. You know something about that?" Art looked at him.

"Maybe. Don't let him back."

Art's frown was real, for just a moment, then slid away into the bland expression he had before.

"Too bad. I liked the man."

What was wrong with Art?

There was an easy answer to that one. Emmanuel was what was wrong. What else could it be? Wynn thought about his own incredible lack of concern not too long ago in the face of danger.

Well, that wasn't good. Wynn hadn't been able to link with Art, but that didn't mean no one could. Emmanuel had a powerful gift.

If Emmanuel could slide into his mind without Wynn being aware of the entrance, then perhaps Emmanuel could enter the mind of someone Wynn couldn't.

Wynn swallowed.

He'd wondered which of them was more powerful. Now he wasn't sure he liked the answer. Hell, maybe Cassie was more powerful than he was, too. After all, she could figure out what had happened to Wynn when he couldn't. Funny how quickly someone could go from feeling proud of themselves to feeling like dirt within minutes.

He didn't like the scared feeling he was getting, either. How was he supposed to cope with this?

"I'll head out then, Art." Wynn figured he sounded casual, unconcerned. "You take care of yourself."

"Of course. Who else will?"

That same friendly smile flashed out. Wynn didn't feel warmed and included this time. Not too long ago he'd felt afraid, annoyed, worried. Now he felt sad.

Art needed to put on his politician act for him now. Art had never felt that need with Wynn before. He shouldn't have to feel that way about Wynn.

Wynn gripped the other man's hand in a quick, impersonal good-bye handshake. Obviously Art knew how to shake hands and move on quickly. Another trick he'd picked up from his job.

Inwardly Wynn mouthed his father's favorite Welsh curses. Why had he let his ambition get him into this? Why had he been kidding himself all these years? You couldn't depend on people but they got dependent on you. That was the biggest flaw with getting close to people in the first place. Not long ago he had been a man on his own, looking after himself, and now suddenly he was saddled with people. Worse, all of these people had problems that Wynn wanted to solve.

Who in their right mind wanted to do that? Why bother? He'd known how he felt about other people and their problems even when he'd been a little gutter rat running from trouble with his Da. You shouldn't care about people because you couldn't depend on them. Those were the words he'd recited like a mantra since he first saw Da creating messes and leaving others with the cleanup.

Obeying those old feelings, he accepted Art's dismissal for what it was, nodded, and started walking away. Walking away was easy.

He could feel the Secret Service agents staring at him as he went. They probably had him marked down as some mysterious threat. That was fine. Let them sniff out threats to Art.

If only he could believe they would figure out where the real threat was coming from and take care of the situation. Bloody hell, he'd love to wash his hands of all this and really take off.

But he couldn't. What sane Secret Service agent would ever believe in the danger Wynn knew existed? And even if some insane one was willing to entertain the idea all this might be true, what would that agent be able to do about it? What could anyone do?

Cassie.

Wynn felt a wash of relief. Maybe he couldn't beat Emmanuel on his own. But he wasn't alone, even though he might prefer things that way. He and Cassie were a team. Together they could at least match if not check Emmanuel.

He hoped.

He needed to talk to Cassie. He was out of ideas but that didn't mean they weren't going to be able to come up with some way to get all of them out of this mess.

He thought about Cassie, about watching her scowl thoughtfully as she concentrated on coming up with a plan. Just the thought of that scowl felt comforting. He needed Cassie right now. She might come up with some off the wall idea, but she'd come up with something. Cassie always did—or she helped him figure out what to do. She wouldn't leave him on his own in this. He could count on that.

Realization hit. Oh, God. Cassie was the person he depended on.

He'd told her he loved her, but he hadn't thought enough about what that meant. What was he supposed to do about her? Whatever it was, he knew he could never just walk away from her. He knew he didn't even want to do that. He depended on her and he cared too much.

Bloody, bloody hell. Everything he thought he'd known about himself was changing because of her. What did you do with all these feelings?

He didn't know what to do about Art and that bothered him. Needing Cassie's help for Art didn't bother him nearly as much as it should. But who could help him with Cassie?

No one. And that answer terrified him.

Chapter Sixteen

"Emily?"

"Cassie! Thank God!" Cassie was a little stunned when her normally unflappable girlfriend ran to her to give her a hug.

"Hey! It's not like I was gone that long!" Cassie protested.

"You idiot! I find Ned being beaten up by thugs in your house, you've disappeared and don't return any calls and then Ned tells me something about you being with this new guy who is bad news. If Ned thinks someone is bad news, I can't imagine how awful he is. What is going on?" Emily's hold on Cassie was changing from a hug to a shake.

"Unhand me and I'll tell you. Just calm down, will you?" Cassie took a step back.

Then she looked at the kitchen that she'd just entered.

Cassie vaguely remembered the large, pristine living room Emily had presided over during her marriage. Good food and drink combined with smart conversation. Cassie had always felt intimidated.

This was different.

"Your kitchen is a wreck!" Cassie said.

"You came here to give me household hints? I know it's a wreck. The oldest is down with the flu, the twins have been fighting and getting into things and I've been lucky to just manage to find time to cook food this weekend. Forget about cleaning up." Emily paused, took a deep breath and then said, "But enough about me. Tell me about your week, dear. Right now, damn it!"

Emily pointed to the one kitchen chair that didn't have something piled up in it. Cassie sat down.

"Actually I can't tell you everything," Cassie started, cautiously. "It's sort of complicated."

"And dangerous." Emily looked grim.

"Dangerous, yeah. I guess you could say it's dangerous."

"And how much of that is this new guy's fault?"

"Well, it's not exactly his fault. Not really."

Emily shut the kitchen door, locked it, and then stood in front of the door, arms crossed.

"I have time. The kids are asleep now. It's either clean up the kitchen or listen to you. So why don't you explain some more?"

Cassie realized her need to reassure her friend and get some reassurance was backfiring. She hadn't thought about what she could and couldn't say before now.

"Wynn isn't bad news, Em. He's a wonderful guy. Ned may not like him because Wynn is competition but Wynn is smart and—and he says he loves me."

"Somehow this doesn't reassure me. Maybe it was looking at those goons' faces when they were with Ned. Try telling me more."

"Um. Well, Wynn works for Senator Hornsby and he's— he's discovered something serious in the course of his job. Really serious." Cassie looked at Emily. "I don't know how much I can tell you, Em! It could be dangerous for you and, well, I don't know how much Wynn would want others to know."

Emily opened her mouth when a large thud came from outside. The two of them turned as another thud hit the door.

"I'm calling the police," Emily said.

She stopped in the middle of the kitchen.

"Damn it, where is the cell phone in here?" Emily snarled. "I can't find anything in this mess!"

Both Emily and Cassie began to pull things off the table and counters, trying to locate the phone. The thuds continued.

Emily held up the phone from under a mound of what looked like children's finger-painting just as the man burst through the door.

"What the hell is going on?" he roared.

"Wynn?" Cassie gasped. "Emily, it's Wynn!"

"Fine. Shall I call the police?" Emily didn't loose her grip on the phone.

"No, he's just upset for some reason. He isn't homicidal or anything, really!" Cassie gasped.

"I am bloody homicidal. I came back and you weren't there. I told myself you were off doing your job. So I waited. Woman, do you know what time it is? It's dark out! I thought for sure Emmanuel had taken you!" Wynn was shouting.

Wynn never shouted.

"I got done and I thought I should stop by Emily's and just tell her I'm all right." Cassie spoke as soothingly as she knew how. "Oh, Emily, this is Wynn. Wynn, Emily."

"Charmed, I'm sure," Emily murmured.

"I'm sorry about the door," Wynn didn't look too sorry. "I'll get it replaced, of course. Lucky for me it was one of those newer, flimsy models. Otherwise I might've broken my foot kicking it in."

"Lucky indeed." Emily stared pensively at the door.

"How did you find me?" Cassie asked.

Wynn looked at Emily and then back at her.

"I could tell when you got here," he told her.

I picked up on your thoughts. What do you think? We need to get out of here so we can talk.

"I'm going to check and make sure the kids didn't wake up after all that noise. I intend to be back in ten minutes or so. Make sure you tell me what is going on. And get your stories straight, will you?" Emily glared at both Cassie and Wynn. "Cassie, I assume you know this guy well enough to know whether he's dangerous. But, mister, if I hear anything going on that sounds like my friend is getting hurt—I mean, anything— I'm calling the police."

"And so you should." Wynn didn't look happy when he told her that. "But I'd never do anything like that to Cassie."

Emily narrowed her eyes, carefully studied Wynn, and then she walked out, still clutching the cell phone.

Wynn let out a long sigh that seemed to let out some of the uncharacteristic temper he'd displayed.

"I probably didn't make the best impression on your girlfriend," Wynn finally said. "But I was worried about you, you know. And I've been feeling a bit unsettled all day. Not having you where I thought you'd be was the last straw."

"That's OK. Emily pretty much has decided my taste in men will always be bad," Cassie told him.

Wynn winced a little. He knew he deserved more than that, though he didn't want to talk about his stupidity at the moment.

"Can we go home to finish this conversation? Your friend will be back in a few minutes. I doubt she really wants to see more of me." Wynn glanced over at the splintered lock on the door he'd kicked down.

"You have a point. I'll just tell her we're going or she'll call the police."

Wynn sighed again.

* * *

"So? What's up? You sounded like you needed to talk," Cassie sounded remarkably calm under the circumstances. Wynn had to give her credit for that.

Perversely, he wondered if he could shake her up with his news. He snapped out what had happened and what he thought might have happened without preliminaries. When he was done, he waited for her reaction.

She said nothing for a moment.

Then Cassie shrugged.

"Now what?" she asked.

"I was hoping you'd know."

His dependable Cassie. Wynn felt his mouth curving up, even as Cassie kept looking at him as if she had no clue.

"This is out of my league," Cassie told him. "Jesus, Wynn, almost everything you tell me is out of my league. How am I supposed to know how to save Art?"

"Because you're smart. Because your gift may even be more powerful than mine—after all, Emmanuel got to me, not you. Because you just will."

"Please. Emmanuel didn't even think I had a—a gift. He never tried to do anything to me. I can't blame him for not knowing. Shoot, I never even had a gift as far as I knew until you showed up. And what does all that have to do with me dealing with a presidential candidate's assassination anyhow?"

"I don't know. You're the college grad, not me." Wynn enjoyed the look on her face immensely.

"Yeah. I can see you need some education in logic." Exasperated, she slung the bucket and mop she had brought in the door close to his head. "I'm taking this to the kitchen. You can bring in the vacuum. That would at least be a sensible plan. I haven't gotten much sense from you so far."

Wynn trailed meekly behind her, still unreasonably—Cassie would say illogically—amused. For some reason being with her could both amuse and calm him. Even when she was being no help to him at all.

"All right then." Cassie put her equipment away and sat down at the table. "Let's strategize."

"Yes, ma'am." He folded his hands meekly on the table as he sat across from her. Pandora came from out of nowhere to leap into his lap. Absently he began to stroke the soft fur.

"You're telling me we have to save Art from Emmanuel and Art isn't going to help. Right?"

"Right."

"Who will?"

"I don't know." Wynn shrugged. "We know everyone around Art that he trusts is Emmanuel's. Or if they aren't, we still can't be sure of them."

"That bites." Cassie scowled and then stood up again.

She saw Wynn smile at her frown and she scowled harder. That didn't seem to stop his stupid grinning at all. The man could be very annoying. Rather than snap at him, she began to make coffee.

"Well, then. If we trust what I saw, then whatever happens will be in a big crowd. A friendly crowd."

"Indeed."

"Before he has nominated whoever it is he's picked."

"That should be really soon."

"Well, can't we go be part of a crowd? I guess we're the ones going to have to keep our eyes open. And our minds."

"We're going to go to every campaign rally Art is going to in the next few days? Have mercy!"

"It's not like I'm excited about doing this." Cassie looked exasperated again. "Do you have a better idea?"

No. He didn't. Damn it.

Cassie went back to scowling again.

"What if Emmanuel hasn't taken over Art's mind? What if you just think he has?"

"What does that mean? You think Art is just so distracted by the campaign—"

"—or maybe by realizing Lida and all his friends are betraying him—"

That he doesn't care anymore? Art had to know how strange things can get by the end of a campaign. He's done a million of them.

That doesn't mean he can't get hurt, Wynn! Besides, this is the biggest campaign of his life.

"Or do you mean something else?" Wynn scowled now. "Cassie, honestly here. Tell me."

"What?"

"You think Emmanuel is messing with me again?"

"Oh, God. You think Emmanuel has taken over Art's head because he's really taken over your head and made you think Art is the problem." Cassie gripped the coffee mug she had just taken out. "Ouch. Now my head hurts."

"We know he can place ideas in my mind. We don't know what, if anything, he can do with Art. It's just Art seemed so—so different. But maybe he only seemed different to me."

"Ouch! Ouch!" Cassie held up a hand. "Stop!"

She was playing the flake for him this time. And she was stalling for time. Wynn was getting too good at figuring her out, with or without telepathy.

"It's possible, isn't it?" Wynn knew what she didn't want to say.

"I haven't seen anything unusual about you lately. I knew last time. Eventually."

"But it's possible."

"Yeah."

"Then hanging around Art is the last thing I should do. I may be a danger to him."

"Well, no one is going to believe me if I go alone and point out a problem!" Cassie yelped. "I'm not Art's advisor! All he knows about me is that I was your messenger girl once. And I bet I wouldn't even get close enough to talk to him anyhow. You're our passport to Art. Damn Emmanuel. Now he's got you second-guessing yourself, and he probably hasn't done anything to you. He doesn't need to."

They were both quiet but Wynn could almost hear the frustration humming between the two of them.

"Back to the original plan. We go together. We both watch out for Art but you also watch for me," Wynn growled. "You're going to bring something along to stop me if you need to."

"What?"

"Surprise me. You're good at that."

And then she did.

In a small voice, Cassie said, "Wynn. Maybe I'm not much of a help to you. What if my gift isn't all that powerful? Hey, what if what I'm thinking will happen is entirely wrong?"

"Huh?"

"I'm not sure I can link up with anyone but you. I could get Emmanuel's thoughts, but only through your mind. Maybe you're the only one I can do this with. After all, I've never done this with anyone but you. Well, I did think once maybe Emmanuel made me call Ned but then I figured I was wrong. I think it's just you."

"I—don't know." Wynn thought about that. "You know we haven't been around many other people in the last few days. Those people we've been with are ones you had to block your gift from. Otherwise it's been just you and me. You haven't had much of a chance to try your gift."

That idea made him uncomfortable. He could be on his own for days without thinking much about it but being with just one other person and not feeling trapped—that was different. That was intimate.

Oh, bloody hell. Was he actually going to have to acknowledge that being with Cassie was different than with other people?

"Anyhow, what difference does that make now? For our current purposes, being able to talk to only me does just fine. Your main job is to be around to keep me in line, right?" Wynn dismissed the uncomfortable ideas Cassie was trying to introduce. "And if what you thought about Art being shot is wrong—well, good. We'll go to hear a few speeches for no particular reason. How can that manage to hurt us?"

Cassie didn't look like she wanted to forget the idea but before she could vent whatever was making her scowl, she relaxed.

"Maybe you're right. After all, just a few weeks ago I didn't know I had any gift. I thought I was nuts."

It's all a matter of perspective, Cassidy.

"Well, if we're going to spend a lot of time wandering around listening to speeches, you're going to have to help me," Cassie told him. "I have houses to clean and a schedule to juggle. How good are you at cleaning toilets?"

"I have no idea."

"Well, Mr. Helper, you're going to find out. We have a lot of houses to make up for. After they're taken care of, I'm going to have to sit down and figure out how I keep running my business and save Arthur Hornsby as well. My customers aren't crazy about having a cleaning person who doesn't clean houses."

Wynn thought over scrubbing dirty toilets with a certain amount of horror. But Cassie had a point. One he could improve on.

"All right. Hire a substitute until you can clean. No—I'll hire one."

"Substitutes can be hired to replace you if they're too good," Cassie said. "And I know a few who are almost that good. But—you're right. This is an emergency. I'll give Lucy and Vi a call and see if they can give me a hand."

"Good. Then maybe we can concentrate on saving a life instead of killing dust bunnies."

Cassie let the sarcasm go. Wynn was right. But so was she. What was she supposed to do when all this was over? She had a life. Maybe her life was mundane compared to political campaigns and possible death but it was her life. She wasn't going to allow this interruption to her usual routine to completely change everything. Even if they saved Art, what would happen if she lost her work?

She looked at Wynn, who had gotten up and gone to the window to stare out. Unless Wynn wanted something else. Wynn could change everything if he wanted to. She cared enough about him that he could—oh, make her move to a new city or change her line of work if that would suit him. She'd never thought of doing that for any man before.

When she'd thought about something like being with a guy at all, she'd always thought she never would be willing to change her life for a man. Now she'd be willing to try.

But she didn't know what he wanted.

Right now he was looking outside like a housecat who wanted to get outdoors and run. Wonderful. That image of a half-wild animal that was desperate to escape didn't make her feel too secure about changing her life to be with Wynn.

Cassie decided to give that line of thought up. She had enough things to concern her already. Things like trying to stay awake during political rallies.

"Cassie. I have something to say."

"Yeah?"

Cassie braced herself. When men said that, it meant things were over. He wanted out. He was going to tell her he was saying good-bye once all this trouble had been resolved.

"Will you marry me?"

"What?"

"You heard me."

"You're serious?"

How could a man who wouldn't even look at her when he proposed be serious?

"Would I ask you if I wasn't?"

All right. Now she had something new to worry about.

"Why?"

Wynn swung away from the window to glare at her. He looked absolutely furious.

"Here I thought I was being stupid because it took me so long to figure out the obvious. Don't you be an idiot. Why wouldn't I? I love you. You love me. We fit together. You know what I mean. We're right together. I could see me married to you. I do see me married to you. Don't you?"

And Cassie could see it. Almost. She and Wynn married. She'd never really thought about marriage—real marriage. Like her dad's? Or her mom's? She'd never wanted either. She'd seen one marrying into a conventional life with all convention's demands and the other marrying to defy convention and then fighting to gain respect and some sort of place in the world. Either way was too draining and unsatisfying.

Maybe that was why she'd avoided getting close to the marriage trap most of her adult life. Ned had been safe. She didn't have to worry about marriage with Ned. But Wynn—that was different. Marriage could almost be tempting with him.

"You're making my head hurt again," Cassie mumbled.

"Is that a no?" His voice sounded as angry as he looked.

"No. I mean, it's an I don't know. Wynn, I do love you, of course, but—"

"You think you couldn't marry me? Someone like me?"

Now she heard the faintest trace of—uncertainty? hurt? Oh, damn.

He was going to start to think about being a freak again and how no one would want him. Even if that idea was incredibly wrong and stupid, she didn't want Wynn to ever start believing she thought that of him.

"No! Of course not! Wynn, saying I'm not sure has nothing to do with you. If I did get married, I'd love to marry you. But I just don't think marriage is worth doing. I've seen my both parents' marriages up close and personal and, trust me, from what I've seen, I just don't want one. You don't, either."

His angry pose changed and Wynn moved closer to her, held her.

She relaxed. He was going to get the message. If anyone could, it was Wynn.

"Hmmm. I don't know. I've never seen a marriage, working or not. My mother died when I was too young and Da never had an interest in marrying again. But I thought we might think about the idea. Just think about it."

His arms were around her. For just a moment Cassie felt trapped and then she remembered who she was with. Wynn would let her go whenever she wanted. This was the guy who was on her side. Besides, she didn't want him to let her go.

Not just yet.

"W-why should we think about that?" Cassie tilted her neck back so he could kiss her throat.

"Everything sort of just hit me right now. I want to marry you because I'm afraid for you. Because I love you. If this works out and we actually get away with everything and live… I want to be sure we're together. I want to be with you, Cassie. I figured that much out. As far as I know, that means something serious. Something like marriage."

"I can agree with that much. Marriage is serious. It's scary, Wynn. And I can't think about it right now. You're right. We could die. We came pretty close before. Let's get out of this mess and then I can have some time to think about other things. All right?"

"As long as you will consider it."

"I will."

And Wynn's finger traced its way from her neck down to one nipple. She shivered. That felt really good. She didn't want to think—but, yes, if she ever did want a husband, Wynn wouldn't be so bad to marry. If she ever did.

Cassie decided to give him a little taste of how good it felt to be touched there. She reached up under his shirt. His male nipple responded nicely as she traced and then pinched it.

But they didn't have to be married to be a team. To be together. Wynn felt they had to do something to show they were united. Personally Cassie thought they had already shown each other how committed they were to each other. For some reason Wynn thought they should make some conventional gesture but marriage was totally unnecess—

"Oh, no, you don't." Wynn's voice was a little breathless. "I'm seducing you here into telling me yes."

"Ye—wait a minute. About what?" It was hard to think about what he meant.

Then his mouth followed his fingers and she knew she didn't want to do any thinking at all. Oh, Lord. When his mouth sucked hard on her nipple she felt like she could come right on the spot.

She slid her hands down to those nice tight buttocks of his and squeezed. Someone murmured approval. Cassie wasn't sure which one of them. She could feel how happy his cock was as it pressed up hard against her.

He began to rock his erection against her, right where she wanted the pressure. Oh, Lord, she was going to come before he even got inside her. She knew it; he knew it. The tension inside began to climb into a joyful crescendo of need—

She moaned into his ear.

The phone rang.

They both jumped. Cassie picked it up without thinking about anything much except getting rid of the intruder.

"Cassie?"

Cassie almost groaned for an entirely different reason. She should have let Joe's answering machine pick up.

"Tash? How did you find me?" Stupid question. She'd called Tash and she knew Tash had Caller I.D.

"Never mind. Where have you been?"

Tash's voice had none of its usual impervious, imperious tone.

"I had to take a sudden trip, Tash."

"Are you all right?"

"Yeah. Why?"

"Why? You tell me some ridiculous story about voices, then talk to me about coming into money and meeting some man and then you disappear for days. Days! Then you expect me not to wonder how you are? Your father and I kept expecting to hear from the police or the hospital."

"I didn't know you cared, Tash." Cassie almost snickered.

Then she stopped. No, she hadn't known Tash cared. Not like this. Tash sounded...concerned. Almost as concerned as Emily had been.

"Cassie. Stop this foolishness."

That was all Tash said.

Cassie stopped. She'd never really thought before about whether people ever worried about her. And she never would have guessed Tash would be one of those people.

"I'm all right, Tash. Really. And I'd appreciate it if you didn't tell anyone about the phone number. Anyone at all. Not even Dad."

"What's wrong?"

"Nothing." Cassie looked at Wynn and could tell he was baffled and annoyed. Of course he was. He wanted sex. And he wanted an answer. Men were like that. He certainly didn't want to have her to sit around and consider his proposal or chat with her stepmother. "Well, something. Now please don't make a big deal about this."

Tash's silence was compelling.

"I'd like you to meet someone. He's important to me. I'm not saying it's a lifetime, forever important. But…" Cassie tried to figure out where she was going with this. "But I'd like you to meet him."

She dropped the receiver before Tash could comment.

Wynn's eyes were lighting up.

Oh, damn. She'd given Tash and Wynn the wrong idea. Why, why, why didn't she ever think things through? They were only listening to her mention the "he's important" part. They'd ignore the maybe not forever part.

But nothing was forever, right?

Cassie thought about explaining that to Wynn, but he moved closer to her, and began to unzip her pants and she lost track of the conversation.

"Cass—"

He was going to want to know just how important he was to her. She didn't want to talk about that.

"You called someone else, didn't you, Cass?" He sounded almost resigned.

"Yes?" Cassie tried to sound innocent.

"We're going to have to move someplace else, aren't we, Cass?" He began to unbutton her shirt.

"Do we?"

"But not just this absolute minute. Let's give it another…oh, thirty or so."

Oh, yeah. That was a guy with romance and marriage on his mind. She could tell he was thinking a lot about her remarks to Tash.

She wasn't sure if she was amused, annoyed or something else. He unhooked her bra.

The something else feeling won.

"How about thirty-five?" she suggested.

Wynn's eyes narrowed. He pulled off her bra.

"I could do that."

Then she was naked. He was dressed and she was naked. Should that embarrass her? She felt hot instead. Sexy and eager and hot.

Wynn looked at her like she was the incarnation of sex as she slicked her hands down her nude body, his eyes watching the path her hands took. He liked her skin. He liked her breasts, her stomach, her waist, her thighs.

Naaaw.

He lusted after them. They both knew how much he lusted. Cassie wasn't surprised when he got on his knees in front of her, still dressed, but with a big bulge in his pants.

So beautiful, Cassie.

She sighed as he began to move his tongue, lazily, up and across her aching clitoris. His hands reached up to hold her legs in place as he nuzzled his face in closer and deeper.

"That's so wonderful, Wynn." Her voice sounded drugged, hoarse.

What had started as a challenge and had been meant to be a quickie was turning into a slow, seductive delight.

Wynn murmured something, the vibrations tickling the sensitive parts of her flesh and making her shiver with the sensation. Cassie's eyes shut but it didn't matter. She could see what Wynn saw, tasted, felt.

He fumbled with his pants, letting them slide down his legs.

Hurry, Wynn. I want you inside me when I come.

He stood and she slid herself up that long, lean body of his and wrapped her legs tightly around the small of his back. She felt a trickle of sweat run down his spine. And then she could feel his big, excited cock slipping into her as if they were meant to be this way, locked together, their breath shallow and desperate.

They stood there for a moment, unmoving. Together.

"You lied, Cassie."

"What?" He began moving, just slightly, the friction making her squirm. She was going to come, any second, any half-second.

"I'm damn important." His movements grew harder and she bit her lip to keep from crying out. Any millisecond. "You know it."

Now! Cassie felt herself cracking open as the wave of lust and heat and sensation rolled over her.

Too important. Too important to say the words aloud.

"Hmmm. I believe we still have another ten minutes or so until the deadline, Ms. Majors. Seeing as how I can make you scream for mercy within minutes, you want to try for a second helping?" Wynn's voice, no longer as urgent or worshipful, brought her back to earth.

Lust and annoyance and amusement all at once. How did the man manage that mix? Cassie licked her lips.

"I believe you were the one screaming for mercy by the end, Mr. Harmon." Cassie made her voice sound as snotty as his. "But I'm willing to go another round to prove it."

We do love each other, my dear flake. A love that means 'til death do us part. I'll prove that to you, too, before we're done.

Chapter Seventeen

Cassie stood, shifting her feet. Damn, her feet were tired. She wondered how politicians did it. They sat down, sure, but they had to stand, smiling and speechifying for hours, day after day. She didn't know how they managed it. She wasn't sure how much longer she could manage to do it. She'd had no idea how long a few weeks could be when she'd suggested this plan.

"...and that's why I want to be president!" Art hit his conclusion hard, just the way she'd heard him do in about three other times the exact same way.

The crowd began to clap. That was when Cassie's boredom began to change. Wynn had told her he could tell when danger was close. Now she could feel it in her gut.

"Wynn—" She touched his elbow.

He looked down at her. He knew, too.

Watch, Cassie.

Watch what?

But he didn't answer. Wynn didn't know what to look for any more than she did.

Then he began to edge away from her and toward the stage. Cassie watched him go, the fear tightening. The crowd was happy, pushing forward. Cassie watched Wynn, his head over most of the horde, moving steadily closer toward Art. Then her throat tightened up some more. She felt as if her brain had begun working properly again after being on half-speed for a while. Now her mind was clear and seeing the whole picture.

They'd missed something before. Something important. Something obvious.

She had never been able to see Lida controlling Emmanuel—to see anyone controlling Emmanuel. Emmanuel's thoughts about women had been much too angry for Cassie to believe he would take Lida's orders. What if Emmanuel was in charge? Emmanuel had been taking everything much too personally.

Deciding who was the real boss didn't matter for her other, more important, insight. She and Wynn had been looking at things the wrong way. If Art had finally become Emmanuel's mind slave, then Emmanuel didn't need Art dead. In fact, he would most definitely want Art alive.

But if Art wouldn't be the one shot, then who would Emmanuel want dead?

Cassie lunged forward.

But Cassie was short. She couldn't push her way through the masses of bodies. She couldn't even see where she was going as the crowd closed in.

Wynn. Oh, God. Wynn.

Emmanuel wants to kill you. Here. Now.

She tried to send him a message but she didn't know if he reacted or heard. She couldn't see anything but someone else's back jammed right in front of her.

"And now I know you've been waiting for this announcement…thought long and hard…"

He was going to announce his running mate. Now. Unless, of course, he was stopped. Oh, God. Cassie wasn't sure what to think now. If Art wasn't under Emmanuel's control, then Art was going to die.

Art or Wynn?

Or both.

If they were both together, wouldn't that be the quick way, the easy way to get rid of two problems? Cassie pushed fiercely at the man in front of her and slithered between him and another body before she could think about any more.

She didn't even know what she'd do when she did get closer. She just knew she had to.

Ironically, somehow, a few feet from the stage, there was a small opening and Cassie looked up to see Wynn speaking to someone on the security detail and then being allowed to get on stage.

No!

But Wynn didn't glance her way. Couldn't he hear her in the crowd? Had she lost her ability somehow as she began to panic?

Stupid bastard. I knew he'd be here.

Cassie sucked in a breath. Well, that answered her question about whether she could only hear Wynn's thoughts. And whether Emmanuel was around. She knew that wasn't Wynn talking.

She turned, somehow knowing where Emmanuel was and saw him in the balcony of the auditorium, smiling his brilliant smile. She didn't see a gun but she didn't need to see it. She knew that it was there. There was someone next to him. Carter? Cassie tried to figure out how she'd get the attention of someone, anyone dealing with security.

And then she heard a shout from the stage and jerked her head back that way.

And she saw Wynn rush forward to pull Art down. His arm knocked the older man down. But just as he did, she also saw Wynn begin to crumple.

"Omygodomygodomy—" And Cassie realized that was her voice.

Some people were rushing on the stage, she saw others running toward the balcony. Cassie somehow managed to hurtle forward and throw herself onto the stage.

Wynn!

And he still didn't answer her.

In the balcony above her she could hear shouting. Men must be wrestling with Carter and Emmanuel. She didn't look. Cassie kept moving toward the group around Art and Wynn. Then on the stage she could hear something else.

A voice. Wynn's voice, steady and insistent, in her head. But he wasn't talking to her.

Tell them. Tell them. Tell them they're wrong to hold you. Tell them you deserve to rule them. Tell them what you think. Tell them what scum they are. Tell. Tell.

Cassie looked up again, involuntarily. The guards had already wrestled Carter to the ground.

Emmanuel was still standing. He might have gotten away but he'd stopped in the middle of the uproar. She couldn't hear Emmanuel's voice but she saw his lips moving. She could tell he was screaming.

She heard one of the Secret Service agents, listening in on his earphone, mutter just loud enough near her for anyone to hear, "Think we've got a St. Elizabeth's candidate."

That was where the man who tried to shoot Reagan was. That was where they put people who were mentally incapacitated. Crazy.

Don't hold back now... Tell them. C'mon, Richie.

That was Wynn's voice in her head but it was beginning to waver in and out, blurring in her mind. Her ability to hear was getting bad? She didn't think so.

Was his inner voice was getting weaker? Was he getting weaker?

The image of blackness was rolling closer and closer in her mind. Something was going wrong. She tried to reach out mentally, to somehow grip onto Wynn before that blackness overtook him. But she couldn't feel anything happening between them.

Desperate, Cassie changed tactics, used her lack of size to her advantage, and dove under some legs. She got close enough to touch Wynn before hands grabbed at her.

"No, she's OK. She's mine."

That was Wynn's voice, thready but still recognizable. The hands let go. Cassie would have been relieved, but then she touched his face and felt blood.

"Wynn, how are you?"

His eyes almost shut and then opened again, slowly. He made an effort and focused on her.

"I've been better. Glad you made it, though."

She wanted to slap him. She wanted to kiss him. How could he have scared her that badly?

Why me? Why me? Don't you understand who you're dealing with? Don't touch me! Don't handcuff me!

Cassie blocked the screaming voice from her mind. She wanted to concentrate on Wynn. She needed to concentrate on him.

Wynn kept looking at her as if he was making a huge effort just to do that. How badly was he hurt anyhow? She grabbed his hand.

"Wynn? Wynn, damn it, tell me what's wrong! Damn, where's a doctor? Hey! He needs a doctor!"

He smiled, crookedly. He opened his mouth and she thought he was going to make smart remark. And then, right in front of her, she saw him shut his eyes and lose consciousness.

* * *

"Why'd you call him Richie?"

Those were the first words Wynn heard when he came back. He scowled, trying to think past the headache. That must be Cassie talking. Who else would ask a question like that?

He could figure out where he was, too. He could feel something in his arm that he figured was an I.V. That must mean he was in a hospital. He didn't like hospitals.

Wynn cautiously half-opened his eyes, but the light hurt and he shut them again. He could see Cassie was there, though. She looked a lot less calm than her voice sounded. He tried to gather strength. He knew he needed to talk to her, to reassure her.

"His name."

"Emmanuel was a *Richie* once?"

"At the Institute."

"That doesn't sound very Godlike to me. I can see why he wanted to change his name."

Wynn wanted to smile but he figured the twist of his lips would send more throbs of pain up to his temples. He hurt. He should be glad about feeling pain since he must still be alive. But mostly he just hurt.

"Well, he's nicely shut up at St. Elizabeth's until they can determine his mental capacity to stand trial. But you made him really lose it, Wynn."

He'd done what he set out to do. Even while Wynn could feel himself black out, he'd hung onto the idea that he had to get into Emmanuel's mind and make him spill his guts. If Emmanuel just said what was on his mind, no one would let him loose. If Emmanuel was declared mentally incapable, he'd be at Saint Elizabeth's longer than he'd stay in jail. No one would ever believe anything he would tell them after that.

And while he was there, Cassie and Art would be safe.

"Good." Wynn mouthed the word.

Then Wynn waited. He heard nothing more. He felt Cassie squeeze his hand. He wanted to squeeze back but he felt tired. Tired and weak.

"Wynn?" Cassie sounded worried. "Wynn, don't you?"

Don't I what?

"Wynn. Oh, damn. You're too tired. That must be why I can't hear you. I know you love me. I love you, too. And I am so glad you're all right."

He felt her kiss him and he slid back into a voiceless, dreamless sleep.

* * *

He wasn't sure when he realized he wasn't all right. At first just having the headache fade was enough. Watching the I.V. come out was a good thing, too. Then came the attention. Cassie was always there, of course. Wynn realized he expected her to be there and she never failed him.

But Art came to the hospital, too. This time the concern Art expressed felt real. The flowers he sent were real, too. Art promised to be back to visit him soon. Wynn thought that, campaign or no campaign, Art probably would visit again. But if he didn't, that was all right, too. Wynn knew the real man—or as real as any potential future president could be—had been in the hospital room with him. That was good enough for him.

He'd had less welcome attention. The press had tried to visit him, too. Cassie and the nurses had been able to deal with that for now. From the coverage the news reports were giving Emmanuel and crew, Wynn could only be grateful they weren't able to scrutinize him. He'd always wanted to spend his life as low profile as he could.

Eventually the concussion headache left completely. He'd gotten that after he pitched forward from the bullet wound in his shoulder. Both the bullet and the concussion seemed like nothing compared to what might have happened. No, they were nothing. He'd probably have been sent home immediately if not for the way he'd gotten hurt. The hospital didn't want to be accused of neglecting the man who rescued Art Hornsby. Unfortunately, except that being in the hospital made it easier to dodge the media, Wynn would have much preferred to leave. Staying in the hospital was much too much like the Institute. If he never entered another similar place in his life, he'd be overjoyed.

On the other hand, he was also nervous about leaving. Once he was discharged he knew he was supposed to be fine. But he wasn't. As his thought processes got clearer, he realized something besides the headache and the bullet had left, too, during his hospital stay. Something much more important to him. Something he was not going to talk to any of the hospital staff about.

It had taken a while to him to understand what had happened. He first realized it when Cassie gave him odd looks now and then during her visits as if he was supposed to reply to something. He understood it even more when he would wake up, feeling oddly expectant, only to realize he felt and heard nothing.

Wynn knew he had to accept that his mind wasn't functioning right.

He'd stayed awake at night, his uninjured arm crossed under his head, listening to the sounds of the hospital and wondering what that would mean for his future. His thoughts made it a very long night.

He finally decided to confront the problem the next day when Cassie was going to take him back to her place. He was officially healed—or at least as healed as much as anyone at the hospital was going to care about. Wynn knew that this was as good as he was going to get. There was no point avoiding the truth anymore.

It was only fair to tell Cassie. He was afraid. He had some faint hope Cassie could figure out the problem and fix it for him, but he kept that stupid hope firmly in its place. No one was going to be able to take care of this one.

Not even Cassie.

He watched silently as Cassie bustled in, kissed him, and then began efficiently throwing things in a suitcase to get him out. Cassie obviously didn't want to waste time. Well, he didn't either.

"It's gone."

"What is?" Cassie picked up his shaving cream and dumped it in the bag as he saw the nurses coming down the hall with a wheelchair for him. He didn't have a lot more time to tell her.

"You know." Wynn saw he was clenching his hands.

How could she not know?

"What?" Cassie looked around as if she honestly meant to gather up the missing item and throw it in the bag with his socks and watch.

He could have shaken her for missing what was so obvious. "My gift. I don't have my gift anymore."

Chapter Eighteen

She didn't answer. She couldn't. The nurses came in at that point and hustled him down the hall in the wheelchair while Cassie went to get her car. They didn't leave where most patients did, in case the press was waiting to pounce.

Wynn watched the car drive up, feeling like an idiot. His shoulder hurt, not his legs, but he had to wait in the wheelchair anyhow. The nurses deposited him onto the car seat, waved, and then he was no longer a patient. He was on his own...except for Cassie.

He waited, but Cassie didn't say anything even then. She just started the BMW and drove them out of sight of the place.

"Well?" Wynn couldn't outwait her any longer.

"Well, what?"

"I don't have my gift anymore. You don't think that's worth even a little exclamation or a 'Too bad' or—"

Cassie's voice sounded hesitant. "I had begun to wonder why we weren't talking anymore the way we did. Are you sure?"

"Of course I'm sure."

"Maybe you just—like, strained yourself when you forced Emmanuel to do what you wanted even though you were blacking out. Maybe you just need to rest."

"I've never had to before."

"All this never happened to you before. Why don't you just put it aside for now? You have enough to deal with."

"The hell with that!" Wynn let his frustration roar out. "I don't have my gift anymore. How do I put that aside?"

"Fine. Sulk. What am I supposed to do about it?" Cassie snapped.

Wynn didn't sulk. He was careful not to sulk.

He fumed instead. He couldn't believe Cassie didn't say any more to him. She acted as if he didn't exist.

She acted as if she didn't give a damn. She wasn't even yelling at him. Fuming stopped.

A trickle of uneasiness set in.

Had she figured out the problem before he told her? Was she thinking of a way to politely tell him that without his gift he wasn't welcome? He already felt isolated from her, from everyone.

All these years he had wondered what it would be like to stop having his gift, and now he knew. He felt wrong. He was used to being the way he had been, blast it!

And Cassie was used to him that way, too. She'd told him she loved him then.

Wynn followed Cassie out of the car, careful not to jar his shoulder. The condo looked the same but he wasn't sure he was as welcome as he used to be. At least Pandora greeted him. She wound herself around his legs and demanded, with a regal yowl, to be picked up and petted.

Cassie dumped his bag upstairs—in her bedroom—he noted with some relief. Then she came down and propped herself against the kitchen doorframe.

"Well, then?" she asked.

"Well, then what?" Wynn put Pandora down.

"You looked ready to go a few rounds with me, Wynn. What about?"

"No. If you want to, though, you can take me back to my place."

"What? Why would I want to do that?"

"I get the feeling I'm not wanted around here." Wynn didn't know what demon of perversity was making him say what he was saying, but he knew he couldn't stop.

"There must be more than one piece missing out of your brain, Wynn."

Wynn almost laughed from relief. That sounded like Cassie. The Cassie who would worry over him and snap at him at the same time.

"Listen, I'm not the one who doesn't want to get married. I'm not the one who still has telepathy."

"Yeah. Great. Anything I want to know I can tap into your mind and find out for myself but it wouldn't be fair to do that if you can't do the same to me. I also finally figured out that I can tap into Emmanuel's. I don't want to do that. So I guess having your gift gone cancels out mine, huh?" Cassie didn't sound overly concerned as she sat down.

But she hadn't grown up with her gift, so maybe it wasn't as much a part of her. Wynn wanted to tell her how he felt but he wasn't sure he could.

Reluctantly Wynn decided to follow her advice and put it aside. Besides, he now had another concern to gnaw over. It was the other thing that had kept him awake and staring up at the hospital ceiling for a long time.

He had to find out. She had to find out, too.

Maybe he should use more finesse, but he wasn't ready for finesse right then. He pulled her up to her feet again. He could tell he had startled her.

"What? What, Wynn?"

She didn't know. She was playing fair. She wasn't checking into his brain. He was sure she would have to know if she did. It was all he could think about.

He opened his mouth and the doorbell rang.

"What?" Cassie asked again, definite irritation in her voice now.

She marched grimly to the door and opened it up before Wynn could yell at her to check through the peephole.

"Oh!" There was almost a note of terror in her voice.

Then people burst through the door.

Wynn tensed until he saw who they were. More importantly, he saw who several of them looked like.

They had to be related to Cassie.

"Darling, we couldn't wait for the telephone call I know you planned to give us any minute." Tash's cool tones cut through the stunned moment. "So your father and brother and I just ran over to see you two for ourselves."

Wynn assessed the people in front of him. There was one grizzled large man, with the same color brown-green eyes as Cassie, one petite older woman holding a bouquet and looking fragile and feminine, and one younger guy who, though he looked like the woman, also had eyes like Cassie.

"How're you feeling, Harmon?" Cassie's father walked over to Wynn, deliberately surveyed him and nodded. "Looks like you still feel like hell but you'll live."

Wynn realized he didn't know what to say any more than Cassie did. He shook hands instead.

"Uh. Right. I'm better."

"I'm glad." Cassie's brother Hank told him, still staying back. "The news reports didn't sound too good. I saw Cassie was there and that's why I wanted us to—"

He stopped and didn't finish his sentence. The silence didn't last long.

"We were terribly worried, of course, and we didn't hear anything from either of you." Tash didn't sound worried. She sounded accusing. "We brought flowers."

Wynn tried not to look as baffled as he felt while Cassie began to fuss with them. Flowers? He'd never had anyone give him flowers before this week. Now he was being flooded with them. What were you supposed to say about them?

What were you supposed to say, period, when you were half-ready to fight with a woman and half-ready to make love with her and then her family burst in?

"Nice flowers, Tash. You have a good eye." Cassie put the last of them in a vase she'd produced from somewhere in her cluttered cabinet.

"Thanks." Wynn finally produced something he knew he should say.

"Those aren't nearly as magnificent as the ones I could get for the ceremony." Tash pushed Cassie aside to fuss with the flowers herself.

"What ceremony?"

"Your wedding, of course." Tash smiled, sweetly. "I'm sure you have something to tell us, Cassie. I saw on the news how you rushed to Wynn's side after the shooting. A woman doesn't do that unless—"

"Unless she's worried about someone." Cassie's lower lip was almost at full pout when she said that. "I can worry about people without marrying them."

What was that supposed to mean? Wynn wondered if he should start pouting himself. Cassie cared a hell of a lot more for him than she was saying.

"Mom, Wynn's had a bad day. We probably ought to go," Hank pointed out.

Cassie almost hugged her brother. Hank might not be a sparkling conversationalist, but he had some good points. Besides, Tash adored him.

She actually thought over what Hank had suggested.

"I suppose so. Glad to see you have recovered, Mr. Harmon." Tasha nodded graciously.

"Oh, yes, he's never been better. Sorry you have to leave and all," Cassie said. "Bye!"

She didn't care if she was ordering Tash and Tash didn't take orders.

* * *

"God, I'm sorry about that, Wynn," Cassie told him.

"I'll live. I have something else to talk to you about, if you recall."

"Oh. Right. Your bad mood. That's OK; a visit from Tash puts me in a bad one, too. So we're even. Let's not push at each other anymore, please. I'll snap at you, and this time it'll be Tash's fault, not yours."

"No." He paused, tried to figure out the best way to approach it, to explain—

There were no words. So he reached for her the way he'd wanted to before.

"I'd love to carry you upstairs to bed."

"Listen, Rhett Butler—" Cassie began.

"But my shoulder is injured." He hesitated. "The hell with it. Hang onto my other shoulder, Cassie."

It wasn't graceful but he managed to get Cassie onto the bed.

She smiled.

"Oh, well, ravish me if you must, Rhett," she replied in a rather good imitation of a southern belle's drawl.

She could make a joke of it, but he planned to do just exactly that. He hoped.

He fumbled a little with the clothes. God, he didn't want to fumble, but this was important. Vitally important. He couldn't help feeling nerves prickling. In the back of his mind, the words *I have to know* kept echoing.

Then for a moment he stopped. Cassie wasn't saying anything. She had stretched out, letting him unbutton and nudge off her clothing. She watched as he stripped. When he finished, they looked at each other a very long moment. And she smiled a welcoming smile.

He could feel the need pounding up from his balls and cock and spread with equal ferocity through his whole being. She could be so welcoming with her tight, soft, wet pussy and her hot, seductive mouth. He wanted to be in her. He had to be in her.

Wynn knew he should wait a little longer, but he knew her body would be as welcoming as her smile. The echoing words he needed to say kept hammering into him as he moved up.

He slid into her and almost gasped. That felt good, maybe the best he'd felt since he'd been shot, but it wasn't the same kind of good as before. He rocked against her while he thought about why.

Oh, God. Of course it wasn't. He couldn't mentally link with Cassie.

Wynn knew he had gone too far to stop. But he didn't know what she wanted! How was he supposed to tell?

Even while he thought that, he slid his hands automatically to the special spot at her collarbone and kissed her. He knew she was sensitive there. That couldn't have changed. She shivered, just the way she always did.

The paralyzing fear moved further away. He knew Cassie. He'd mapped out her body and its pleasure spots by now. Mind-link or not, he knew what she liked.

He slid his fingers down, toyed with one nipple, then the other. Sure enough, her breath caught again. She swallowed hard. So did he.

Cassie. Already slicked up with sweat and trembling. He could do this. He wanted to do this. He had to do this or he was going to die.

When he heard her first little whimper he thought he might burst then, in a mix of lust and triumph. But he didn't want to right away. He could get more out of her than a whimper.

He suckled one breast and she twitched gently. He did it again and she moved less gently.

He knew he could finish then and satisfy them both, but suddenly he was sure that wasn't what she wanted. And if Cassie didn't want that, he didn't either. They could make this better yet.

He moved as quickly and smoothly as he could and then Cassie was on top, laughing a little breathlessly at him. She hadn't laughed while they made love in what seemed like a long time. The laughter felt good, too. She positioned herself so he could just feel the entrance to that lovely pussy of hers but couldn't enter.

"How did you know it was my turn to make you crazy?" Cassie murmured.

Was letting her on top taking the easy way out? Cassie could still read his mind. She knew what would make them both happy. All he needed to do was lay back and enjoy the show—Cassie touched his cock with her hand and he nearly tried to throw them both off the bed. Cassie wasn't going to let him just relax and enjoy. That was all right too.

He had to—he had to—he took his hands to position her and then slid her hard down on top of him. She moaned just a second after he did.

He could still feel and smell and watch Cassie and that was damn exciting.

Just as he thought that, for one short moment, there was a flash of almost blinding light and he was sure he could link again. God knows the two of them must be generating enough electricity that Cassie could see that light with her mental link. He watched it burst in front of his eyes and then-then there was nothing.

Just that one flash had been enough, though. He heard her sobbing now, saw her shivering. Now. Wynn arched up and emptied into her.

She stretched out on top of him, her arm curled up against his body. The weight felt good. He felt good. Again. Cassie bloody knew how to do that to him.

Wynn thought about that brief flash and his jubilation subsided a little. Was that the last of his telepathy? He shut his eyes. Gone. Gone in one last burst of light.

But he could feel Cassie. She wasn't gone. He smiled, a lazy smile. He'd done that much anyhow. He'd satisfied her and he'd satisfied himself without his gift. That light had been a little bonus at the last moment.

If that was the last link he would ever feel, it wasn't a bad way to have it end. He hadn't needed his gift to make her happy. He could handle things. He could manage without his mental linking with Cassie.

He opened one eye. Cassie was still collapsed against him. He'd exhausted her, but he knew in his gut that she had some energy left.

He could do it again. He could do it forever.

"God, you're a fantastic lover." Cassie muttered the words against his chest. "And, God, I'm glad you're still around to be one."

Wynn swallowed. He wasn't going to ask if she was being truthful. He wasn't going to be one of those losers who asked women for reassurance.

Besides, he knew she had meant what she said. She *must*. Cassie never lied. And how could she lie about something that made her cry and shudder the way she had?

"I love seeing you watch me while we make love—" Cassie stopped.

She meant telepathically. Wynn was sure of it. He'd loved doing that to her, too, back when he was able to.

Gone. His gift was gone but she could still use hers.

Wynn got up, abruptly, from the bed. He moved toward the window to look out. Naked or not, he needed at least the illusion of space and freedom. The bedroom suddenly felt confining.

Wynn pushed aside his sudden resentment. If Cassie could use her gift to enhance lovemaking, then he ought to be glad. He was glad. He was still the one who made her feel the way she did when they made love. She'd said he was fantastic. Cassie'd meant it. He was deep-down sure of that.

He could still make love with her and it was more intense, more special than it had ever been with any other woman. He might have lost some of his abilities, but he hadn't lost that one.

He thought about the last time he'd looked out the window instead of at Cassie. He thought about what he'd asked her then.

Those words were hammering inside of him, demanding an answer. Without thinking any more about whether he should wait longer, Wynn said the words out loud.

"So. Are you?"

"Am I what?" Cassie asked, still sounded rather sleepy and satisfied.

"We're not going to die anymore. At least not immediately. You've had time to think about it. Are you going to marry me?"

Jesus. He was standing, literally and figuratively, naked in front of a woman and asking her the biggest question of his life. Hell, he might as well go all the way. Why not face her to see what she was going to say?

He turned from the window to look at Cassie.

Cassie looked odd. How funny. After all these years of feeling like a freak because he had his abilities, of longing to feel ordinary, he wondered if Cassie would refuse him because he didn't have his gift anymore. Maybe she was used to the old Wynn, too. Maybe she wouldn't like the new one.

Besides, what did this Wynn have to offer? He'd remade himself once, using determination and his gift. Now he was back to nothing again—he didn't have much more to offer Cassie than his naked self—and he only had one of those original assets left. But he had a hell of a lot of determination.

"You really want to?" Cassie asked.

Was she scared? God knows he was.

Wynn knew he couldn't hesitate. He didn't want to have her agree out of pity but all of a sudden he was positive that having her say yes was the only thing in the world that would help make him feel better about becoming…well, normal.

"Absolutely."

Cassie looked like she was bracing herself. "All right then. Let's."

"Soon?"

Wynn wasn't going to let her get away with a long, indefinite engagement. That would be a little too close to whatever she'd had with Ned.

"Sure. If we're going to, we might as well get it over with."

"Ah, yes, now that's the way I like my bride-to-be thinking." Wynn moved closer to her.

He couldn't tap into her mind, but when he kissed her he could tell she wasn't as reluctant as she had sounded. He could feel a spreading warmth inside him. He'd done the smart thing, the only thing. Maybe he didn't have much to give but it looked like he had Cassie anyway.

She began to kiss him back, tentatively at first, and then more possessively.

Wynn was feeling better. This was going to be all right. In fact, this might have been the most all right thing he'd ever done in his life. Absolutely.

Cassie opened her eyes, smiled dreamily at him a moment, then murmured, "But you have to break the news to Tash and my dad. I don't want to hear Tash gloating."

Chapter Nineteen

Things were not all right. Cassie smiled and tried not to sweat too much in her designer silk dress. Tash had insisted on buying it for her engagement party. Tash had insisted on an engagement party. In fact, Tash had pretty much taken over their engagement.

To make matters worse, Cassie was wearing the pearls again.

"Darling, I'm so impressed with your young man," her stepmother cooed to her when they met at the dessert table. "I can't believe he advises Art Hornsby. And that the senator was willing to show up at our party, especially with the elections so close!"

"Yeah, well, I don't know how much longer Wynn is going to keep advising Art," Cassie told her. "I have a feeling Wynn won't have that job for long."

"Well, if he doesn't have anything lined up, I'm sure your father could find a spot for him at one of his companies,"

Natasha refused to acknowledge concern. "He seems very impressed with Wynn as well."

"Wynn working for Dad?" Cassie wanted to laugh and then stopped to consider the idea.

Maybe Wynn would think it was a good idea. Dad certainly paid well and it was a very—steady—sort of thing, working for Dad. Very settled and married. Wynn might like that sort of thing. He was the one pushing for the settled and married routine after all.

She was just the one who said yes because—well, she didn't know why she had said yes except that Wynn seemed to think it was so important to him. She knew he was feeling a little lost and confused right now and she hadn't wanted to add to that by refusing to marry him.

But marriage was starting to feel more and more like a bad idea to her. Not Wynn. Not at all. He wasn't a bad idea. Just marriage.

Cassie opened her mouth to tell Tasha that and then shut it again. Tash actually looked happy with her tonight. She might be the world's most insufferable snob and Cassie knew that in any contest between Cassie and her father or brother, Tash would favor the man but—Tash did look happy. That emotion was rare enough for Tash that Cassie decided not to destroy the mood.

If Cassie tried hard enough, she could imagine Natasha was actually happy for Cassie. That was nice. Someone ought to be happy for Cassie at her engagement party.

* * *

Wynn could tell Art wasn't happy. He was learning to read body language more now that he had to rely on that to gauge emotions and thoughts. Judging body language was a much trickier business without mind-reading to aid him, but then he was used to Art.

"I appreciate you coming tonight." Wynn meant it.

"I appreciate that you allowed me to be alive to come here tonight." Art sounded like he meant it, too.

"Ah. Well. I was doing what I said I would." Wynn resisted an urge to shuffle his feet in embarrassment.

"That's more than most people would do." Art nodded to someone. "I'll be glad when this is over."

"The polls say you'll win?"

"The polls? They say I might lose. I got a little upsurge in a sympathy vote when the news first came out but that's smoothed itself off now. Guess I should have been shot a little later."

"Oh. Well. Polls can be wrong."

"Wynn, for the first time in my life I can tell you I don't give a damn. Winning or losing won't change much."

Art sipped at the glass of white wine in his hand.

"What does that mean? Of course it will make a difference."

"Not for me. For my lifestyle, maybe. But either I get to go on doing what I've always done or I do a little more of it than before. I'll still be the same old bastard I've always been. And the people around me will be the same old sharks as well." Art stared into the cup. "I'd appreciate it if you were around, Harmon."

"Art. I'd be of no more use to you." Wynn was glad he could get that out. He still wasn't sure how to phrase it so he would be believed. "When I got shot—something happened. That's the truth. I can't do what I used to for you. I don't have the ability anymore. Um...my sources of information have dried up."

Art let out a brief laugh. Wynn knew it wasn't a happy one.

"Damn. My one honest advisor gone. You haven't lied to me before so I'll have to believe you."

"Please do. I don't need any special visits from any of your people asking for favors or checking to see if I could help. I'm being straight with you. I can't."

"Yes. Yes."

"If you ever want me around—uh—as a friend, I'm here." Wynn wasn't sure how to say what he wanted. "An e-mail away."

"That might be...pleasant. Thanks, Harmon."

"My pleasure, Senator. I wish I could have continued to help you."

"Don't lie. You started hating this long before I did. Maybe you're lucky you can get out." Art hit him lightly on the unwounded shoulder and then turned to an eager-looking woman who had appeared at his elbow.

* * *

Wynn thought about that. Maybe he was glad about being out of the whole situation. He thought about going back to his old life, drifting until he found another chance... But he didn't have his gift to help him out. His old life wasn't going to be so easy to regain. Maybe he was going to end up like his Da after all, just a two-bit con man.

Even that life didn't seem as bad as he used to think it was. He'd come to accept that his idea of becoming something important would never have happened anyhow. Art couldn't afford to let someone like him become too prominent. In many ways he would've remained what he always had been—a mysterious consultant who could be summoned when needed and dismissed when he wasn't. He never would've been openly acknowledged. Art would never show Wynn how he was important to him.

At least now Wynn wasn't going to have to worry about losing his life or having people demand more of his time and energy than he could give. Yeah, compared to Art and his life, maybe he was a lucky man.

He looked over at Cassie. Maybe he wasn't so lucky after all. Something had changed, gone wrong, since he told her he was missing his gift and then asked her to marry him anyhow. She wasn't like herself anymore. He couldn't reach her.

She didn't even look like herself anymore. He stared at the silk sheath and the pearls. She looked tasteful. Expensive. Hell, her stepmother had even gotten her to pose for some engagement photo for the newspaper. None of that was Cassie.

She complained about her family, long and bitterly, but right now she looked like she fit in just fine with the rest of them. Probably she expected he would fit in, too.

He'd done his best tonight. Cassie had laughed as he went over and over which tie to wear for an engagement party. He thought back to their earlier conversation.

"What difference if it's black or red?"

"It's important to look right." Da had taught him that. Once you looked the part, you acted the part and everyone believed you.

Oh, damn. This wasn't a part. This was his new life.

No, he wasn't going to be allowed to slink back into his old life. Cassie would expect more than that. She should expect more. Wynn wasn't sure he was going to live up to expectations.

Maybe marriage was supposed to change you completely. Wynn brooded. If so, Cassie wasn't going to like what he had told her father not half an hour ago.

Could he work for Bill Cassidy if Cassie expected him to? Wynn went and abruptly got some more white wine.

He didn't have to work immediately, of course. If Emmanuel's goons hadn't trashed his rental place, he had some antiques he could sell. That would stave off making any decisions for a while. He might not have to tell Cassie or her father anything for a long while if he worked it right.

Still, what if that was what he'd have to do? Settle down. Settle in. Especially now that he was going to be a father.

Wynn almost sloshed the wine out of the plastic cup.

Where had that come from? He and Cassie hadn't talked about that. Except for that one time that Cassie had said *maybe* she could get pregnant. Maybe. But he could feel the conviction growing inside that he was going to be a father.

Oh, hell. Was that why Cassie was acting so strange? Cassie knew. She must know. She hadn't told him yet, but she knew. Oh, hell and blast. Was that the only reason why she had agreed to marry him?

* * *

"Hey, Dad." Cassie put her cheek against her father's.

Enough champagne and wine had gone down everyone's throat that she didn't feel awkward making that gesture. Maybe she hadn't been drinking herself, but she knew no one else would mind what she did by this time in the evening.

"Hello, daughter."

Her father actually put his arm around her. This was an unusual evening. "How're you enjoying yourself?"

"Well, not much. But this evening wasn't for my enjoyment, was it? It was to show me off. Me and Wynn." Cassie couldn't help saying that, no matter how mellow the alcohol was making him feel.

"I like him. Much better than the last one."

That approval would have been the kiss of death to any potential boyfriend once. Cassie would like to think she'd matured a bit since her teenage and college years.

But the words still made her uneasy. She'd seen Wynn and her father together. At first Wynn had eyed him over as distrustfully as always, but within the hour the two of them had been talking to each other and she'd seen Wynn visibly relax.

That's when Cassie realized the truth.

The man was actually going to fit in with her family. She'd never brought home anyone able to do that. Give him another few days and he'd be inviting Tasha over to pick out the brand of china they'd ask for at the bridal registry.

Cassie restrained a shudder. What really was awful was that she loved him so much that she'd even let something like that happen if Wynn wanted to.

This was so strange. She'd done what she thought her mother would have wanted and because she had, now her father and his family were getting closer to her than ever. Maybe that was good.

She didn't know what to think anymore. All her usual perceptions about life were shifting.

"Why, Dad? I mean, yeah, he's better than Ned as a husband, but that isn't saying much. What makes Wynn worthwhile to you?"

"He loves you."

Her father looked as sincere as Cassie could ever remember seeing him.

"Oh."

"He refused my offer of a job, though. Tasha says that he isn't going to be working for the White House even if the election goes the way I assume you two would want it to go." Her father leaned against the balcony wall and smiled at her. "You have any future plans?"

"Um. I don't know. I suppose I could try law again."

Where had that come from?

Cassie couldn't believe she was saying that. She had never wanted to return to law. She still never wanted to return. "Maybe be a public defender or something. I wouldn't go back to a big firm. Ever."

Not even if she got married to a man who didn't want to be married to a mere cleaning person. She didn't know how he felt about her job. They'd never talked about that. They'd never talked about a lot of things.

"A big firm might not be the best thing if you plan on children, I'll admit. Or at least not right now." Her father's voice was indulgent. Frighteningly indulgent. He'd never before allowed for the possibility that Cassie might have any law career other than one on the fast track. "You ever thought of going corporate?"

"Only if I turned my cleaning business into a corporation," Cassie retorted, then caught herself. "If I kept up with that business, I mean. Are you offering me a job now, Dad?"

She was getting all tangled up in what she wanted and what Wynn wanted—might want.

"I could."

"No, thanks. I mean, I guess I should talk to Wynn. But, no, I don't think so." Cassie knew she couldn't go corporate again. Wynn hadn't consulted with her when he turned her father down, so probably she didn't have to talk to him either. Damn, this was tricky.

"Well, I'm sure you two have plans. Speaking of which, what about children?"

Cassie jumped. How had he known? She hadn't even told Wynn yet. She barely had acknowledged the news to herself. She had spent a long time in front of the bathroom sink this evening before they left, staring at the home pregnancy test.

Cassie had looked up into the mirror and seen one terrified face. Then she'd gotten dressed and to the party without saying anything about the results. For the first time she'd been almost glad that she and Wynn had lost their mental bond. She hadn't wanted to tell him.

She didn't want to confirm that she was pregnant by telling other people. Things were already changing way too much as it was. Cassie wasn't sure what she should do about those changes. She wasn't even sure what she wanted to do about them.

"Children would be fine. Sometime." The words brought up something Cassie had been thinking about and she decided that would be perfect to change the subject. "Hey, Dad, I have a question along that line. Did Mom ever talk to you about—about—"

"Yes?"

This might be harder to discuss than Cassie thought. She couldn't really think of a way to tactfully ease into the subject so she took a deep breath and just asked.

"Did she ever have any special abilities? Oh, man. I mean, could she use telepathy or something along those lines?" Cassie rushed the words out, waiting for the laughter to start. But she'd been thinking about genetics a lot lately.

"No." Her father looked surprised. "No, she didn't. In fact, she always envied me my ability to do that. I think that was what made her interested in me in the first place, to be honest."

Cassie stared at her respectable, conventional, businessman father.

"You? You, Dad?"

"Yes. I never talked to you about it because—well, it's so unusual, I suppose. I was sort of a late bloomer with that anyhow. Never got any unusual insights or flashes until I was in college. Your mother was very supportive when I first realized what was going on. I'm not necessarily very good at it, but I must say it has come in handy a time or two during business deals."

Her father looked just the way he always did. He sounded like he always did. But what he was saying was simply extraordinary.

Then he smiled at her. That grin was youthful, mischievous and just a little sly. After all these years Cassie could finally see just what her free-spirited mom had seen in him. Her dad looked a little like Wynn.

Then she had a really bad thought. Maybe her dad had been a lot more like Wynn before he got married. She had just been allowed to see the last remnants of her father's old personality before marriage destroyed them.

"You've been getting some flashes yourself?" he asked. "I can't imagine why else you asked."

"Yeah. Yeah. That's what you could call it."

"That could be damn useful in my corporation, honey. You sure you want to turn me down?"

"Yeah. Very sure. You know, Dad, I never would have guessed this stuff came from you." Cassie still couldn't believe it.

"You made assumptions, dear. They were very—conventional assumptions on your part." Was her father laughing at her?

"You're right. I've been doing a lot of that lately. This engagement thing has kind of thrown me."

"No need to be thrown, dear. You and Wynn will do just fine." Her father looked a little hesitant and then came and hugged her again. Twice in one evening. "Sounds to me like you and he need to talk a few things out. Like how you both intend to make a living, for example."

That sounded more like Dad. That was also a relief since nothing else seemed to be going the way she thought things would between them. Was her dad mellowing or was she? Well, it damn well better not be her.

"You have a point," Cassie admitted. She risked a kiss and then headed for her young man.

She might as well get the discussion over with now. The hesitation and uncertainty was killing her. She'd been going crazy ever since she took that pregnancy test and got the results. No, she'd been going crazy ever since she agreed to this stupid engagement party.

She'd had enough of trying to do things the way people expected fiancées and mothers-to-be to do things. Doing things the right way was driving her further and further from Wynn. She didn't know what either of them wanted anymore. She'd suffocate if she kept trying to meet expectations.

If Wynn thought she was going to do marriage the way most people did, he was in for a big surprise.

On her way she unclipped the strand of pearls and dumped them in her purse. She wanted to dump them in the trash, but then she decided Tash would probably see her do it, have an unholy fit and then scoop it up out of the garbage to inflict that necklace on Cassie's kid when she turned twenty one. She had to start thinking like a mother and protect her child. Cassie decided a dumpster on the way home would be the way to go in this case.

"Cassie. Hand over the jewelry."

Cassie whirled around at the familiar voice, clutching her purse.

"Nope. You'll take care of them or something."

"Exactly." Emily crooked a finger at her, her other hand holding some champagne. "Come on, Cassidy."

"But, Em, I want to get rid of them. I want to get rid of everything associated with this evening."

Em smiled knowingly at her.

"I knew you had that 'I'm trapped' expression on your face. You want to get rid of everything, including Wynn?"

"Maybe. Yes."

"Then you're an idiot. Wynn is perfect."

"You like him? You never like my boyfriends." Cassie felt almost betrayed. "You threatened him with the police."

"Now that he isn't kicking my door down, I can take a second look. I like him for you, Cass. He adores you. He's gorgeous. And I can tell you and he are on the same wavelength. I always thought that would be impossible. Up until now I figured you were one of a kind. Now I see there are two of you. A matched pair."

Cassie snickered.

"Yeah, Wynn and I are on the same wavelength all right." Cassie hesitated. "But Em, I was sure you'd never approve."

"Of Wynn?"

"Of marriage. Didn't you get kicked in the teeth from your marriage?"

Emily hugged her suddenly. The champagne sloshed a little over both their shoes. Cassie figured she didn't mind if Emily didn't.

"Yes, I guess so," Emily agreed. "But ending the marriage wasn't my choice. If it had been, I probably would still be Jim's wife. I suppose it's lucky that it wasn't up to me because now I know that particular marriage wasn't right."

"See?" Cassie said, but she didn't feel triumphant.

"No, Cass. I'm not so crazy about Jim anymore, but marriage is wonderful. I like being with someone, sharing jokes with him. I like sex with love. I like watching a guy shave in the morning and knowing he'll come home at night."

"I can do that without marriage," Cassie pointed out.

Emily sighed, as if her friend was a particularly stupid two-year-old and continued. "I like feeling like I'm accepted into the adult's club. That acceptance is what you get from the world when you're married. How can I explain this? Cassie, I really want all the stupid sentimental things you always sneered at when we talked about weddings back at school. I want to promise to belong to someone in front of everyone and to know he'll always belong to me."

"Still?"

"Still. Even with all the arguments, all the childbirth, all the hurt that comes along with the promises. Oh, Cassie, give the whole thing a chance. I can see you married to Wynn. I couldn't see you with any of the other idiots you picked to be with. Take David. All I can say for David was that at least he wasn't Ned."

Cassie hesitated.

"Besides, Cassie, when else will I get to be your bridesmaid or matron of honor or whatever? You are going to have me be in your wedding, aren't you?"

"I don't want there to be a wedding! I really think you're wrong this time, Em."

"Cassie, don't be impulsive. Think. Besides, have I ever been wrong about you, ever? Honestly, the only thing I'm sorry about with you and Wynn is that even Ned has figured out that with Wynn around you're gone forever. Ned's looking for a substitute, Cassie. I may have to adopt him if he hangs around my house much longer. But I don't need five kids."

Cassie laughed as she left, but some of the angry energy was gone. That didn't mean she'd changed her mind, though. And the only important person she needed to convince was Wynn.

Chapter Twenty

"Wynn, listen to me—"

Cassie swept up to him while he was chatting with her brother. Wynn was almost relieved, even though he could see she was ready for war.

He didn't know why she wanted a battle but anything had to be less boring than talking job prospects—Hank's, not Wynn's. The conversation had really dragged since Wynn knew he had none of his own and couldn't exactly contribute much to the conversation.

"Oh-oh." Hank might be boring, but he wasn't stupid. He ran for cover without bothering to say good-bye.

"Yes, darling?" Wynn tried for a mild tone but he could see that wasn't going to do.

Well, they hadn't had a fight in a while. He could feel a little surge of anticipation and adrenaline kick in. Would Cassie start one in public? At their own engagement party? She swept him away to another, deserted room and he was almost disappointed.

She looked different, he realized. Well, different from the start of the evening. She was more like his Cassie—with her hair a little bit wild and sparks snapping in her eyes. And no pearls. He wondered if she'd lost them. That wouldn't be a surprise for the old Cassie.

"Listen to me, Wynn Harmon."

"Always, dear."

"Don't start. I have some important things to say to you."

"Me, too."

"If you think I'm going to settle down and just be—be married, you're wrong. I know Dad is going to ask you to take a job with him again. I know you're probably feeling a little lost, trying to figure out what you can do now that you aren't the same as before. I know you are getting to like the man. Listen to me. Don't you dare consider it! If we have to, we can live off my cleaning job. At least until you figure out what you want to do."

"Fine. That's what I planned. Well, not the living off you part. I'm not sure what I can do, especially now that I've—changed—but I can keep us both afloat with my acquisitions for a while."

"Fine. Hell, maybe you can stay home for a while and take care of the baby. You know as much as I do about how to deal with one."

"Whoa. Whoa. Ah, I take it that means you are—"

"Yes, I am, but that isn't the important thing just now. I love you, Wynn. Just the way you are, all right? We don't have to be just regular married folks. How could we be? After all—"

Neither of us are regular folks, married or not.

"Neither of us...are...Wynn?"

Blessed Jesus Christ, I believe I've got it back.

Cassie stopped in mid-tirade and threw her arms around him. He was happy to let her.

"Oh, Wynn, I know how much that was bothering you! I'm so glad!"

"Me, too."

And he was glad Cassie was laughing, and holding him and giving him her declaration of independence. For some reason that was even more important than regaining his gift. "Cassie, you should know we aren't going to be conventional. We're freaks, right?"

"If you want to call us that."

"What do you say we leave and discuss what we are elsewhere?" Wynn kissed under her ear. She always liked that.

Oh, she liked that all right.

Cassie's eyes promptly half shut and she almost purred out her response. The sound of her voice, all throaty and excited, made him feel like a hell of a stud.

"Sure. My house? I mean—our house?"

He thought about her house. Their house. He'd said once he could find another home. There his home was, waiting for him.

His new place wouldn't be at all like the old one. He'd planned to create a stir with his old place. He'd planned to impress colleagues with how important he was by his surroundings. After all, he'd planned to have an image to maintain. None of that would happen where he was about to live.

His old house had been a quiet refuge. This new home would be cramped and cluttered and eccentric. Cassie would probably be in his face all the time. The kid would, too.

Maybe the place would be just a little unsettled for a staid married couple and a kid. And he would definitely have to get rid of the antiques. They wouldn't fit her house or a small baby's life. Oh, hell. Maybe he could store a few until the kid grew up. Who said they'd be in one place forever anyhow?

In the meantime, Cassie's place would be fine. Any place with Cassie would be fine. With Cassie and the kid, he wouldn't have to create an image to show he was important.

For the first time in his life he was going to be as important to someone else as they were to him. Someone who was going to stay.

"I don't know. We have the rest of our lives to be there if we want. For now why don't we just leave the party and go see where we end up? We can get in the car and go. Just for old times' sake?"

"Sure."

She didn't hesitate. Wynn smiled. He threw his arm over her shoulder, ready to sweep her out the door and into something unpredictable.

Then he paused to nuzzle one stray lock of hair. He could feel her shiver. He nuzzled closer. Maybe he could stretch this out a little more. He liked waiting when he could feel Cassie getting more excited with each moment they lingered.

"By the way, Cassie, I thought you should know I've one thing planned for when we do stop."

"Oh?"

"I've been having this fantasy I hoped you could help me out with."

"A fantasy, huh?"

"Mmmm. It involves scarves. But I thought this time it would only be fair if we switched roles. Or, if that bothers you, maybe we could just pretend. But I definitely think it's my turn to dominate. My fragile male ego can't handle things any other way. At least not until I've had my turn."

"Your turn?"

"I bet I could get you all wet and moaning those little cries of yours while I tie you up with your legs spread nicely apart. And while I tell you how pretty that pussy of yours looks all wet and welcoming. And when I lick it. I hear some women get extra horny when they're pregnant. You'd love the way my tongue would work its way all over you. When I stopped, just to tease, you'd moan and twitch enough to make me keep going. Longer. Harder. You'd probably beg me to do it that way all the time before I'm done with you."

"Beg? Well, that might be—different." Cassie's face looked sweetly thoughtful but her eyes showed she was amused and interested. And she shifted, just a little, like she was getting excited by her thoughts.

"I don't think married people are supposed to do things like that, you know." Wynn did his very best to look innocent, too, while he pointed that out.

Cassie broke down first and snickered. Then she turned to give him a long, slow, serious kiss.

Somewhere in the middle of that kiss he realized he might not be able to wait to take a long drive to anywhere with her.

In fact, Wynn figured he had just about enough self-control left to get her out of this house and into the car without shocking too many of the guests—as long as she stopped doing that within the next few seconds.

When she didn't stop he dimly began to think about locked dark closets, rearranged clothes and quick hot sex. The scarves could wait. His new fantasy now involved getting to a bathroom or anywhere nearby with a locked door. Quickly.

Suddenly he knew that things were going to work out. He couldn't see what their life would be like exactly, but neither of them wanted it that way.

Cassie, are you happy about the kid?

I'm not sure. I still can't quite believe it yet. What about you?

Yes. I can't believe it yet, either, but yes.

Cassie stopped thinking about Wynn and getting him naked. At that moment she had entirely different image in her head. Cassie imagined holding a small baby with dark, intent eyes.

Her grip on Wynn's shoulders tightened. She knew that Wynn had imagined the same thing just then. That was when the baby became real to her at last.

And that was when she finally did know how she felt about having a baby.

This baby wasn't going to have to spend any time feeling left out or wondering if Daddy really loved his own child. Cassie had wondered plenty about that when she was growing up, but Wynn was different from her father. Their baby was about to be lucky enough to get the perfect dad.

She didn't know how he managed it, given his own dad, but Wynn was a father who, whether he realized it yet or not, was already ecstatic about his baby's future arrival. Cassie could feel the joy bubbling inside of him.

Because she loved him, she couldn't begrudge him that joy or selfishly wish she had Wynn all to herself for just a little bit longer. Maybe some of that joy sort of flowed over to her too, because she could feel a smile forming.

I'm starting to get happier about things now, Wynn. If you're sure.

What Wynn was sure of was that they'd still be a bloody secure family, no matter where they went or what they did. The baby was almost certain to inherit their gift but with Cassie around he had a feeling the kid was going to always see that as a welcomed present. She'd make the perfect mother for a kid like that.

He almost hoped the baby inherited her flaky moods.

Almost.

She pinched him.

"I heard that, buddy."

"Now what, Cass?" He wanted to give her—well, something amazing. It was like the stupid songs. The stars didn't seem enough.

Wynn stared at Cassie's face. She was happier than he'd seen her in days. Happier than he'd seen her since she'd agreed to marry him.

"All right, then. After weeks of being a dutiful fiancée, dressing and doing what I'm supposed to do, I've declared my independence. The pearls are finally gone. What next?" She thought for a moment. Then Cassie's eyes glittered with amusement. "I hate this dress. I'm not going to wear it anymore, either."

Cassie began to wiggle the tasteful and expensive dress off, suddenly laughing. The old Cassie was back with a vengeance. Wynn hastily glanced around but no one was nearby. When he looked back at her, his mouth went dry.

Cassie's dress was gone. Now she looked tasty instead of tasteful, and instead of expensive she looked—not cheap…

She looked fuckable. Damn fuckable. His fantasies, momentarily frozen from amazement, came roaring back. Cassie's dress might be conventional, but her underwear wasn't. Had he ever seen her with silk stockings and a garter before?

"Um—are you planning to leave like that?" Wynn really wasn't sure what would happen next. But things were looking up.

"No, silly. Give me your jacket."

His conventional suit jacket just skimmed her thighs and the lapels formed a low V to show her cleavage. The cleavage that her—her bra-like thing that had been driving him crazy was pushing up to overflowing. Wynn swallowed hard. In his jacket and her high heels, she looked…she looked…she looked like he had to get her the hell out of the house and into the car while there was still time. Before he got into her right there in the hall. "Come on, Cassie."

"Just a minute."

Cassie began to tug at something else.

Wynn stopped, all his X-rated thoughts suddenly fleeing. "No."

Cassie paused, her hand on her engagement ring.

"But, Wynn, I thought you said we didn't have to be respectable married folks!" she protested. "I don't want to be."

"The engagement ring stays, Cassidy."

"Why? We're going to be together forever, right? What difference does it make if we're married or not?"

"The difference is—because—"

Because he needed them to be married. Somehow that didn't seem like a good enough reason.

How was he supposed to argue with her when she looked like that? If those buttons came undone, he wasn't going to be able to remember his name, much less put a sentence together. A sentence that would convince Cassie they needed to be married.

"Well?" Cassie challenged him.

"Because…because I'm going to show you we can do things differently married. Better."

"Better than what, ace?" Cassie asked.

"Better than your folks did. Better than mine did. Better than anyone in the whole world has ever or will ever do. I promise." Wynn knew he was promising more than he was sure he could deliver. Right now he didn't care. Call him weak, but even if everything else came off Cassie—a prospect he wouldn't really mind at all—that ring was going to stay on. Somehow. "It's going to be different and exciting and you're going to love being married to me."

Wynn, I'm scared. What if we make each other miserable? What if this doesn't work?

Cassie, don't we always work better together than alone?

"But—" Cassie looked like she wanted to protest and then she looked at him again. He wasn't sure what she saw there other than his desperation, but her face softened. "Tell me the truth. Why do you want to marry me?"

He wasn't sure how the words came to him. He was sure Cassie wasn't feeding them to him from her head. She probably didn't even know the answer. But Wynn did. He even knew the right words. Or at least he knew the words he needed to say. The words he meant from the heart.

Now they just had get them forced out his mouth. Wynn cleared his throat.

"I always wanted to be important. I thought. But that wasn't quite what I needed. I really needed to be important to someone. I didn't know before, that to get there, someone has to be important to you. You are."

This was worse than when he was naked and proposing. He'd rather be naked. He'd only do this for Cassie.

For a minute he thought he'd done things wrong because she looked like she was going to cry.

"You promise?" Her voice wavered.

"I swear it." He'd said things the best way he could and Wynn figured it was time for action. He picked Cassie up, threw her over his shoulder—getting a fascinating view of her delightful rear—and headed out the door. He saw the glint of the engagement ring on her finger. "But I think I'd rather show you. Quickly."

When he heard her laugh, he knew he'd won.

"I'm only doing this because you're such a smooth talker and you're so sexy and you want to marry me so badly." She twisted her head up to whisper the words in his ear. "This is totally against my better judgment."

"Honey, you don't have any better judgment available than mine," Wynn told her. "Certainly not yours."

He looked at the view again.

Oh, why not?

He slid his hand onto that tempting rear and then explored a little more. Her ass cheeks were so pretty. He slid one finger past the crack of her rear and then tested the waters, so to speak. He let out a little whoosh of air when he felt her wet pussy. He could tell he wasn't the only one who wanted to get to someplace moderately private quickly.

She pinched him again.

He yelped, even while a wave of relief hit him.

He managed to open the door with Cassie draped over him and then kicked it open the rest of the way. As he hauled her outside he knew Cassie was finally with him on this marriage venture now.

I don't know why you picked me for this, but since you did, Wynn, we're definitely in it together.

I'm counting on it, Cassie.

Treva Harte

Treva Harte claims taking care of the family's neurotic miniature dachshund and raising two prepubescent kids is a full time job itself, but in addition she works as an attorney in a city with many other attorneys.

She and her husband both like writing in whatever time they have left, so they often fight over--sorry, since they are attorneys they NEGOTIATE--keyboard time. No wonder Treva's particular brand of sensual romance is a bit offbeat and usually mixed with fantasy.

Treva is multi-published with several e-publishers, a member of WRW, RWA, and PAN and winner of the CAPA 2003 award in the "Erotic Fantasy Romance" category.

NOW AVAILABLE In Print

ROMANCE AT THE EDGE: In Other Worlds
MaryJanice Davidson, Angela Knight and Camille Anthony

CHARMING THE SNAKE
MaryJanice Davidson, Camille Anthony and Melissa Schroeder

THE PRENDARIAN CHRONICLES
Doreen DeSalvo

COMING SOON in Print

HARD CANDY
Angela Knight, Morgan Hawke and Sheri Gilmore

FOR THE LOVE OF...
Kally Jo Surbeck

Printed in the United States
38438LVS00003B/103-510

9 781596 321304